THE WARATAH INN

The Waratah Inn, Book 1

LILLY MIRREN

Black
Lab Press

To the generations who sacrificed lives and love so we could have freedom.

THE WARATAH INN SERIES

The Waratah Inn
One Summer in Italy
The Summer Sisters

Christmas at the Waratah Inn
(a standalone novel)

AUGUST 1995

BRISBANE

The wind clutched at Kate Summer's straight, brown hair blowing it in wild bursts around her head and into her green eyes. The ferry lurched forward. She grabbed onto a cold, metal handrail with one hand and held her flyaway hair against her neck with the other. Then she stepped through the doorway and into the City Ferry cabin. The rush of wind in her ears quieted, replaced by the dull murmur of conversation between commuters as they huddled together in clumps throughout the cabin.

The Kangaroo Point terminal faded out of sight behind them as the ferry chugged across the sluggish, brown Brisbane River toward the city centre. Kate tugged her coat tighter around her body and inhaled a steadying breath through her reddened nose. It'd once been smattered with freckles, but time had faded them to a pale remnant of their former selves.

Sighing, she sank into one of the hard chairs that were lined up like so many church pews, smoothed her hair with one hand as best she could, and set her purse on the empty seat beside her.

She had to get to work on time today. Marco was stressed out about the new menu. He'd called her at home to tell her he wasn't entirely convinced it was a good idea to take the restaurant in a new direction, what with the economic climate the way it was. She reminded him the economic climate was fine and it was the perfect time to try something new, as they'd discussed a hundred times over the past six months. That he'd named her head chef at the *Orchid* for a reason and should listen to her ideas.

He'd agreed and hung up. But she'd heard the tension in his voice. He hated change. She knew that well enough, having worked for him for five years. But five years of creating food that was expected, safe, the same as it had always been, was more than enough for her. If he didn't want to make the change, then she would. Her creative spirit itched for something different.

The ferry pulled to a stop, growling back and forth until its ramp lined up with the dock. When she stepped onto solid ground, she couldn't help one wistful glance back at the river. She missed the water. The ocean had been like a second home to her once. She'd spent so much of her teenage years diving under the waves, floating on her back, and staring up at the sky on a calm day, or surfing the break when the wind was up. But since she didn't live near the beach these days, she had to make do with the river. It wasn't the same but paddling a kayak or riding the ferry brought a measure of peace.

By the time she reached the restaurant, she'd already run over the menu again in her mind and was convinced they were doing the right thing by reinvigorating their offerings. It was fresh, unique, delicious — it would bring diners into the restaurant in droves. She was sure of it.

Or it would drive them away.

Her stomach tightened at the thought of what Marco would say if it didn't work the way she hoped it would. Reputation was everything for a chef, and in a small city like Brisbane, failures weren't something you could hide.

"Morning chef." Her Sous Chef greeted her with a warm smile. "Ready to change the world?"

She chuckled. "Ready as I'll ever be."

Fresh groceries from the market lined one of the bench tops along the wall. She always placed her orders the day before. Fresh produce, direct from the farmers, was the best way to make delicious meals, and the write-ups she'd received so far in the local newspapers showed it. She'd sent one review to Nan.

What she really wanted to do was drive down to Cabarita and bring Nan back with her, so her grandmother could taste the food for herself. Not that she was such a big fan of Asian fusion cuisine. Nan preferred her meat and three veg, like most Australians of her generation. Still, Kate wanted her to see the restaurant, see the career she'd built for herself over the past decade. She was proud of what she'd achieved and wanted someone to share that with.

Just thinking of Nan and the inn put a twist in her gut. She hadn't been back to see Nan in months, and when she'd gone the last time she'd only visited briefly. Nan had made her promise to stay longer on the next trip, but with everything she had going on, the visit never happened.

If the new menu didn't work out, Kate would have plenty of time on her hands to visit Nan and the Waratah Inn. Maybe she'd be a permanent guest there. She shook her head, her pulse accelerating as worry over the future, her career, and personal life washed over her again. She was used to it, this anxiety. It clogged her thoughts, put knots in her gut and sent waves of adrenaline coursing through her veins.

The new menu *had* to work. It was the first time Marco had given her complete control over what they'd serve. If people didn't like it, he might never offer her the chance again.

She wasn't ready to concede defeat and move in with her grandmother yet. But a holiday, a beach holiday, was a great idea. Davis had been bugging her about getting away together, away from the city and their crazy, hectic schedules, ever since he proposed six months earlier. She'd suggest it when she saw him that night after work. They often met up late for a light meal, since she worked when most people were done for the day. He didn't like it, but what could she do? It was her career. He'd said they should take a vacation, but they hadn't spoken of it since. Perhaps it was time to raise the subject together. They could both do with some time off. And more than that, she missed Nan.

CABARITA BEACH

The sand squelched between her toes, wetting the soles of her feet with a cold that sent a shiver up her spine. The grittiness of it, the scent of salt in the air, the warmth of the sun on her face — all were familiar feelings, sensations she'd grown to love. It'd taken time to embrace this place, but she had. For years now, it'd been home.

Home.

The word reverberated through her soul and her smile lingered as she brushed the strands of white hair from her eyes. When had it turned white? She'd have described it as salt and pepper not so long ago. Now there wasn't any pepper left; it was more the colour of snow.

It'd taken an age to allow herself to call it home here. Home had been so far away. Such a different place, a different time. But this was Edie Summer's home now. Adjusting to change was part of life, though some changes you never grew accustomed to.

Even her name had once been foreign to her, had caused a little pain in her heart that couldn't be shaken whenever anyone called her by it. "Have a nice day, Mrs. Summer," they'd say, and her stomach would clench. "Nice weather we're having, Mrs. Summer," and her head would spin as pin pricks of light danced before her eyes. Now, her name was as familiar to her as the lines that lingered on her face long after her smile had faded.

A pair of seagulls trotted along in front of her, just out of reach. Their red-rimmed eyes watched close as each head craned from side to side, feet scampering in a steady rhythm. She picked up the pace and they launched into the air, a rapid flapping of wings taking them above her head in no time, their cries drifting back to her on the breeze.

She watched them go, her eyes squinting against the glare of the rising sun. One hand tented against her forehead, her gaze followed them out over the spray of a dark wave, then they disappeared into the bright colours of the sunrise.

Pink, orange, and yellow. Glowing fingers reached from the horizon toward her, shooting bright blue lights high into the sky overhead. It was beautiful in a way that made her heart sigh. How many more of these would she see? How many had she ignored or simply slept through in her youth?

She glanced along the length of the beach, studying the dark outline of Castle Rock as the dawn pulled it from the shadows, surrounded by froth and bubbles. A wave hurtled itself at the rock, and salt spray shot into the air, raining down in droplets on its black surface.

Perching on that rock was one of the things she'd loved to do most, back when scrambling out beyond the waves wasn't such a chore. She'd dive beneath the curling lip, water rushing against her ears and pummelling her body. Then both feet would plant in the sand and her head would break free of the water's surface as she gasped for breath, in time for the next breaker to lean over her.

A frown creased her forehead. That was before her body slowed and diving through waves became a hazard, or at least that's what Jemima told her. Back when so many things were easier to do. Maybe she should never have given it up. Mima had become too cautious, except when it came to love. She wasn't cautious about love.

Edie smiled and let her eyes drift shut a moment, the sun playing a kaleidoscope of lights through her eyelids. A play formed in her mind as the lights danced, the cast so familiar to her and yet seeming unreal in their youthful beauty, with broad smiles on handsome faces. Smiles unchecked yet by grief, suffering or loss. Smiles full of love and the prospect of life to come.

Her own smile drooped as one image filled her mind's eye. His face was no longer so clear as it once had been. Wisps and vapours gave him smudged edges and his eyes, at one time so clear to her, seemed distant. Still, her heart squeezed as memories poured over her like deep water through narrowed shores.

With a cough she cleared her throat and her eyes blinked open, taking a moment to adjust to the burgeoning daylight. So many memories. She could spend the entire day wrapped up in them and never leave the beach, but there were things to do. Always something needing her attention.

She pushed a hand into one of the pockets of her loose-fitting culottes, searching, and pulled free a piece of paper, a newspaper clipping. An article about a chef in Brisbane whose restaurant had surprised the critic with its vibrancy and unique artistry. "A breath of fresh air," he'd written — a cliché but it'd warmed her heart, nonetheless. She read it again in a whisper, repeating the words over as one finger traced the outline of her granddaughter's cheek.

Kate was so beautiful, as all her granddaughters were. So much like her father, in so many ways. Edie's eyes misted, and she swatted at them with the back of her hand and with the impatience of having cried too many tears too many times.

Her stomach clenched and she wondered if the milk she'd added to her coffee that morning had been too far gone after all. Bile rose up her throat. She shook off a dizzy feeling and strode through the sand, shoving the article back into her pocket as she went.

There were guests to wait on, people to serve, rooms to tend. Not so many as there'd been in years gone by, but still, they were there, and they needed her. The life of an innkeeper was never dull.

It wasn't a life she would've chosen in her youth. She'd had so many dreams for herself back then, but that was before her eyes had been opened by horror and violence, to the possibility that life should be more than what others laid out for you like freshly ironed clothes on the bed.

When she was young, all she'd known was the path followed by her mother, grandmother and the generations of women that surrounded her then. She knew what she would be, and she relished the thought. Treasured it. Looked forward to a life of domesticity in the town of her birth, with icy winds nipping at her nose and children mewling at her breast.

Then she'd grown, and her dreams had grown with her. A career, something for herself. A path to sharpen the mind and leave behind a legacy. It was difficult to remember exactly what it was that had driven her. Likely the same energy and optimism imbued in young people everywhere before the world snatched it away.

Puffing lightly, she stepped out of the sand and onto a hard-packed trail through the dunes. It wound, rose, and fell, soon becoming a track of loosely connected timber slats, dusted with sand that rose and rose toward the green hillock ahead.

When she reached the hillock, she paused to catch her breath. Walking had become more difficult in recent days. She'd done so much of it in her life she had no desire to slow down now. She knew how to push through the pain. To keep going even when she didn't feel like it.

With one calloused palm resting on a handrail made of sun-bleached timber, she glanced back over her shoulder. The sun had popped over the horizon in its full glory now, remnants of pink glistened within its bright, yellow rays. The entire beach was bathed in light, sand warming, and crabs finding their way back to holes that hid them from the heat of the day. The waves, no longer dark, sparkled azure.

Her breathing slowed and she climbed the stairs at a brisk pace. Sandals awaited her at the top, lined up neatly side by side. She slid her feet into them, then marched through the short grass.

The inn rose tall ahead of her. Shadows from a grove of pandanus mottled the peeling pink paint. The gutter on the rear side of the building sagged and smoke sputtered from the small chimney above it.

She stopped to study the building, inhaled slowly, and smiled to herself. It'd seen better days, but then again, so had she. To her it would always be the place she'd found herself. The place where her wounded heart had discovered a refuge.

Her thoughts returned to her granddaughters. They'd spent years living here, with her. Would they treasure it the way she had, or would they throw it away and go on with their busy lives? She knew she shouldn't care. When she was gone, she'd have no way of knowing what any of them did, or what became of her legacy. Only, she wanted them to find each other again, her wayward girls.

Perhaps she should've told them why it meant so much to

her. Already Nyreeda had suggested she sell the place and retire. "Relax," she'd said. "You've worked hard all your life. Sell the inn and get some rest." Bindi was the only one of the three who'd objected. But she'd always been the fondest of the inn, probably because she'd spent the longest part of her childhood within its paint-chipped walls.

Relax. *Pshaw.* What did she know about relaxing?

At some point in your life you had to give up and do what you knew how to do, and she knew how to take care of people. It was what she did, what she loved. They might as well bury her now if she couldn't do that.

But the girls — they didn't understand it. Didn't understand her. And perhaps it wasn't their fault. She'd kept so much of herself from them. Had it been a mistake?

She'd only wanted to protect them. To give them some semblance of stability. But they were grown women now. Maybe it was time. The next visit, she'd sit them down and tell them all about why this inn mattered. How it'd saved her. Why she was the way she was. What she'd been through, what she'd kept hidden. Yes, it was the right time. They were ready, and now she had no reason not to break open the past and let its secrets spill out like stagnant water from an old vase.

❧

KATE WASHED HER HANDS AT THE SINK, THEN EXAMINED the produce, turning the vegetables over in her hands, her mind running through all they had to get done before service began that evening.

One by one, the kitchen staff filed in. They greeted her, then chatted together as they set about doing their various tasks. She missed the camaraderie of being one of them. She was the boss, and as much as she'd worked to make that happen, she hadn't realised it would be such a lonely job.

The phone on the wall rang, a high-pitched jangle that pierced the air and reverberated off the white, tiled walls. One of the staff answered, then met her gaze with the earpiece extended toward her.

"It's for you, chef."

She set down a bunch of greens with a frown. Who would be calling her at the restaurant? It could be Davis, he didn't call often, but maybe he'd had a change of plans and couldn't meet her tonight for tea. Irritation bristled over her skin. He'd been doing that a lot lately, canceling on her. How did he expect them to enter into a lifetime of wedded bliss if they never saw each other?

She took the phone and pressed it to her ear, already considering the things she'd say to Davis if he canceled again. She'd be calm, mature, but firm. He couldn't keep backing out of their plans last minute, it wasn't fair to her or to them. They were building a life together and he should prioritise that.

She wouldn't raise her voice or let her temper flare up, the last thing she wanted to be was some shrill housewife demanding her future husband spend more time with her. And Dad had always told her she should begin as she intended to go on, in relationships and in business.

She'd be kind, patient, loving, but make sure he understood that she wouldn't stand for second best when it came to their relationship. Either she was his priority, or she wasn't. In her mind it was simple. She hesitated for a moment before speaking. What if he decided she wasn't his priority? Her stomach twisted into a knot.

"Hello? This is Kate Summer."

"Kate? Is that you, Kate?" The soft, wobbling voice threw her.

"Yes, this is Kate. Who is this?"

"Oh good, I'm glad I found you sweetheart. It's Mima, from the inn."

"Mima? Wow, it's good to hear your voice. How are you?" Unexpected tears pricked the back of her throat. She should visit them more often. She hadn't realised how much she missed the entire crew from the inn. After all, it'd been her home once.

"I'm good honey. Not as spry as I once was, and one of my knees has been playing up. But otherwise, I'm fit as a fiddle."

"I'm glad to hear it. I hope everything's okay." Why was Mima Everest calling her at the restaurant in the middle of the day? Her stomach knotted as she waited for Mima's response.

She heard a rustling sound. Mima cleared her throat, soft at first then with a loud, grizzled cough that hacked at her lungs. She was about to speak again, when Mima's voice echoed down the line.

"Look, sweetheart, there's no easy way to say this." Her voice broke, and Kate turned away from the kitchen to face the wall, her breath caught in her throat.

"Your Nan died this morning. She's been having some trouble with her ticker as you know, and she took a walk along the beach, like she always did, but as she was coming up the path to the inn she fell over. Thankfully, Jack saw her and came running to help. We called the ambulance right away, but it was too late I'm afraid. Jack performed CPR, and mouth-to-mouth, he knows about all that stuff from being a lifesaver for years. But she was gone just the same." Mima sniffled and coughed again. "I'm so sorry, sweetheart. I know how much you loved her. We all did."

Kate's breath finally released, and she inhaled again with a sharp intake of breath. "No," she whispered, squeezing her eyes shut.

"Sorry, what was that, love?"

"Nothing, nothing. Thanks for calling to tell me, Mima."

"You okay, sweetheart?"

No, she wasn't. How long had it been since she'd seen Nan's sweet face? Christmas at least. She'd gone to the inn for Christmas but hadn't stayed for New Year. Davis had wanted them to go to some party at one of his colleague's fancy penthouse apartments. Anger burned in her gut. Why hadn't she stayed longer? Nan had asked her to, but she'd turned her down. There was always next year, she'd told herself, only now there wasn't. There never would be again.

"Kate?"

She realised she hadn't answered Mima's question. "I'm... I don't know, Mima. I'm wishing I'd come down there. I didn't know about her heart. Why didn't she tell me?"

Mima sighed. "I thought she had told you. She promised me... but you know your Nan. Stubborn as the day is long." Mima chuckled, but the sound faded away.

The sounds of the kitchen hummed behind her and Kate rested her forehead on the cold wall beside the phone. She squeezed the earpiece until her fingernails dug into the flesh of her palm.

She cleared her throat. "Have you spoken to Reeda or Bindi yet?"

"I talked to Reeda a few minutes ago. I have to dig up Bindi's phone number. I couldn't find her at work. I tried you earlier, but I guess you weren't there. No one answered."

"I just got in," Kate responded.

"That makes sense. Reeda's hopping on a flight to the Gold Coast airport tomorrow morning. I don't know when Bindi will be coming."

Kate's head spun. They were unveiling the new menu; everything was riding on her. Marco was counting on her.

And she had to go to Cabarita Beach to say farewell to her grandmother. Her stomach roiled.

"I guess I'll go home now and pack. It shouldn't take me more than a couple of hours to make the drive. I'll be there before tea."

"Okay, love. I can't wait to see you, sad circumstances notwithstanding."

"You too," Kate replied, numbness filtering through her body.

She hung up the phone, but stayed still, her forehead pressed to the wall. She pushed her hands against it as well, and hovered there for several long moments, willing her body to move.

"You okay, chef?" asked a voice behind her.

She nodded. "Fine." And pushed herself back from the wall.

❧ 3 ❧

AUGUST 1995

CABARITA BEACH

Leaving the city had frayed Kate's nerves. The ferry ride back to Kangaroo Point. The walk to her unit where the lift wasn't working and she had to climb eight flights of stairs, then leaned, puffing against the door before she could extract her keys from her purse in a haze of oxygen deprivation.

She'd packed a bag without a clear thought. She threw in a bikini before remembering it was the middle of winter and she wasn't likely to want to swim, then thought perhaps she should keep the bikini after all since her surfboard was stored at the inn. She wondered briefly if it was bad form to think about bikinis and surfing when her grandmother had recently died and slumped onto the bed with her hands pressed to her face.

Her thoughts were tangled, and she struggled to extract a strand long and straight enough to focus on getting out the door and into the car. After that, she'd run into a traffic jam, and it'd taken three hours to drive from Brisbane to Cabarita Beach. She'd tried to find a radio station with soothing music to help slow her heart rate, but all she could find was something called *Trance Dance*, and another pumping out a loud, alternative rock song where the vocalist's almost on-pitch nasal growl tugged on her frayed nerves.

She switched off the radio, letting her thoughts wander. Her mind kept flicking through a slideshow of images. Nan in her rocking chair laughing over something she and her sisters had done. Nan marching along the beach in her gumboots, waving a stick at a seagull who'd had the nerve to steal a hot chip from Nan's hand. Nan sitting astride her favourite chestnut mare, then digging in her heels to send the animal into a gallop over the golden sand.

She was only a few minutes away from Cabarita and her pulse accelerated at the thought of what she'd find there. The Waratah Inn, with no Nan.

The sun set in a lazy haze beyond the distant mountains. Shadows lengthened over the straight, narrow road that was called a highway but was really only wide enough for two cars to squeeze by each other with dust and gravel flying up beneath the tires that tickled the edges, and her stomach was clenched in the same knot it had been ever since she took that phone call from Mima.

Rolling dunes undulated toward the blue sky to her left with hardenbergia, dianella, and lomandra plants dotted here and there and lining the uneven edge of the bitumen. To her right, squat casuarina and banksia trees shielded a fragile grassy plain and hid the road from the bulk of the sunset's blinding rays where they shone through the breaks between foliage in bursts.

Kate chewed a fingernail, the other hand holding tight to the steering wheel of her blue Honda CR-V. She'd taken her first trip down this road the year she turned eight. Her parents brought her and her sisters up from Sydney for a visit. They'd hired a car at the airport and taken this road to the inn. She recalled her father's words, as he leaned forward to peer at the narrow stretch of bitumen over the steering wheel, his knuckles white.

"I mean, what were Mum and Dad thinking moving all the way out here? Good Lord! I know I grew up here, but I didn't realise it then: we're in the middle of nowhere. Where are we?" He waved a hand with enthusiastic abandon toward the windscreen. "You'd think they'd want to see their grand-children occasionally, but no. They're so caught up in taking care of other people, making sure strangers have the most tranquil beach holiday of their lives, that they can't spend time with their own family! I was sure they'd have given it up long ago."

Her mother had sat mute through his tirade, one elbow resting on the car windowsill, her hand pressed to tight lips, an unfolded map occupying her lap. They'd been studying it earlier, looking for things to do on their holiday.

"And..." her father had continued, "do you know what she said when I asked her about it? She said they couldn't leave the inn for long anymore, because it couldn't run without them and was getting busier every year, that it was time for us to make the trip. Can you believe it? I mean, when I pointed out that retirement was supposed to involve relaxation, maybe a trip to Europe, she laughed and said, 'To each their own, my darling boy'."

He'd huffed in frustration then and pointed out that the map they were using didn't have the road the inn was on. "What kind of place isn't on the map?"

Kate remembered being quietly fascinated by her own grandmother then. Her father was right, she hardly knew either of her grandparents, since she often only saw them once or twice a year. And every time had been either at their home in Sydney, or at a campground halfway between the two locations in Scott's Head on the verge of a long, horseshoe beach with soft rolling waves.

She loved the idea of moving to a remote beach as they had, to a place that didn't show up on the map and starting a new life. A life that didn't involve stop and go traffic, private school, or boys that pushed you over in the playground and laughed when you grazed your knees.

Instead they could live in a mysterious inn that wasn't on the map, along a road with not a single car anywhere in sight, fringed by waves. That kind of life would be fine by her.

And that was her first memory of admiration for Nan. There had been so many times since that she'd lost track, and at some point, she'd begun to take her grandmother for granted, assumed she'd always be there, and stopped wondering, stopped being fascinated by the details of her out-of-the-ordinary life. She was just Nan. The woman who baked the most delicious cinnamon tea cake in the state, or the most scrumptious scones. The woman who loved to sing to her chooks while she scattered seed on the ground for them to peck at. And the woman who loved the ocean almost as much as she loved her granddaughters. Almost, she'd always remind them with a wink, but not quite.

Kate's eyes misted and she wiped them with a quick movement, peering through the tears to find the road's uneven edges and make sure to keep her car firmly between them.

Her mother had made some comment then. Something wise in her kind, patient voice. Something that'd soothed her father's nerves and made him smile, wiped the anxious lines from his face. She'd always done that. Been able to smooth his uneven edges. Then she'd turned to look back at her three girls, wedged side by side into the back seat of the car, smiled and patted their knees one by one. She didn't have to say anything. Kate knew what it meant. She'd had a special way of making Kate feel as though everything was all right. So many years later, she hadn't felt that way in a long time.

⌘

THE CR-V'S TIRES SLIPPED AND SKIDDED AS SHE PULLED the car into the inn's driveway. She'd almost missed the turn, distracted by a possum's last-minute twilight dash across the road. She pulled the car onto the verge, her breathing ragged. A cloud of dust swept over the car, enveloping it like smoke from a campfire, the headlights dimming in its midst.

Kate's eyes squeezed shut a moment and she exhaled with slow deliberation. An image of the startled possum barely escaping her tires flashed across her mind's eye. She shuddered. Just as her heart rate was about to return to normal, a thud on the car's bonnet sent a bolt of adrenaline through her body.

In the dim dusk light, she saw a familiar face. Jack, the handyman who'd worked at the inn for almost as long as she could remember and who had to be at least seventy years old, grinned at her from beneath a worn, tan Akubra hat. Behind him, a lop-sided timber sign painted in a gaudy dark pink announced *The Waratah Inn, Beachside Bed and Breakfast*.

She pushed the car door open with a smile. "You scared the life out of me."

He chuckled, then stepped forward with open arms to embrace her. She wrapped her arms around his waist, enjoying the familiar scent of fresh cut timber, leather, and Old Spice.

Her memory flashed back to another time. Jack had taught her to ride. The horse's name was Janet. She'd laughed about that at the time and asked him what kind of person called a horse Janet. He'd told her it was as good a name as any for a horse, and besides, didn't she look like a Janet?

He'd held the reins while she and Janet walked around the yard. Then he'd shown her how to hold on with her legs and use pressure from her heels to urge the horse forward. Finally, he'd given her a lesson on how to hold the reins in her hands, loose but firm enough to be able to communicate with the animal about where she wanted to go and when she wanted to slow down or stop.

That had been a good day during a time when good days were few and far between. After the accident, Nan had remained in her downstairs bedroom for weeks, unwilling to come out and face the world. Mima and Jack had been the ones who'd comforted Kate and her sisters, taken them to town to buy groceries, watched as they swam or ducked waves, and helped them buy the school uniforms they'd need to start attending the new school.

When Jack brought Janet up to the inn, Kate had been sitting on the verandah, staring off into the distance, thinking about all the things she missed. All the things she'd never have. She'd smiled at the sight of the horse, then felt immediate guilt over that smile, wiping it away and replacing it with a scowl. He'd pretended not to notice, and patted Janet's long, brown neck instead.

"Isn't she a beauty? I was hoping you might help me with her. She needs someone to take care of her, and I'm so busy with everything around here..."

She hadn't needed a second invitation. With a few bounds she was down the stairs and standing beside the bay horse, her hand pressed to the animal's fine fur coat.

"She's so soft," she'd said. "What's her name?"

Jack had been the one to help her onto Janet's back, and ever since, she'd loved horseback riding. It was an escape, an adventure. And she'd be forever grateful to him for introducing in her a love of the majestic animals.

He faced her now with a smile, his eyes gleaming. "Good to see you, love. I hope the drive wasn't too bad." He shifted his hat back with the tip of one finger.

She shook her head. "It was horrible, but it's over now. I'm glad to finally be here."

"Let me help with your luggage."

"I should move the car, I'm in the way here," she said, scanning the winding gravel driveway that encircled the inn's front yard.

"I'll help you inside then move the car to the parking lot for you."

"Thank you, Jack."

He patted her on the back, an awkward but sweet gesture that made her throat smart.

"You're welcome, hon. I'm glad you're here. We've missed you."

Jack was a fixture at the Waratah Inn. He repaired anything that needed it, and Nan counted on him to help her keep the place running. Generally, he kept to himself and barely uttered a word to anyone. These few words of greeting were the most he'd said to Kate in years, and they meant a lot.

She couldn't speak as a wave of sorrow washed over her. She'd been gone too long. Nan had asked her to visit, maybe she'd even suspected she was sick but hadn't wanted to say anything. Now Kate would never know, and she wouldn't see Nan's smiling face or bouncing grey curls as they marched along the sand together, arm in arm, ever again.

She slung her handbag over one shoulder and stopped to stare at the inn. Peeling pink paint with white trim. The verandahs that encircled the first and second floors were lit up with the soft glow of lamplight. Inside, a couple of the rooms were lit as well, but the rest of the regal old building had fallen into darkness.

With a grunt, Jack slung her suitcase up onto one shoulder and marched toward the inn. Her brow furrowed. The man was a machine. There was no slowing him down. He carried her suitcase as though it weighed nothing, boasting the physique of a much younger man.

She hurried after him, with one worried glance back at the CR-V. Its headlights illuminated the driveway, the boot door hung wide open and the bell dinged in a perfect rhythm to let her know the keys were in the ignition. Still, she couldn't think straight. The inn was drawing her to itself, like a bee to honey. She had to touch its weathered timber, feel the hard, cool boards beneath her feet, see the rooms that held so many memories and so much of her heart.

As she climbed the first few steps, her pulse quickened. Nan wasn't there to greet her at the door. She remembered a similar feeling when Pop died. She'd been eleven years old at the time and came to Cabarita with her family for the funeral. She'd ascended this same set of steps to find only Nan inside waiting for them in the large, high-ceilinged sitting room. The room had felt empty and Nan looked shrivelled, seated in the large, leather wing-backed armchair. She'd realised her grandmother was getting old. That was seventeen years ago.

She paused at the top of the staircase and inhaled a deep breath. The screen door slapped shut behind Jack and he disappeared into the inn, taking her suitcase with him.

How could she stay here without Nan? The Waratah Inn was Nan, it shouldn't exist with her gone.

The door flew open, and two lined hands stretched toward her.

"Kate! Sweetheart! You made it. Come on inside and I'll make you a cup of tea. You must be freezing!"

Kate accepted the embrace Mima offered, almost getting

smothered in the process by the woman's ample bosoms and purple knit cardigan. Only in Cabarita would someone define a balmy twenty degrees Celsius as freezing. Her eyes filled with tears, and she smiled as Mima patted her back and kissed her cheek.

"I'm fine, thanks Mima. It's good to see you too. Tea would be lovely."

Mima bustled her into the kitchen, pulled up a stool for her to sit on, and set about boiling the kettle, all the while regaling her with a moment by moment account of her day. The woman's wide hips swayed with each step. Her salt and pepper curls were pulled into a bun on top of her head but couldn't be tamed, instead tumbling down on each side of her face. Her blue eyes sparkled as she spoke.

"We've still got two guests. Can you believe it? They know what's going on, and yet they stay. The other couple that were here checked out right away, after giving their sympathies, but this couple. Wowsers!"

Mima set two mugs on the bench. "So, I guess we'll shut the place down for a while as soon as they leave. But that's something we can discuss later."

She pulled a teapot from the overhead cupboard and measured a tablespoon of tea leaves into the pot. Then, filled it with boiling hot water. "And do you know, I was in the breakfast nook this morning, reading my Home and Garden magazine... I get one every month dear, I know it's pointless since I live at the inn these days and don't really have my own home or garden, but I like the decorating tips and I always thought that maybe one day my cooking might earn me a featured article."

She set the lid on the pot, turned it to the right, then to the left, resting her hand on top of the pot while she continued. "But that's neither here nor there, you don't want to hear about the silly dreams of an old woman. Now, where was I? Oh yes, the lizard..."

"Lizard?" Kate gave her a confused look. Mima's tales were famously long and winding.

"Yes, the lizard! It came creeping into the breakfast nook. I don't know where exactly it came from. It was one of those blue-tongued ones, you know? And it scared me half to death because when you see the head, it looks like a black snake. It's not until the tiny little legs come into view that you can breathe again.

"So, I thought we had a black snake, and a pretty big one at that, in the breakfast nook. And of course, I don't eat my breakfast until after everyone else has finished and gone about their day. So, I was all by myself. I didn't scream, mind, I gasped. Because, after all, it's not my first run-in with a snake. They're common enough around here. But I tell you, I was relieved to see those little legs when it pushed past the chair it was hiding behind.

"I like to sit in the breakfast nook to eat my breakfast, and usually Edie... uh... your Nan, would come join me after she'd finished her morning walk. We'd sit there together every day and have a cup of coffee and talk about everything going on in our lives. She'd do the crossword, and I'd do my knitting. So, I knew something was up this morning when that lizard came in, and once my heart had recovered, I looked down at my watch... and Edie wasn't there. That's when I went looking for her and found her on the path that leads down to the cove. Oh dear, I've made you cry. I'm sorry, love. And now I'm crying too. I can't help it you know, I'm a sympathetic crier. If I see tears, I join in. It's the way I am."

Kate let the tears fall. She hadn't cried more than a few tears since she'd heard the news about Nan's passing, and the pain in Mima's voice was more than she could withstand.

"It's okay. I'm fine. I hope she didn't suffer..." She sniffled into her jacket sleeve.

Mima set down the teapot and waddled to where Kate sat, and embraced her all over again. Tears streaked the old woman's face and her bottom lip wobbled before she crushed Kate's head to her chest. "No sweetheart, I don't believe she did. She looked as peaceful as can be."

Finally, Mima released her hold on Kate.

The inn felt like a part of her. She didn't visit often enough these days, and with Mima and Jack sitting in this sturdy old kitchen, she was at home, loved. She scanned the room, her eyes misty, taking it all in as an ache filled her heart. Peeling white paint, an ancient steel stovetop, and racks of drying herbs hung with string beside silver pots and pans with blackened bottoms.

This kitchen stirred up memories of hot chocolate with tiny marshmallows, bacon and eggs with toast, and soft hugs that smelled like woodsmoke and chocolate chip biscuits.

"It's good to be home," she said.

Mima poured tea into two mismatched, floral print china cups with a smile. "You're home, sweetheart, and even though there's grief in my heart, I've a bubble of joy working its way up in there for seeing you."

KATE SAT AT THE VINTAGE DRESSING TABLE AND SPUN slowly on the chair. The room Mima had led her to after their cup of tea was the same one she and her sisters had shared as young girls. Only now, it was decorated as a guest room.

A single queen-sized bed with an outdated, floral bedspread squatted in the middle of the room. Dark, antique side tables sat on either side of the bed, one with a blue lamp, one without.

The rug beneath the bed was worn but looked to have once been a shade of pale blue. On another table by the window, a small bowl held an assortment of seashells and sun-bleached coral. Beside it, a cream coloured vase was filled with fresh cut flowers, no doubt from Nan's beloved garden.

As a girl, whenever she couldn't find Nan, she knew to run to the long, rectangular garden out the back. She'd find Nan there, dressed in a pair of denim overalls, with an old straw hat perched on top of her head, wispy, every-which-way hair flying out beneath the brim. She'd wear yellow gloves and carry a pair of secateurs or a small shovel in one hand. Her boots would be caked with dirt, and she'd always say, "Damn this sandy soil, it's so hard to grow anything." Then she'd smile and wave Kate in through the rickety gate that guarded the rows of vegetables, flowers, and seedling plants from the rabbits and possums.

"Come on in love, you can help me figure out how to make these waratahs grow." Then Kate would pull on a second pair of gloves, much too large for her small hands, and together they'd spread fertiliser, or lovingly trim Nan's waratah shrubs.

Kate sighed and walked to the window. She fingered a piece of coral in the bowl and stared out through the second-story window and into the darkness. She could make out the familiar outline of the garden shed, and beside it the chook pen. The garden was there too, though she couldn't make out much other than a shadowy fence and the tops of a few bushy plants.

A scratching sound overhead caught her ear and she frowned at the ceiling. Did they have rats in the inn? Then, the scratching turned to a gnawing and her stomach clenched. Something was eating the building from the inside out. Waves sighed, crashed onto the sandy shores of the nearby beach, drowning out the soft shuffling overhead bringing a sense of peace to her soul.

She was fifteen and living at the inn when the rhythm of waves first soothed her nerves. The funeral had passed in a blur, and life had returned to some semblance of normality, though Nan still kept to her bedroom. She, Bindi, and Reeda were crammed into this room with one set of bunk beds and a single for Reeda by the window. Kate had been grateful at the time that the inn was so busy they all had to live together in one room. They clung to each other in those days as though letting go might mean never seeing each other again.

Kate rested a hand on the windowsill and strained her eyes in the direction of the cove. The path that led down to the sand was there, a little overgrown, but she could make it out in the moonlight. Then, it was obscured by undergrowth and bushes. She knew beyond lay the dunes. Rising mounds of sand where she and her sisters had spent countless hours, pretending to be princesses from far off lands and rescuing each other from unnamed monsters, or imagining they were jillaroos, rounding up a herd of wild brumbies and bringing them home to break and train until they ate from the girls' hands, nuzzling their open palms softly with whiskered snouts.

Kate shook her head and turned away from the window. Those days were such distant memories now, like whispers of a time past that would never come again. Whispers that couldn't be caught, and if she grasped too hard at the memories, they'd disappear like a vapour.

When was the last time she'd seen Nyreeda? Her older sister hadn't come up from Sydney for Christmas. She'd been busy. At least that was what she'd told Nan and Nan hadn't seemed inclined to be pushed on the subject.

"Your sister has enough to deal with," was all she'd say, and when Kate asked what she meant by that, she'd simply smile.

"We all have our own stuff, my love. That's why it's important to show people compassion even when you don't understand why they do what they do."

The memory caught Kate off guard. What had Nan been referring to? From all she knew, Reeda was a highly successful interior designer with her own business in Sydney. Her services were in demand with the upwardly mobile elite of the northern beaches. And she was married to a handsome surgeon who, from what Kate had seen, seemed to adore her.

What "stuff" had Nan been referring to? And why wouldn't Reeda talk to Kate about it herself? She knew the answer to that one at least. Reeda didn't talk to her about anything, not anymore. They'd all but lost touch over the past five years, and if not for Nan, may not have seen each other at all.

And there was Bindi, who seemed lost in a world of her own. She'd been there with them at Christmas, at least physically, but she'd been quieter than usual, and spent a lot of time on her own at the beach.

Why did the passing years have to mean that relationships changed? They'd been so close as girls, and yet from the first day after Reeda left for University, those bonds had stretched, then frayed, and finally snapped one Christmas about five years earlier when the three of them had a blow up over something trivial. She couldn't remember what it was that'd started the argument, only that they'd all yelled things at each other, and she'd said things she wished she could take back.

When it was her turn to graduate from Kingscliff Public High School, she'd been so focused on getting away from Cabarita Beach and starting a new life, she hadn't taken the time to think about the fact that nothing would ever be the same again. She could never return to that life — a life of peaceful warmth, with Nan cooking scrambled eggs over the ancient stove top when she padded down the stairs in her pyjamas. Or sitting in her rocking chair, knitting, and glancing at Kate over the top of half-circle black rimmed glasses, as Kate read out her homework, nodding every now and then to something she'd said.

Kate's throat tightened, and a lump filled it so that it was hard to breathe. Why couldn't she have appreciated everything then? Now it was too late.

❧ 4 ❧

CABARITA BEACH

Kate plodded down the wide staircase, her slippers slick on the hardwood boards. She'd slept late. She hadn't been able to get to sleep until well after three a.m. Anxiety over all the tasks that lay ahead had kept her awake, thinking through lists of to-dos and questions, like what are we going to do with the inn now? And if we sell it, what will happen to Mima and Jack? Not to mention the horses, the chooks, and the cat that showed up from time to time and drank milk from one of Mima's saucers without Nan knowing about it, since she'd be darned if she'd take on a cat as well as everything else she was managing.

Though of course, Kate had seen Nan feeding the cat herself often enough and checking over her shoulder to make sure Mima didn't catch her.

She chuckled at the memory, then pushed the birds nest her hair had become with all her tossing and turning, out of her eyes. In the kitchen, she made a beeline for the espresso machine. A luxury they didn't need and couldn't afford, according to Mima, but something Nan had insisted on buying. The two of them had argued over the purchase innumerable times, until finally Nan had said it was for the guests, and that was that.

Kate and Nan had enjoyed many a cup of hot, steaming coffee together whenever she visited. Nan always said, coffee was for the mornings when you couldn't rub the sheet marks off your face. And that was how Kate felt. Her eyes were half-lidded, her body felt heavy, and her head thudded with sinus pressure. She hoped she wasn't coming down with anything. That was the last thing she needed. Right now, a clear head, logical thinking, was the best thing.

Someone had to organise a funeral. She assumed the task would probably fall to her, unless her sisters materialised sometime soon. Then, perhaps they could do it together, if they didn't kill each other in the process.

She poured coffee into a large mug, then cozied up to the bench, feet resting on the bottom rung of the stool, to sip it gingerly.

The kitchen phone rested in its cradle just above her head. She eyed it with a stab of guilt. She hadn't given a single thought to her fiancé since she arrived at the inn. She should at least try to call him and tell him she'd made it there safely. He was probably worried about her. Though she couldn't be sure, since she'd never seen that particular emotion in him. It didn't really match his dark, tailored suits, perfectly coiffed hair, and chiselled features. When she pictured Davis in her mind, it surprised her all over again that he'd chosen her. Men like Davis, the Chief Technology Officer for a large, lifestyle company in downtown Brisbane, usually chose women who wore designer gowns with décolletage fighting to burst free from the neckline, and diamonds glimmering on various parts of their body.

That just wasn't her. She usually wore her chef's jacket,

black and white chequered pants, Doc Marten boots, and her hair pulled back into a messy bun on top of her head with a hairnet holding the whole thing in place. Her look didn't exactly prompt the word "glamour" to come to mind. And yet, he'd asked her out after they met outside one of the corporate functions she'd been asked to cook for, and he'd attended as a guest. He'd been smoking on the balcony, and she'd been looking for a breath of fresh air at the end of a long night. She'd quipped about the health benefits of fresh air, he'd laughed, and the chemistry between them had ignited.

Still, she couldn't help wondering sometimes if perhaps he deserved someone else. Someone who fit him in all the ways she didn't. They were supposed to be getting married, but she'd postponed the wedding date three times. She said it was because they were both so busy, but when he hadn't seemed to mind, she wondered if perhaps her fears that they weren't suited to one another had some kind of merit.

She tugged the phone from its cradle and punched in his office number. Pressing the receiver to her ear, she waited, drumming her fingers against the bench top. The phone rang out, and she hit redial to try again.

This time, he answered. "Yyyello."

She smiled. "Hey, it's me."

His voice softened. "Kate, I was wondering when you were going to call. How'd you go?"

"I got here late last night. The traffic was horrendous. But everything's fine. Reeda and Bindi aren't here yet, so it's me, Mima, Jack and two guests who haven't found the good sense to check out yet for some reason." She scrubbed a hand over her face.

He chuckled. "You should kick them out."

"I don't think Nan would want us to, but I might if they don't leave soon." She groaned. "And now I have to think about funerals, and plans for the inn, and all kinds of things I don't want to think about."

"Won't you sell the place?" he asked.

She grimaced. "I'm sure we will. I don't see how we can keep it running. That is, if she's left it to us girls. We haven't seen the solicitor yet about her will, so there's really no point thinking about things like that. Knowing Nan, she probably left the place to Mima and Jack. And honestly, that would be fine with me. If I don't have to take responsibility for figuring out what to do with it, then I can simply organise the funeral, say goodbye and go back to my life in Brisbane. And back to you, back to normal."

His voice sounded more distant. "Look, hon, I have to go. Work is crazy right now and I've got a million things to do. I'm sure you'll work it all out."

"We'll probably have the funeral next week. Do you think you can make it down?" Kate took another sip of coffee and scalded the end of her tongue. She gasped, then blew on her tongue as best she could, setting the mug back on the bench.

"Ahhh... I'm not sure. As I said, we've got a lot going on, and I really have to be here for it, since I'm the boss. Pick a day, let me know, and I'll see what I can do. Okay?"

Her brow furrowed and she chewed the inside of one cheek. He knew how much Nan meant to her. She was basically Kate's parent, the only one she had left anyway. "Okay."

"Look, I'll call you later, hon. Love you."

He'd hung up before the words "Love you," had left her mouth in response. Her eyes narrowed, and she stared at the receiver a moment before pushing it back into its place on the wall.

Footsteps echoed in the living room, then Mima rounded the corner and into the kitchen.

"Ah, there you are! Good morning, sweetheart, I hope you slept well."

She shook her head with a glum smile. "Nope. But I have coffee." She raised her mug as though in salute.

Mima rolled her eyes. "You and Nan with that coffee! Pfft! A good cup of tea is what you need. Coffee clogs your arteries."

Kate bit down on her lip to keep from laughing. Mima always railed against the evils of coffee. That and surfing. She couldn't understand why anyone would stand on a flimsy board and trust a wave to carry them to shore when God gave them a set of perfectly good feet and land to stand on.

"Are you hungry? I made a batch of scones, and they're cool enough to eat. Your Nan's recipe." Mima pulled a dish-cloth from a tray of soft, golden-topped scones, cooling on a rack.

"Um... I haven't eaten breakfast yet so maybe I shouldn't."

"Good Lord, rules are for fools, my girl. Eat what you want, when you want. That's what I say." She giggled, as she patted her rotund rear end. "Perhaps I've found the source of the problem," she whispered, then laughed out loud as she refilled the kettle from the tap.

Kate laughed with her. "No, you're right. I don't have to follow the rules, I can be flexible, footloose and fancy-free..."

Mima flicked the switch on the kettle with a chortle. "Uh-huh. Sure you can, sweetheart."

"No, I can. Let's do it. Scones for breakfast. I'm breaking all the rules today. I slept late and now I'm eating scones with jam and cream for breakfast. Who knows, next I might go upstairs and mess up all the books on the bookshelf so they're out of order."

Mima waved her arms over her head. "Hallelujah! It's a miracle!" She laughed as she put scones onto a plate. "Let's go to the breakfast nook. It's so nice in there this time of day."

SUNLIGHT FILTERED THROUGH THE PLANTATION SHUTTERS casting dancing prisms of light over the pale blue seat cushions and making the painted white timber furniture look new again.

On closer inspection, Kate could see the cracks in the paint and the dark smudges of mould and grime growing in out-of-reach places beneath table tops, close to the bottom of table legs, and in between the black and white tiles that covered the narrow floor in the breakfast nook. It'd once been a covered porch off the back of the Waratah Inn, and had since been enclosed when Nan decided it would be the best place to sit in the morning to have her coffee and ruminate over the early morning's activities and what was to come.

Nan always considered the inn her home and the staff who worked there her family. When guests came to stay, they were invited unceremoniously and with great affection into the family for the duration of their trip. Nan and Pop had decided early on that the inn was their retirement plan and treated it accordingly. They worked hard in the early hours of the day, rested until evening, then set to work again to make their guests comfortable. All the hours in between were for them to relax and enjoy themselves in what they called their little corner of paradise.

Kate had asked Nan once, only a few years earlier, why they didn't close up the inn for guests when they hit retirement age. They could've lived a quiet life, Pop throwing out his fishing line in the cove, Nan walking on the beach or puttering in her garden. Why bother waiting on guests. She'd told Kate it was their dream, their crazy little dream. No one understood it but them, they never had. And what would she do with her days if she had no work to do? She'd go stir crazy sitting around with no one but Pop to talk to. Much as she loved him, she'd added with a wink.

Kate sat in one of the chairs across from Mima, who

lowered herself with a huff of air and a grunt into her own. She smoothed back the grey hair that was pulled into a tight little bun at the nape of her neck. Wisps and tendrils had escaped and were flying free around her face in loose curls, the grey streaked with more white than Kate remembered from Christmas.

Between them sat two cups of tea on matching saucers, and a plate of warm, soft scones, with side dishes of cream and strawberry jam.

"Made from the strawberries Edie picked in her garden in autumn," Mima said as she pushed a spoon into the chunky jam. "So, how are things with that handsome man of yours?"

Mima sliced open one of the scones.

"Things are good, I think. I mean, we've postponed the wedding again; we're both so busy."

Mima didn't say a word, just smeared jam on her scone.

"We'll get there, we have to be sure the timing is right," added Kate.

Mima nodded. "You do what you feel's right to do. But can I ask you something?"

"Okay." Kate wasn't sure she wanted to hear whatever it was Mima had to say.

"When it's right, you know it is. You don't have to wonder or wait for the right time. If he's the man for you, you'll be tripping over your own feet trying so hard to get to that altar."

Kate dropped a dollop of cream on her own scone, irritation boiling up from within. It wasn't anything she hadn't thought before. But hearing it come from Mima's lips didn't help her feel any better about it, and she bit back a defensive retort.

Mima had been single for as long as Kate had known her, and as far as she knew, had never married. What did she really know about love?

"He's the right man for me. We're busy. That's all it is."

Mima smiled. "Of course he is. And the two of you will be the most beautiful couple around. Him with his dark hair and suave suits, and you with those big green eyes and killer figure."

"I have a killer figure? Hardly." Kate rolled her eyes as she bit into the scone. It practically melted in her mouth.

"Please, sweetheart. Enjoy what God gave you because Heaven only knows it doesn't stay that way forever. You're beautiful, and you should know that. We women waste far too much of our youth wishing it away, envying everyone around us, and before we have a chance to stop and enjoy our freedom, our looks, our energy and strength, time has ripped it all away." Mima shook her head. "Don't spend your young years wishing, sweetheart. Enjoy them."

Kate nodded. "You're so right. I'll try to, I promise. And by the way, these scones are amazing. I could eat a dozen of them."

"Well, don't stop on my account. I can always make more. And you're practically skin and bone."

Kate laughed. "Thanks, Mima. Hey, I was wondering — do you know what Nan wanted, what her final wishes were?" This was an awkward conversation to have. Mima and Jack lived at the inn, but Kate still didn't know what Nan had decided to do with it, if she'd decided anything at all. Looking back, she realised they should've had a discussion about it years ago, but none of them had imagined Nan would leave them so soon. She'd always been so youthful, strong, and vibrant.

Mima's brow furrowed and she tapped one cheek with a finger bent by arthritis. "Let me see, I know she wrote a will, because Jack and I witnessed her signing it. She has a solicitor somewhere in Kingscliff, I've probably got his number in the rolodex back there in the office. I didn't get to read the will, mind you. So, I can't tell you what's in it. But I know there's a copy around here somewhere, and some other things she wrote down for you girls as well."

"What about funeral arrangements; did she have anything to say about that, do you remember?"

Mima smiled, her full lips pulling so wide that her eyes almost disappeared beneath her wrinkles. "Now, that I *do* know. She wanted us to have it in the cove and sprinkle her ashes in the waves. She was pretty clear about that."

Kate nodded, her throat tight. "That makes sense."

A tap on the door frame caught Kate's attention and she swivelled in place.

"Anyone home?" called a familiar voice.

Mima lurched to her feet, her eyes lighting up. "Bindi! You made it, honey. Oh, just look at you."

Mima embraced Bindi, pressing her sister's head into her bosom the way she did with anyone she hugged. Bindi's wispy sandy-blonde hair was pulled into a ponytail and sagged beneath Mima's hug. Bindi wore a pair of jeans, a long-sleeved flannel shirt and a pair of chunky boots. Her green eyes looked tired and freckles stood out across her pale nose and cheeks.

Kate stood slowly, brushing scone crumbs from her lap as she did. Her heart thudded. Bindi had always been good to her, but she'd never been one to keep in contact much. It was hard to stay in touch when you worked nights, weekends, and everything in between as a chef. People counted on her, and for the past decade everything and everyone else in her life had come in second best. Guilt washed over her as she took in the sight of her youngest sister's tired face. She didn't know anything about her — what was she doing, was she in love, healthy or sick, happy or sad?

"Hi Bindi, it's good to see you." She offered open arms and Bindi stepped into them.

With an awkward pat to her sister's back, she smiled. "How was the flight from Melbourne?"

Bindi shrugged. "It was fine. You're looking good."

"Thank you. You too."

When had things become so stilted between them? They used to be able to talk about anything, laughing together until their sides hurt. If she remembered rightly, there'd been a time Bindi had peed her pants when they were playing tennis one evening and laughing over some nonsense or other, unable to stop. They'd had the kind of connection other sisters envied. And now they were behaving like strangers.

"I'm going to take my bags upstairs and grab a shower, if that's okay, Mima. I'm pretty tired." Bindi ran a hand over her eyes, and Kate studied her. She looked tired. Something was going on with her little sister. Or maybe this was how she was these days.

Mima excused herself to walk Bindi up to her bedroom. Kate slumped into her chair and picked up the scone. She took another bite, then set the pastry back on the plate, her appetite gone. Sadness balled like a fist in her chest.

Without Nan, she was all alone in the world.

"Helloooo!" called a voice from the reception area.

Kate hurried to greet whoever it was, and to tell them the inn was closed to new bookings. With Mima busy upstairs, and Jack out doing who knew what somewhere on the property, she was the only one available to meet an unexpected guest. She glanced down at her pyjamas in dismay and smoothed her flyaway hair back as best she could. She pushed out her chest and stepped through the arched doorway that lead from the sitting room.

"Good morning, I'm sorry to say that the inn isn't open to new bookings..."

A woman stood in the reception area, her back to Kate. She wore a narrow grey pencil skirt that hugged her lithe figure, offset by a pink knit jumper. Long, straight hair swung like a waterfall with each movement. Perfectly manicured hands pressed to her narrow hips and she spun about on stiletto heels to face Kate with a smile. A thick blunt fringe that brushed against her eyelashes, almost entirely obscured her eyebrows but accentuated wide, brown eyes

"Kate, how lovely to see you. You look... nice." Nyreeda's gaze swept up and down Kate.

"Reeda, wow, we weren't expecting you yet. I'm sorry, I literally just woke up... rough night." Kate kissed her eldest sister's cheek, then stood back to study her.

"You look like you stepped off a runway, and not the airport kind," said Kate, cocking her head to one side.

"Thanks. Where is everyone?"

"I don't know where Jack is, in fact I'm surprised he didn't meet you at the gate. He was hovering close by when I glanced outside earlier. Bindi arrived a few minutes before you, so Mima's showing her upstairs. You must've missed her at the airport by a hair. I'm sure she'll be down soon."

"Bindi's here? Great, I guess we're all here, then." Reeda drummed her fingers against her hips.

"Want me to walk you upstairs? I'm actually not sure which room Mima has you staying in, but she can tell us that." Kate crossed her arms over her chest, painfully aware of the contrast between her fashion model sister and the vagabond look she was currently sporting.

"Thanks. It's so strange to be back here. Isn't it?" Reeda scanned the room, her eyes softening. "And Nan's not here." The last was almost in a whisper, so that Kate couldn't be entirely sure she'd heard the words.

Kate inhaled sharply as another stab of grief hit her unexpectedly. It came in waves. If she forgot Nan was gone for a moment, the realisation crushed her anew each time it hit her.

"Yeah, I know. Really strange." She pursed her lips. "Come on, let's go upstairs and find Mima."

❦

KATE PEEKED INTO THE SMALL, UNTIDY OFFICE THAT WAS wedged behind the inn's kitchen and beside the tacked-on laundry. It felt strange to pry in Nan's office; it'd always been the place she'd come to sit with Nan while she ran over the bookwork, her black-rimmed glasses perched on the end of her button nose.

Where would Nan have kept her will?

A small, rusted filing cabinet was pushed up against the wall behind a worn timber desk. That was a good place to start looking.

She squeezed in behind the desk and sat in the swivel chair, since there wasn't room to do anything else. After a few minutes of rifling through files, she still hadn't found anything. She sighed and spun around in the chair to face the desk, massaging her temples with her fingertips. The beginnings of a headache had set in, and she suspected it had something to do with her sisters' arrival. Tensions between the three of them ran high these days, and none seemed able to shrug things off the way they had in the past.

An old-fashioned black rotary phone sat on the desk and she eyed it. She really should call Marco, find out how things were going with the new menu. She'd been dreading making the phone call, since she'd abandoned them right when the restaurant was rolling out a menu she'd designed. Marco had put his faith in her after so many years of tightly controlling every aspect of his restaurant. She'd been so excited to show him what she could do. Now that might never happen.

She dialled the restaurant's number, her anxiety growing with each ring. After a minute of ringing, one of the kitchen staff finally answered. She asked for Marco, then sat chewing a fingernail while she waited for the call to be transferred to his office.

She could see him, seated behind his large, hardwood desk, hunched down in his expensive ergonomic chair, his small, black eyes fixed on the computer screen in front of him. He'd mutter over the figures he was collating, about how many guests had attended the restaurant the night before, what the takings were, tips distributed, staff numbers and everything else. His business ran like clockwork, and he knew every last detail about it, down to how many napkins were used and needed laundering. He was the most fastidious restaurant manager she'd ever worked with, and his tight control over every detail of the business made it a challenge to work with him, especially when it came to creative risk taking.

"Hello?"

"Hi Marco, it's Kate."

"Kate, I hope your trip is okay. I know how hard family funerals can be."

She nodded. "Thanks Marco. Actually, I was calling to see how the new menu worked out and to tell you again how sorry I am that I couldn't be there for the first night."

He hesitated and she could hear the rustle of papers. "It didn't go well, Kate. I'm sorry to say it, but I've had to roll back to the old menu."

Her mouth fell open. "But..."

"It was a complete disaster, Kate. The kitchen staff couldn't pull it off without you, and we had more complaints than ever from customers. The scallops were overcooked, the salmon undercooked, there was too much soy sauce on the crab... you name it, they got it wrong. We needed you here, Kate."

She squeezed her eyes shut and pinched the bridge of her

43

nose with two fingertips. "I'm sorry, Marco. I wanted to be there."

"I know, and I get why you couldn't be. But you have to understand, this is my business, my livelihood, and I can't risk it for a new menu that my staff can't deliver. I thought it was a good menu, and perhaps one day we can try it again with you at the helm, but it didn't work. Not this time."

She scrubbed a hand over her face. This couldn't be happening. "I'm really sorry to hear that Marco."

"So, can we expect to see you here on Monday?" His voice was gruff.

She could feel the tension pinching a nerve in her neck, and the headache that'd been building in the base of her skull reverberated through to her forehead. "Um... not Monday. I'm going to need to take a bit more time off. We've still got to arrange the funeral, and I'll have some loose ends to tie up. We don't know what Nan wanted to do with the inn yet, so I'll have to meet with her solicitor, then figure out a way forward."

He wasn't going to like it, but there wasn't much she could do about it. She hadn't prioritised Nan the way she should've while her grandmother was alive. She certainly wasn't going to make the same mistake after her death. The least she could do was to give Nan's final wishes her full attention.

"I see, well you know I need a chef in my kitchen, Kate. So, I'm going to have to put you on unpaid leave so I can hire a temporary replacement."

Her breath caught in her throat. "It's only for a week or two, Marco."

"That's fine, Kate. Take the time you need, but I have to replace you, the kitchen can't keep operating without someone in charge. I've been stepping in, but it's been a long time since I managed a kitchen and I'm a bit rusty. I need a pro in there."

She nodded silently, her eyes blinking. "I understand."

"Give me a call when you're ready to come back," he said.

When he hung up the phone, Kate lowered her pounding head onto the cool desk. After five years of loyal service, she'd expected more from Marco. Though knowing him as well as she did, she knew she shouldn't have. He was as cutthroat in business as he was pedantic. She'd never seen him show an ounce of sentimentality, why would she think he'd start now?

5

CABARITA BEACH

The waves in the cove chuckled as they drove and bubbled to shore. Sheltered by the outcropping of rocks at each end of the cove, and Castle Rock, they were never as rough or wild as the waves along Cabarita Beach itself. Those were waves that dragged in from the depths of the ocean and rushed at the sand as though launching an attack.

Kate watched them for a moment, the bottoms of her pants still damp from where she'd waded only moments earlier. This was one of the things she missed now that she lived in the city — early morning walks along the beach. And today she'd walked for hours.

It was mid-morning, and she'd taken her time, pushing herself until her breath came in hard, short bursts, then stopping to admire shells on the waterline, or dig up pippies with her toes in the wet sand. She'd shoved the pippies into her pockets, their wet, black shells rubbing together. When she

47

got back to the inn, she'd put them in a bucket and set them aside for later.

She felt an overwhelming urge to go fishing, something she and Nan had often done together when she was a kid. Nan loved to fish in the cove. She'd stand on the rocks at the end of the beach in her gumboots, or scramble to stand atop Castle Rock, and cast the line out as far as it would go. Then whistle or hum, while she waited for a fish to bite, casually dragging the line back in, one slow turn of the reel at a time.

Casting one last look at the ocean, Kate headed for the sandy, winding path that would take her from the beach, through the dunes and up to the incline to where the inn perched, overlooking the cove. Pop had built a set of custom, timber stairs for the last part of the climb, the steepest part that took the path up an embankment to the grassy hill beyond. He hadn't been the most talented craftsman. Still, the stairs were sturdy and perfectly aligned. He'd boasted they'd outlive him, and they had. Kate paused, puffing hard, on the second to last step, to run a loving touch over the handrail. She missed him, though it'd been so long she'd grown used to the feeling. Besides, there were so many more people to miss now, the ache had become familiar.

On her way back to the inn, she passed the chook shed. No one had let the chooks out yet, and they crowded the wire-mesh door, heads darting, feet strutting as they crooned and clucked in her direction.

"You want to get out, huh?"

Kate released the latch on the door, flicked it open and stood aside as the crowd of about two dozen chooks hurried out and set off around the yard to find things to peck. A bucket hung on the outside of the door, and there were a few remnants of chook food in the bottom. She reached in a hand and flung the seeds over the patchy ground. The hens darted in every direction, working frantically to consume as many of the seeds and grains as they could before they were gone. Kate hummed a quiet rendition of "Tenterfield Saddler", one of Nan's favourite tunes, under her breath, then laughed at herself. She didn't have Nan's steady alto voice, but the chooks didn't seem to mind.

They strutted around, the hen in charge chasing a few of the others away from a nice sized haul of seeds that'd all fallen together in one place. Kate watched them with a grin. Some things never changed.

Inside, Kate took a shower, washing off the sweat and salt from her beach walk. The hot water felt good against her skin, and she scrubbed her hair with shampoo, before standing in place to let the water pummel the aching muscles around her shoulders and neck.

She'd tried calling the restaurant the previous evening but hadn't been able to get a hold of Marco. When she called Davis, his assistant had told her he'd left the office for the day. Yet his home number went straight to the answering machine.

She felt so cut off from the rest of the world in Cabarita. The inn had a computer and dial-up modem, but she didn't know her grandmother's logon, so hadn't progressed far in her attempts to send emails. The stress of the funeral, living in the inn with her sisters, and not having contact with anyone from her life back in Brisbane was manifesting as tension in her shoulders. She massaged them with her fingertips and rolled her head from one side to the other.

Her plan for the day was to spend time in Nan's room in the hope of finding some photographs for the funeral, and possibly a copy of her will.

She dressed in a pair of black, stonewashed jeans and a long-sleeved blue and white flannel shirt, with her standard caramel Doc Marten boots. Then she ran a brush through her wet hair and headed down the hallway to the staircase. The second and third floors were crowded with guest bedrooms, but Nan's room was downstairs on the ground level. As the master suite, it was the only bedroom on that level, apart from the small room that jutted from one side of it, and the spacious suite had its own bathroom and walk-in closet.

She peered up toward the empty third floor, thought she heard a scratching sound in the roof, then with a frown of irritation skipped down the staircase to the ground level.

෨ඁ෪

NAN'S ROOM WAS DARK. THE DOOR WAS SHUT, AND WHEN Kate inched it open, it creaked, sending a pulse of adrenaline through her veins. She'd never spent much time in Nan and Pop's room. It'd always been something of a mystery to her and her sisters.

She'd snuck into the room once when she was playing a game of hide and seek with Bindi and Reeda. They'd searched everywhere for her and hadn't thought to look in the large, draughty room. It was so quiet and dim in there that she'd huddled, wide-eyed in the bottom of their closet. When a tree branch scratched against a windowpane, she'd leapt to her feet and run from the room screaming. When Nan found her, she'd buried her head in Nan's apron, wailing until finally she relayed what'd happened. Nan had laughed softly and stroked her hair until everything felt better. But she hadn't been back to Nan's room since.

Inside, it smelled musty. No one had cracked open the curtains since Nan passed, and it was colder than the rest of the inn, being located in the back, away from the sunlight that streamed through the windows on the other side of the building.

She stepped through the door and scanned the room, taking in the dark, timber, king-sized bed on one side, the small sitting area against the windows, with two armchairs and a round table between them. Nan's knitting hung over one arm of the chair, the latest shawl, scarf, or blanket she was working on. Kate couldn't remember a time when Nan would sit with idle hands, she always had something to do — knitting, crossword puzzles, reading the latest mystery novel, or scratching words in her unmistakable elegant cursive handwriting, into one of the black bound notebooks she carried around with her.

Kate's throat tightened as she walked to the armchair and fingered the rows of wool. Knit and purl, knit and purl. She remembered Nan's soft voice, as she'd sat once with Kate, patiently explaining the process to her. Kate hadn't taken to it, instead preferring to go outside and ride Janet. But Nan hadn't minded. She understood, she said. Little girls were meant to ride horses the way old women had to knit. She didn't make the rules, she'd said, she only followed them. Then she'd grinned and offered Kate a knowing wink before ushering her outside.

Next, Kate peeked into the bathroom. It hadn't been remodelled in at least twenty years. Bright orange curves looped over brown circles on wallpaper that Kate found difficult to focus her gaze on. She scrubbed both eyes with her fingertips, then wandered over to the bed. There was an armoire beside the bed, maybe she'd find something useful in there.

She tugged open one of the doors on the armoire and found a stack of photo albums, of all shapes, colours, and sizes, side by side, wedged into two of the shelves. *Bingo.*

She pulled one of the albums free, then two more, and carried them in a bundle back to the bed. Seated on the floor with the bed behind her, she opened the first album and began to thumb through it. There were photographs of her and her sisters when they were teenagers, living at the inn together.

Her on Janet's broad, bay back in a swimsuit and a pair of shorts, her hair wet against her scalp and Janet's coat dripping with sea water.

Reeda, sprawled and fast asleep in Pa's hammock, a book open on her chest, her eyes shut. Kate smiled — Reeda always had a book in her hands back then. She'd been more interested in reading than in outdoors adventures, something they hadn't seen eye to eye on.

Bindi, soaked to the bone, her wetsuit half shucked and hanging around her waist. Her yellow bikini top, tiny and without much to hold onto, bright against a backdrop of squat pandanus trees. Directly behind her, the brilliant red flowers of Nan's waratahs stood out. Bindi had a surfboard under one arm, and the other hand wrapped around the stem of a waratah flower. A grin lit up her young, freckled face.

Kate's chest tightened, and she bit down on her lower lip.

Memories washed over her, filling her throat with a lump. She inhaled slowly as the lump grew. When had she let herself forget about these moments? She'd gone on with her life, determined to make something of herself, and let the past stay where it was.

She rarely thought about that life, the one she'd left behind when she moved to the city all those years ago. And when she did, the nostalgia was tinged with so much pain that she'd pushed the thoughts down, squashed them until they were hidden deep in the recesses of her mind. But there'd been good times too, times like the ones in these photographs. She should remember them, hold onto them; the good times with Nan and her sisters. A season when life was a simple sequence of activities, instead of the ever-turning wheel of responsibilities, duty, and confusion that adulthood had brought.

Tears wound down her cheeks and she didn't stop them or wipe them away. Another page turned, more memories to jolt her away from the present and back to the past.

This time with Mum and Dad, and the old Ford Falcon station wagon they'd driven up from Sydney that one time over the Christmas holidays. They'd stayed for a whole month that year, one of the best times of her life. She traced the outline of Mum's face with the tip of one finger, tears still leaking from her eyes.

There was a knock on Nan's bedroom door and she glanced up in surprise to see Reeda's face poking through the gap. She wiped her tears with the back of a sleeve and forced herself to smile.

"Hi," she whispered.

Reeda grinned. "We wondered if you'd like a cup of tea with your snooping?"

The door swung wide and Bindi stood beside her, carrying three empty china cups, and a plate of Tim Tams. Reeda held a teapot and a potholder to set it on.

Kate chuckled. "That would be perfect. Thank you. And I'm not snooping, well not exactly. I'm looking for something to use at the funeral, some photographs or home videos. I thought I might see if I can find a copy of Nan's will, as well."

Bindi and Reeda joined her beside the bed. Reeda sat next to her and curled her long legs up beneath her. Bindi sat across from her, cross legged.

"Good idea," said Bindi.

"What's this?" asked Reeda, peering over Kate's shoulder.

"I found these photo albums. Look at this one of you eating an ice cream with Dad, it's run all down your chin."

Reeda laughed. "Wow, I'd forgotten all about that trip. That was a good holiday."

"It was the best," agreed Bindi.

"The last one at Cabarita with Mum and Dad before..." began Kate, then swallowed the rest of her words when her voice broke.

"Before the accident," finished Reeda, a muscle in her jaw clenching. She sighed and reached for one of the unopened albums.

"Let's see if we can find photos of Nan to use. I thought we might have one enlarged to set up on the beach, and maybe another one to print on the Orders of Service," Kate used her brisk, business voice to change the subject.

Reeda hated talking about the accident, it sent her into a mood. For the two years she lived at the inn with them after Mum and Dad died, if anyone brought up the topic of car accidents or anything to do with their parents, she'd disappear into her room and not talk to anyone for weeks at a time.

"You don't have to do that, you know," snapped Reeda, her eyes flashing.

"Come on, let's not..." began Bindi, in a conciliatory tone.

"I'm sorry," replied Kate, "I didn't mean to bring it up."

"I'm not going to break down," Reeda insisted. "I can talk about it."

"Okay. That's good to know." What could she say? How about the fact that every time they'd discussed it in the past, Reeda had disappeared into a haze of grief and anger?

"We all know why it happened, and after so many years, I think I can face it, face up to my part in it."

Bindi poured them all cups of tea with her eyes fixed firmly on the task at hand.

Kate's brow furrowed. "What do you mean, your part in it?"

Bindi handed around the teacups. "Aren't these cute?

Look at mine with the aqua-coloured flowers, and yours is pink."

Kate and Reeda ignored her, their gaze connected.

"I mean, the part I played in the accident. It was my dance eisteddfod. My fault we were out on that road at that time of night."

Bindi's gaze travelled from the cup in her hand to find Reeda. Kate's mouth fell open. "What?"

Reeda's voice broke. "Come on, everyone knows it, I know it. Let's talk about it like adults. It wouldn't have happened if it wasn't for me. They'd still be here, and everyone would be happy. You've both hated me for it ever since, don't pretend you haven't."

Bindi and Kate exchanged a horrified look.

"I don't hate you," began Bindi, her voice soft.

"How can you say that?" Kate's voice was full of tears.

A tear rolled down Reeda's cheek and she pushed out her chin. "It's true."

"You were seventeen years old, Reeda. It wasn't your fault, it was an accident," Kate sniffled.

Reeda rubbed the back of her hand over her cheek. "I know it was an accident, but if it wasn't for me..."

"And you were injured too," added Bindi. "You were there, you had to go to the hospital."

"I know. I remember," spat Reeda.

"It wasn't your fault," continued Bindi, laying a gentle hand on Reeda's arm.

"Definitely not," agreed Kate, looping an arm around her big sister's shoulders.

Reeda swallowed.

"I don't blame you for it. I worry about you..." said Bindi, her words soft.

Reeda blinked. "Really?"

"Yes, really," added Kate.

Bindi picked up another photo. "Do you remember this? We all rode our bikes to Coolangatta to see a movie, and you forgot your glasses, Reeda. You had to wear your sunglasses inside, since they were prescription."

Bindi held up the album and Kate laughed at the sight of the three of them, young, thin as rails and standing beside three beat up bicycles with wide grins splitting their faces in two. They'd asked a stranger to take the photo and had been relieved to see it wasn't blurred when they got the processed pictures back from the chemist.

"That was so fun," Kate said, remembering the feel of the wind on her cheeks and the honk of horns as cars passed them on the highway. "And dangerous."

Reeda tugged a tissue from the box on Nan's bedside table and blew her nose. "I remember. I couldn't see a thing. The movie theatre was so dark, and with sunglasses on, I only saw a flash of light every now and then. It was ridiculous."

They chortled together.

"That was right before you moved to Sydney to go to uni," added Kate.

Reeda inhaled slowly. "Yep."

"Everything changed after that," said Bindi, nodding her head.

"Again," confirmed Kate.

"Yes, everything changed again."

"Do you ever think that maybe we should've held on a little longer, a little harder?" asked Kate. How had they all moved on with their lives so quickly and forgotten about what they'd had together? Was the pain of their loss too much to look back on, or had they simply been excited to get started on a new adventure?

"All the time," whispered Bindi.

Reeda nodded. "I guess I wanted to make a clean break.

To put the past behind me. I couldn't go back and change anything. I felt responsible, whether it was right or wrong. I needed to move forward. And I haven't stopped since... always moving forward."

Kate's stomach clenched. What did Reeda mean? Sometimes she felt as though she didn't know the woman seated beside her at all, and other times she'd flash back to their childhood and feel a sense of complete understanding, as if they each knew everything about the other.

Behind Kate something sharp poked into the small of her back. While Reeda and Bindi continued scrawling through photographs, bent over an open album, she spun about to look under the bed. She pulled the patchwork quilt that covered the bed high enough to peer beneath. There were two squat lockable boxes shoved in there, and one small timber one. She tugged the timber box free and was grateful to see it didn't have a lock. She pulled up the lid to reveal three notebooks, like the kind Nan carried around in her apron pocket or scribbled in when she had some spare time in the breakfast nook.

There might be something helpful in one of them they could use at the funeral. She didn't have time to look through them right now, so Kate decided she'd take them back to her room and look through them later. She closed the lid and pushed the box to one side, admiring the carvings on the lid and sides — a horse on top and birds, in full flight around the outside. The box was chipped in a few places, and she'd had to tug hard to get the lid to come free. It was obvious the box had been around a long time; dust had settled into the crevices where someone's knife or implement of some kind had whittled the carvings in the wood.

Kate turned her attention back to the pile of albums, intent on finding a picture that summed up Nan's vivacious, adventure-loving personality in a single snapshot. How could you sum up a life with a couple of photographs and a few tearful words on a beach? It didn't seem possible, yet, somehow, they had to find a way to do it. They owed Nan so much, the least they could do was to plan her funeral well, and find a way to honour her final wishes, whatever they were.

🧩 6 🧩

CABARITA BEACH

Black clouds skidded across the sky. A sly wind whipped up suddenly, tugging Kate's hair into her face. She pushed it behind her ears and strode along the water's edge faster still. Her arms pumped in time with her footsteps, and her breath huffed in short gasps.

She wanted to make it back to the inn before the clouds opened above her head. It'd rained most days since she arrived in Cabarita. Today's sky threatened with a growl, and she picked up the pace to a jog as she made her way from the hard, wet sand and into the dry, soft sand, then up the steps toward the inn. Smoke curled from the chimney, the cool air fragrant with its acrid scent.

As she hurried past Nan's garden, she couldn't help noticing it looked a little drab. Most of the produce was dotted with splats of mud from the rainfall, some had been pummelled into the ground. The flower beds looked sodden and sad. No flowers this time of year and the greenery seemed patchy.

She stopped and rested both hands on the bleached timber fence to study the garden. It'd been Nan's pride and joy, and though Nan had only been gone a few days, the garden had suffered from neglect in that time. That, along with the cold and rain, had given it a haggard look. Not much of a gardener, Kate wasn't sure if the look was normal for a garden in the last month of winter, but she didn't remember ever seeing it look so bad before.

With one hand, she pushed open the garden's gate and stepped inside. She stooped to study some of the plants and noticed they looked as though they'd been cut off at ground level. She frowned, pressing her hands to her hips.

A fat drop of rain landed on her head and her head jerked upward to stare at the sky. This time a raindrop landed right on the tip of her nose. She shook it off, then broke into a run as the heaven's opened, pulling the gate shut behind her and heading for home.

Kate shook the raindrops from her coat and hung it on the coat rack inside the back entry. Mima was in the kitchen, a white apron tied around her waist, stirring something in a pot on the stove.

"Phew! It's wet out there," said Kate with a shiver. Then she peered into the pot. "What're you making?"

"Custard," replied Mima, "To go with the apple crumble that's in the oven."

Kate sniffed the air and her stomach growled. "Mmmm. That smells delicious. I can't wait."

Mima chuckled. "I thought we might like something hot to eat with the weather we've been having. Something to warm us, body and soul."

Kate sat on one of the worn timber bar stools that lined the other side of the bench, ran her hands through her hair and watched as droplets of water rained onto the off-white laminate surface.

"Something's been at Nan's garden. Half the plants have been eaten down to ground level," she said with a grunt.

Mima arched an eyebrow and kept stirring. The wooden spoon moved in a slow arc around the saucepan, never stopping. "It's probably possums."

"Mima, that reminds me: do you know if the inn has a rat problem?"

Mima's brow furrowed. "I should hope not!"

"It's just that I was upstairs in my room the other night and I heard a scratching sound in the roof cavity, and then something that could've been chewing — you know, on the timber beams."

Mima laughed. "Oh that, that's our ringtail possum."

"Our possum?" Did possums chew on timber?

"There's a possum living in the roof. She doesn't bother us, so we let her be."

"But she's chewing on the timber beams... that could be a problem." Kate ran a hand over her face. Well, wasn't that wonderful? Now she had a vermin problem to deal with as well, that was, if possums could be called vermin. Although, if one was living inside the roof and eating the inn piece by piece, that seemed to qualify her for the category.

"Don't worry about her, she won't eat much."

Kate stared at Mima in astonishment as the cook returned her attention to the pot on the stove. No wonder the place was falling apart, none of them seemed to care about keeping it all together.

Kate's mouth puckered. "Do we have any possum traps or anything like that around here? I can't believe it's eating up Nan's garden. She loved those plants, it's like... they're a part of her."

Mima shrugged. "She loved it, that's true. But Edie's gone, so if we want to keep her garden, someone is going to have to take it on, and it's a big job to keep something that size in shape. Even without the possums."

"How is it getting through the fence, that's what I want to know?" Kate groaned, then covered her face with both hands. It seemed everything was coming undone. Her boss was replacing her, her fiancé hadn't returned her calls, and now Nan's garden was dying right in front of her eyes.

It was that darned possum. If she could catch it, then it'd all be over. Nan's garden would survive, and she could focus on getting through the funeral and back to her life in Brisbane.

"There's probably a hole in the fence somewhere, you'll have to investigate."

They'd have to do something about that possum. They couldn't have her living in the roof cavity, chewing up the supporting beams, destroying Nan's garden. She was an outlaw living on borrowed time. And like all outlaws, this possum had a reckoning coming her way.

"What's got you so fidgety?" asked Mima as she moved the saucepan away from the heat and onto a cork pad.

Kate hadn't realised her fingers were drumming on the bench. She laced them together with a sigh. "I don't really know what to do with myself."

"Oh?" Mima chuckled. "Not a feeling you're accustomed to, I'd say."

"Not at all. My life is so full, so busy, I rarely have much time to do nothing. And when I do, it's usually after a long shift at work, and I'm exhausted, so I lay on the couch and watch television or read a book."

"Now there's an idea," said Mima with a wink. She checked on the apple crumble, then straightened, one hand pressed to her lower back, her face pinched.

"Are you okay?" asked Kate.

"My back is playing up. Nothing out of the ordinary.

Getting old isn't as much fun as you'd think." She winked again and Kate couldn't help smiling.

"It's just that, we don't know what's happening with the inn — we still haven't found Nan's will, or her solicitor. I really wanted to get everything sorted out before I go home." She hesitated. "And my sisters — we haven't spent this much time together in years. I don't feel like I know them anymore. Not really."

"Sounds like there's a lot going on in that head of yours," replied Mima, setting her hands on her hips. "If you ask me, you need to relax a little bit. It's good that you're spending some time here at the inn, saying your goodbyes. No one doubts Nan left the place to you girls. We'll find the will, but in the meantime, you should probably assume it'll be yours. And you *do* know your sisters — they haven't changed as much as you might think. You're all still the same little girls that used to visit and sit on my knee while I read Enid Blyton books to you or showed you how to make the perfect choc-chip biscuits, all those years ago."

She brushed a strand of wet hair from Kate's face with two bent fingers. "You're going to be fine, love. Just fine."

Something caught in Kate's throat and she swallowed, her eyes blinking back tears as memories swamped her. "I feel so lost."

Mima's arms wrapped around her and pulled tight. "You're not lost, love, you're grieving. It happens to the best of us. Grief makes us look in, to see if we're on the track we want to take. If we're not, we can adjust our course. Losing someone gives us back the perspective we need, if we let it."

Kate sobbed, her head spinning. She hadn't thought she was off track. The drive to succeed, to chase her career goals, to meet and marry the perfect man, all of it had been what she wanted. Those things *had* been her dreams. All she was doing was pursuing her dreams. Wasn't she? Something inside her tightened and made her want to cry harder. She inhaled slowly, then dabbed the tears from her eyes.

"I'm going upstairs to rest."

Mima beamed as if Kate had given her a gift. "Good idea. And when you come down for lunch, there'll be apple crumble with custard. Dessert makes everything better."

THE MATTRESS WAS SOFT, PERHAPS A LITTLE TOO SOFT, AND Kate flung herself from one side to the other, trying desperately to fall asleep. After an hour of restless thrashing, the bed looked like it'd been through a war zone and irritation burned in her chest. There was no point, she wasn't going to get to sleep no matter how tired she felt.

She swung her legs over the side of the bed. A scratching in the roof caught her attention. She glared at the ceiling, her eyes narrowed.

"That possum again," she hissed. Anger burned in her cheeks.

Her left calf muscle contracted and spasmed. She grabbed hold of it with a yelp of pain. Cramps happened often enough that she was used to them, but the pain always caught her by surprise when it first hit.

She slid onto the floor and got to work doing the stretches she always did whenever her calf muscles cramped up. Usually the cramps came while she was sleeping and jolted her out of a dream or deep REM cycle. This one wasn't so bad. It subsided quickly and soon was gone. Only a dull ache reminded her it'd happened at all.

She set her hands on the floor to push back up onto her feet, then noticed a small, timber box beneath the bed.

Nan's journals.

She'd forgotten she put them there. She tugged the box

from beneath the bed. A sliver of light fell through the curtains and lit up the box, highlighting its age and the dust motes disturbed by her movements, floating through the air above it. She leaned back to reach the curtains and tugged them fully open, flooding the room with daylight. The rain had stopped, yet still dripped from the gutters. Sunshine peeked between the clouds, and everything smelled fresh and new.

With her back pressed to the side of the bed, Kate opened the first journal. Inside the front cover was written a date.

1985 - 1993

She frowned, set down the book and opened another. This one was dated as well.

1967-1984

How far back did they go? With a gentle push, she upended the box and let all four notebooks fall to the floor. Something silver caught her eye. It dropped to the hard timber floor then rolled under the bed with a faint tinging sound. She set the box on the floor by the pile of journals and crouched low to peer under the bed. What was it? Something small, maybe a ring? She couldn't be sure; she'd only caught sight of it out of the corner of her eye.

With her head held as low as she could get it, she inched forward on her stomach, leveraging herself under the bed. It was a tight fit, and she huffed and puffed her way forward little by little until she could reach it if she stretched her arm out as far as it would go and held her breath. Her fingers closed around it and she let out a squeak of victory, unable to do more. Then, she backed out from beneath the bed, knocking her head on the side slat as she did.

She groaned and held a hand to her head as she sat up, pushed the hair from her eyes, and stared at the thing she'd recovered. It was a ring, but not like any she'd ever seen before. It looked homemade, and it didn't sparkle or shine but had a dull, silver look to it, and was tarnished with a brownish hue.

Why would Nan keep something like that? It was obvious the ring wasn't valuable, and yet there it was, in a carved timber box with her diaries. Kate pushed it onto her finger and found she couldn't get it past the knuckle on any but her pinky. With a shrug, she set it back into one corner of the box. Then, she stared at the pile of journals.

The bottom book had a black cover, like the ones she'd seen Nan carrying around. Another had a purple, floral cover. She reached for the most tattered book on the top of the pile. A few pages fluttered free when she opened it, and she did her best to put them back in place. The hard, dark-green cover was made of fabric and had frayed in places. The leaves of paper that filled the book were yellow and stained, and filled with Nan's looping scrawl, though the letters were less jagged than she remembered them being.

When she turned to the first page, the date set her heart racing.

1935-1950

As she calculated the figures in her head, her mouth fell open. If the dates were true, Nan would've been ten or eleven years old when she wrote the first words lining these pages.

She flicked slowly through the journal. Each page was covered in Nan's handwriting. Black ink scratched across the page in lines, filling front and back with words, dozens of exclamation points, and a few sketches.

Her heart in her throat, she turned back to the first page and began to read.

I went riding today. Eliza propped when I tried to send her up a hill.

She can be stubborn at times, but in the end, she gave up and did as I asked.

Mother made roast lamb for supper, which was a treat. I could do without eating mutton ever again in my whole life.

Tomorrow it will likely be rabbit stew since Bobby went shooting with Charles Jackson today. Charlie has the bluest eyes and smiles a lot when he talks to me.

I think I will be a hairdresser when I grow up. Mother says it's not a fit career path for a lady, but I think it would be nice to make people pretty and talk all day long. Still, there wouldn't be any horses, so maybe I'll have to think more about it before I decide...

❧ 7 ❧

JULY 1935

BATHURST

Edith Watson was ten years old and the best hack in the Bathurst area for her age. At least she was in her own mind, and that was all that mattered. Horse riding was the thing she loved more than anything else in the world. Well, besides Mother and Father. They were her parents, so she loved them most. Actually, according to the minister at their church, she was supposed to love God more than anyone or anything else. So, after God, Father, and Mother, she loved her bay mare, Eliza.

Eliza was a young horse, so of course that meant occasionally Edie lost her seat. With Eliza's disposition, anyone would. When Eliza decided to buck rather than gallop, even the best rider would be thrown. Father said so. At least she hadn't broken an arm like Arnie Merriweather, riding that big black thoroughbred with the white star on his forehead Arnie's father had bought at auction. She was certain it'd been a race-horse before it found its way to the Bathurst livestock auction, by the way it pulled at the bit whenever he tried to bring it to a stop.

Eliza clip-clopped up the hill behind the small, white timber farmhouse on a narrow trail, worn bare by sheep and horses over many years. Two days off from school. She'd ride as much as she could, though Mother would insist she help around the house. There was also a cross-stitch project Mother was pushing her to complete, though Edie couldn't see the point of it. Cross stitch didn't seem to her like a good use of her time, but according to Mother, every young woman should learn it. For some reason or other. Edie thought horse riding a far more valuable skill for anyone, young woman or not.

She raised a gloved hand to her face and rubbed a cheek. It tingled, numb from the cold. Mother didn't like it when she rode so early in the morning. She said it gave her dry skin and red cheeks. Still, it was the most beautiful time of the day to be outside, even if the air was so clouded by fog in every direction you could barely see what you were coming upon until you were there.

She heard the dogs rush someone on the driveway. There must be a visitor at the farmhouse. The dogs' baying echoed, caught in the thick, cold air. Eliza's ears pricked and she pranced a few skittish steps sideways.

"Hush, Eliza. It's nothing to worry about," she admonished.

She found her brother, Bobby, beside the house with his friend from town, Charlie Jackson. Charlie was twelve, but not much bigger than Edie herself. He and Bobby hadn't had their growth spurts yet, according to Mother, who liked to talk about such things with their neighbour, May Hobbes, when she thought Edie was busy with her cross stitch.

She pushed Eliza into a canter, steering her directly at the boys. Then, pulled her up when they drew close. Charlie had a rifle slung over his shoulder, one foot rested on the pedal of his bike, the other planted firmly on the ground.

"Hi, Edie," said Charlie.

She smiled, her chest tight. He always seemed to make her feel that way, a mixture of butterflies and breathlessness.

"Hi Charlie, where are you two headed?" She slid from the horse's back and threaded the reins over his head.

"Going shooting," replied Bobby instead, with a toss of his head. "Tell Mum, will you?"

"I'm not telling Mum, you tell her. She'll be mad as anything if you go out shooting without asking first."

Bobby groaned. "She knows I'm going, she's with the milking cow, and I don't feel like going over to the shed to tell her I'm leaving. Just tell her all right?"

Edie rolled her eyes, and she let out a huff of air. "Okay, jeez, I'll tell her."

Bobby ran around the side of the house and soon returned wheeling his bike. He slung a rifle across his back and climbed onto the seat. "See ya later."

Charlie's gaze met hers. "So, I suppose I'll see you tomorrow."

Edie nodded. "See you then, Charlie."

He grinned, his blue eyes sparkling beneath a long blond fringe and the cap of his wool hat, then he pushed off, peddling, his breath forming white clouds in front of his face.

The two boys cycled down the driveway together.

Edie watched them go, her heart jittering in her chest. Charlie seemed nice enough, but he made her nervous. She headed for the shed. Time to put Eliza away and go inside to thaw by the fire.

🌿 8 🌿

CABARITA BEACH

Kate chewed the end of the pen as she scanned the kitchen. The inn was a spacious, regal structure, and hadn't been renovated or painted in years. Jack was too old to be the only one responsible for the entire property's upkeep, and for some reason Nan hadn't taken the initiative to bring in anyone else. She couldn't help wondering why and had never thought to ask. Although she hadn't noticed before now how bad things had gotten.

The wide, timber floorboards were scuffed and in need of polishing. The paint was chipped and stained in places. There were scuff marks on the walls and some of the tiles that lined the kitchen above the bench were broken or had fallen away. The old stove seemed to be in decent shape, but the refrigerator and freezer were old and constantly emitted a loud buzzing sound at opposing pitches.

Mima sat at the kitchen table, a ledger book open in front of her, pen poised above it. She was putting together an order list for groceries for the week and told Kate she wasn't accustomed to feeding so few.

"Did you say you're doing a stocktake?" asked Mima.

"Um... yep." Kate studied the notebook she held in one hand, then scribbled a few notes.

"What exactly does that mean?" asked Mima.

"Well, we still don't know Nan's final wishes for the Inn, and I was talking to Davis last night about it — he suggested I write down everything I find around the property, so at least if we sell, which we haven't decided yet, we'll know exactly what we're dealing with."

Mima's lips tightened. "You think you'll sell?"

Kate inhaled a slow breath. She knew what it would mean for Mima and Jack and hated to put them in that situation. But if Nan left the inn to her and her sisters, then there was no way they could keep it. She didn't know how much the upkeep would cost, and none of them had the faintest idea of how to manage an inn, let alone the fact that all three of them lived in different cities. "We don't know for sure yet, but it's a definite possibility." She lay a hand on Mima's shoulder. "I'm sorry Mima, I know you and Jack both live on the property, but Reeda, Bindi, and I don't know the first thing about running the place, and even if we did, we don't live nearby. I'm not sure how it could work."

Mima nodded. "It's okay, love. Jack and I will find our own way, don't worry about us."

"Where does Jack live, by the way? I don't think I've ever seen his place?"

"He lives in a little cottage at the end of the cove. It's right on the edge of the property line. We have about ten acres of scrub land and beach front property here. It's a bigger parcel than most realise."

Kate spun the pen between her fingers, her lips pursed. For some reason she hadn't understood that. She'd always thought the property line only stretched as far as the horse paddock, down to the beach and back to the road.

"No wonder the place is so rundown. That's a lot for Jack to manage."

Mima chuckled. "Don't tell him that. He thinks he's still in the prime years of his life. Come to think of it, I do too, until I try to walk, and my hip gives me grief." Mima slapped her left hip and grimaced.

Kate wandered around the inn, peering into every room. The last of their guests had finally checked out that morning, so the entire place was empty, apart from the rooms she, her sisters, and Mima occupied. The housekeeper, Milly Wood, came from her home in Kingscliff each morning to clean, but was always gone by two o'clock. So, the only other person left on the property was Jack, and according to Mima his cabin was some distance from the inn. Kate was curious enough to want to take a look at it sometime. But for now, she had a job to do.

She wrote a list of furniture, guessed at room sizes, and noted the damage she found. She counted bedrooms and bathrooms and was surprised to recall that although the inn had eleven bedrooms, there were only three bathrooms. That was something guests wouldn't be too keen on when making travel plans in the nineties. And as far as the decor went, the inn was firmly stuck in the nineteen sixties.

By the time she reached the sitting room, she was on the third page of notes. She found Bindi and Reeda there, each holding a hand of cards.

Bindi stared at the cards, fanned out in front of her, feet extended to rest on an ottoman as she leaned back in an over-sized, tartan patterned armchair.

"It's your turn to make a move. Come on, you're the slowest card player I've ever seen in my life," complained

Reeda, slapping a hand to her forehead and slumping in her own matching armchair.

A small, round table stood between them, with a pile of cards in the centre.

"Wait a minute. I'm thinking."

Reeda groaned. Then, she caught sight of Kate. "Kate, can you please tell her this is not rocket science?"

Kate laughed. "What are you playing?"

"Twenty-One," replied Reeda with another groan. "Come on, Bindi. You're killing me."

Bindi poked out her tongue in Reeda's direction, then fixed her gaze on Kate. "What are you doing? You wanna join us?"

Kate pursed her lips. If she were being honest, one of the reason's she'd decided to do the stocktake now was so that she could avoid spending too much time with her sisters.

Time together almost always resulted in some kind of confrontation, and she wasn't up for it. There was too much going on, too many other things to think about and deal with. She couldn't take an argument on top of it all. Ever since they lost their parents, Reeda had grown a biting tongue. She used it to slice pieces from her sisters and Kate had shrunk from her, in response, widening the gap between them with every passing year.

"Ah... I'm making a note of everything in the inn. You know, in case we have to sell."

"Why would we have to sell?" asked Bindi, sitting straighter in her seat.

Reeda grunted. "Because, if Nan left it to us, we're hardly going to move to Cabarita to run an inn. Are we?"

Bindi shrugged. "Maybe. Maybe not."

"We don't have to make a decision yet, because we have no idea what Nan's wishes were. I'm going to call the solicitor today and make an appointment, if I can find him." Kate sighed, if only she'd shown a little more interest in Nan's life, maybe she'd know details like who wrote Nan's will. So far, a quick search of the office hadn't turned up any copies. Mima had checked the rolodex with no luck. She'd have to do a more thorough search later.

"I'll locate the solicitor," said Reeda, still eying her hand of cards. "Do we know his or her name?"

"All I know, is that he's a him, according to Mima. But she couldn't remember his name. He has an office in Kingscliff, but that's all I've got. I was going to do a more thorough search of the office to see what I could find after I've finished with the stocktake."

Reeda shrugged. "I can do it. No worries."

"Thanks."

"What should I do?" asked Bindi. As the youngest, she'd always been the one everyone else took care of, and whenever they were together, it was the role she naturally filled. Or was it that they naturally fell into the role of carer where Bindi was concerned?

"Maybe you could look over Nan's books... see how the place is going... you know, financially."

Bindi nodded. "Great, I'll get started as soon as I've crushed Reeda."

Reeda chuckled. "Good luck with that."

Finally done with her stocktake inside the building, Kate stepped outside. An empty saucer sat by the back door; a few drops of milk had spilled where the cat's tongue had slurped up the bowl's contents. Mima still didn't admit to owning the creature and only fed it when she thought no one was looking. Nan hadn't been a fan of cats and had banned them from the inn because of the way they killed the native wildlife, but Mima never could resist a pair of hungry eyes.

She held a hand to her forehead to shield her eyes from the glare of the sun. The first place she visited was the garden shed. It crouched dark against the patchy grass of the back lawn. Pandanus trees sprang up around it, branches held aloft like clutching hands. Beside the shed, a long, rectangular fence line marked out the space where Nan had spent so much of her time digging, planting, and tending her garden.

Kate stepped inside the garden shed. It had dark timber walls, faded by the sun, and rows of tools hung above sacks of fertiliser. Drums of what she knew to be chook food and compost, lined the back wall. She wrote down everything she found, as best she could. There were bags of seeds she couldn't identify, but most of the items in the shed were recognisable. And it was kept in good order, with everything neatly stacked and hung in its designated place.

Next, she made her way to the garden and looked out over the neat rows of dirt. Most waiting for the spring planting, some winter crops, like strawberries, onions, and peas, hugged the near end of the enclosure.

Kate's hands trembled as she clutched hold of the top of the fence. She half expected to see Nan, back bent as she pushed a trowel into the soft, sandy dirt. She'd straighten, press a hand to the small of her back with a grimace, then wave in Kate's direction. Only she wasn't there. A lump formed in Kate's throat and she swallowed around it.

The stables were her final stop, and she'd deliberately been putting off her visit. Janet, her horse from childhood, had passed on years ago. Ever since, she'd kept her distance from the stables. Not wanting to grow attached to the newer horses who filled the stables, taking the place of the animals she and her sisters had grown up riding. And besides, she hardly had time to spend with Nan, let alone go riding when she came home to the inn. Still, seeing the timber railings of the yard where she'd first learned to ride atop Janet's wide, bay back, and the stalls where she'd fed her carrots, oats, or the occasional cube of sugar when Jack wasn't watching, warmed her heart.

She'd missed the place more than she'd known.

Inside Janet's stall, stood a tall, chestnut mare with a long streak of white down the length of her head. Kate stepped closer and reached up a hand to stroke the animal's nose.

"Well, aren't you beautiful?" she whispered.

The horse nudged her arm, moving closer for more. Kate laughed, and ran a palm down her sleek neck. "I guess you liked that, huh?"

"Her name's Ginger. She's a biter, although she seems to like you. Is there something I can help you with?" The man's deep voice startled her.

She spun around to face him, guilt creeping through her chest. Why she should feel guilty for walking into Nan's stables wasn't clear, but something about the way his voice reverberated through the stalls made her feel as though she'd been caught out by the school principal.

"Uh hi," she said, extending her hand toward him. "I'm Kate Summer — Nan's granddaughter. Well, at least, one of them, anyway."

The crease lines on his forehead faded, and his lips pulled into a gentle smile. "Ah, right — of course. Pleased to meet you Kate. I'm Alex Cannon, I help Edie out... uh, helped Edie out with the horses." A flash of grief passed over his face but was gone before Kate could process it. Why had Nan never mentioned him?

He wore a long-sleeved, blue- and white-checked flannel shirt, with the top few buttons undone, and the sleeves rolled up to his elbows. A pair of snug, blue jeans hugged a pair of athletic legs and riding boots completed the ensemble. The Akubra hat perched on top of his head was pushed back and his light brown hair stuck up in all directions in front of it, wet with perspiration above a pair of intense, hazel eyes. He held a soiled rag in one hand.

"I'm sorry, I didn't know anyone was out here. I thought Jack was taking care of the horses."

He shrugged. "I've been doing it for a few years, but I'm not here all the time. Edie said she needed help, and I was looking for some casual work, so..."

"Maybe she thought it was all a bit much for Jack..."

He stared at the rag in his hand. "I was oiling the tack."

"Well, don't let me get in your way."

He nodded, raised the rag as a kind of wave and disappeared back into the storage room behind the stables. Kate stared after him, her eyes narrowing. She needed more information. After all, nobody had mentioned there was a man working in the stables, taking care of the horses. How had Jack and Mima both managed to gloss over that information?

She followed him into the storeroom. He stood beside a saddle stand, perched on top of a low bench. As she watched, he dipped the rag into a can and then ran it over the seat of a saddle that was balanced on top of the saddle stand.

"Um... actually, do you mind if I ask you a few questions? I'm doing a stocktake for the inn, and I thought you might be able to give me some insights about the horses."

He shrugged but kept his back to her. "Okay."

His wide shoulders almost taunted her. Was he being intentionally rude?

She inhaled a slow breath. "How many horses do we have on the property?"

He paused, then spoke over his shoulder. "Four. But one of them is old Zaney, and he's not really fit for guests to ride these days. Two of the others are getting on in years, and that chestnut you were patting, she's got a mean streak when it comes to strangers. She's all sunshine and sugar cubes when she's in the stable or the paddock, but set a saddle on her back and you'll find out soon enough how good your seat is... She's a lawsuit waiting to happen."

Kate frowned. "So, we have four horses, but only two that guests can ride?"

He nodded.

"Do we have tack for all four?"

Another silent nod, as he continued rubbing oil over the rest of the saddle.

Her lips pursed. It was like pulling teeth to get any information out of the man. "Okay, well thank you."

He faced her and crossed muscular arms over his chest. "The stables need work too. They're practically falling down. I found termites back there in the corner of the storeroom, and it won't be long before it'll be dangerous for the horses to stay in the stalls the way some of those boards have come loose."

His words had a tone of accusation, as though somehow all of this were Kate's fault. As though she was the reason the inn was in disrepair.

She nodded. "That's good to know. Thank you for your honesty. Unfortunately, I'm not sure what we can do about it right now. We don't know what the inn's future looks like, who will own it, whether it'll be sold or closed... it's pretty up in the air, and we don't have the money to sink into something that might or might not have a future."

His face registered understanding. "Oh."

"Is there anything you can do for now, you know, to keep things going?"

He shrugged. "I could do some of the repair work, if you want me to. I have a mate who works construction, he could probably get me timber offcuts."

"That would be wonderful. Thank you. I'll be happy to help out with whatever I can as well... while I'm here."

"How long are you planning to be here?" he asked, his hazel eyes fixed on hers.

She shook her head. "I don't know. Long enough to take care of everything, I suppose. I have to get back to Brisbane, back to my job and my fiancé."

"In that order?" he asked, a twitch in his cheeks, almost like he'd stifled a smile.

Kate's eyes narrowed. "No, not in that order." Now he was being downright rude. He didn't know her — didn't know anything about her relationship.

He held Kate's gaze for a moment longer, then turned back to the saddle.

"Okay, well I'll be here most afternoons. You can come and find me, help out, whatever you like. Doesn't matter much to me either way. I'll see what I can do about the repairs."

She studied his back, irritation burning in her gut, then marched out of the storeroom. Just before she was out of earshot, she heard him call, "Sorry about your grandmother. She was a real beaut lady."

❧ 9 ❧

BATHURST

The Carillon City Music Club will hold their September recital at the Red Rose café on Sunday evening next, and looking over the programme they have on this occasion gathered together a very fine array of artists, so that patrons should enjoy one of best programmes this progressive club have yet submitted to a music loving public (Town Tattle, The Bathurst National Advocate).

Edith Watson tugged the last rag from her hair and the strand rebounded into a long, blonde ringlet. She smiled at her reflection in the looking glass and turned first to the right, then to the left. Satisfied with what she saw, she smoothed down the skirt of her pale blue cotton dress.

She wished it could've been a light-grey silk gown like the mayor's wife wore to church last week. But silk wasn't for farmers' daughters, as Mother told her when they'd bought the bolt of cotton for her own dress. Her skirts were dotted with small, white flowers and the dress puffed lightly in the sleeves making her look older than her fourteen years. At least she thought so. It cinched tight at the waist, showing off her slim figure, or as Mother said, her hourglass. Though she didn't see much of an hourglass in her reflection. She was petite with narrow hips and thin limbs and hadn't changed much in appearance like so many of the other girls her age had. Mother had only sewn her a set of cotton brassiere's and camibockers to wear under her petticoats a year earlier.

"Edie, are you ready yet?" Mother's voice echoed up the narrow staircase.

"Coming, Mother!"

She gave her hair one last primp with her fingertips, then hurried downstairs, her black and white Oxfords clacking on the timber boards.

"We'll be late for the recital if we don't get moving. Father says he'll drive us to town in the truck. Isn't that a treat?" Mother's eyes sparkled as she adjusted the pins holding her curls in smooth waves around her face.

"Mother, you look beautiful." Edie stopped to stare. She never saw her mother dressed up this way. Even on Sunday mornings Mother wore three-quarter-length cotton or wool dresses to church with sensible coats and shoes that could walk the two miles to town and back, since Father said the horses needed to rest on Sundays too, and he didn't think it was right to drive the truck when they each had perfectly good legs to carry them.

"Well, well, there are times to make an effort, and I have to say this is one of them. I haven't been to a recital in years. You know, I used to play piano at recitals when I lived in Sydney as a young girl. But then I married your father... and well... I'm looking forward to it, I can tell you." Her cheeks coloured as she fidgeted with the seam of her ankle-length purple cotton gown. With ruching over the sleeveless shoulder straps, drawing into a smooth waistline that showed off Mother's curves, and a flowing skirt that almost brushed the floor, she looked to Edie like a princess.

She leaned forward to kiss her mother's rosy cheek.

"Come, my darling girl, grab your coat. Let's see if your father is ready to drive us into town."

Her mother wasn't much for affection or making a fuss. Still, the pink in her cheeks gave away her pleasure at the compliment and the kiss.

"Bobby! We're leaving. You know where your tea is, don't you?"

Bobby's head poked around the doorway from the lounge room. He yawned. "Yeah, I know."

"Yes," replied Mother. "Not yeah."

Bobby huffed, but not loud enough for Mother to hear. "Yes, I know where tea is, and I know how to heat it up when Father comes in."

"Why aren't you outside helping him with the fence line?" Mother's brow furrowed.

"I hurt my foot when I was digging a hole for a fence post earlier." Bobby's face crumpled into a grimace that was convincing enough for Mother.

"Fine. Do you need me to get the first aid?"

He shook his head. "I'm resting it."

"All right. We might be home late, so please, go to bed."

When Mother turned away, Bobby pulled a face at Edie who poked out her tongue and crossed her eyes. He giggled softly against the palm of his hand. Then waved. She waved back and followed Mother out the front door as they shrugged into their overcoats.

When they reached the *Red Rose café*, people were already lining up at the door. Most arrived on foot, since they lived in town, and nothing in town was very far from anything else. A few pulled up to the café on bicycles and left them leaning against the outside of the café before joining the line to buy a ticket.

A bubble of excitement welled up inside Edie. She shivered against the chill spring air as a breeze gusted up the street, then died down again just as fast. She'd brought a cardigan with her to wear inside but had no intention of putting it on if she didn't have to. The dress was new, and she planned to show it off.

A hand squeezed her arm, followed by a squeal of delight. She spun to face her best friend, Jemima, with a grin.

"I can't believe it. You're actually here, for something other than school and church," declared Mima in a conspiratorial whisper.

"Shhh Mima..." admonished Edie with a giggle. "Mother will hear you."

"I'm serious, it's like you're a prisoner out on that farm. I miss having you around. It's boring, I need you. When are you going to be allowed some independence?" Mima pushed out her lower lip.

"Well, I'm fourteen now. So, if I ask Mother can I ride the bicycle to town on my own, I think she might let me. I haven't been game to ask yet. But she agreed to the recital, so you never know."

Mima linked her arm through Edie's as the line began to move forward. They stepped in time together.

"Hello, Jemima," said Mother, her tone more school-ma'amish than usual.

"Hello, Mrs. Watson. How are you on this fine evening?"

Mother arched a perfectly plucked eyebrow. "I'm well, thank you, Jemima. How is your mother?"

"She's wonderful, thank you. She's a few people ahead of us in the line."

"Oh really? That's lovely, would the two of you like to sit with us for the show?"

Mima nodded. "We would love that."

As Edie and Mima walked into the ballroom behind the Red Rose café together her pulse quickened. The lights were dim, and people were filing through the rows of seating, looking for a place to sit, smiling, greeting one another, and exclaiming over the chandelier, the plush carpet or the brocade on the deep red curtains that shielded the stage.

They found their seats on the left side of the room. Only three rows separated them from the front row where the performers sat with the event organisers. Edie and Mima discussed everything they saw. They marvelled over the location of their seats, the beautiful dress worn by one of the performers, the number of people in the audience, and the delight of having an entire Sunday afternoon of music and performance, with the best part being that they were seated together, hand in hand.

"I can't believe your father let you come to a recital on a Sunday afternoon," whispered Mima, as she squeezed Edie's hand.

Edie nodded. "I know. I can't believe it either. But Mother said she wanted to do it, and you know he never tells her no. Not for anything."

Mima laughed softly. "Your mother is an impressive woman. One day I'll have to ask her how she does that."

"Do you think you'll get married someday?" asked Edie, suddenly serious.

Mima frowned. "Of course I will. Why on earth wouldn't I get married?"

"No reason. I'm sure you will. I'm not sure I want to... you know, marry someone." Edie sighed and tipped her head to one side. "I think instead I'll train and breed horses, and I'll become world famous for my amazing Andalusians. Or maybe I'll be a scientist and discover a cure for something."

"Amazing Andalusians? That sounds like a great name for a stud farm." Mima laughed.

Mother shushed her, and she clapped a hand over her mouth.

"Well, you can train horses, and I'll get married and have a dozen babies, and whenever I need help with them, I'll call for you," decided Mima with a determined nod of her head.

"Sounds just about perfect to me," said Edie with another sigh.

Edie scanned the room. It was practically full, and the large, round clock on the wall showed that the recital would begin in a few minutes.

She recognised most faces in the room. There were kids from school, half the Baptist church was there, as well as her teacher. She frowned. It was strange to see Mrs. Flannigan out of the classroom and wearing her hair in soft waves around her face, rather than in the severe bun she usually sported.

"Mrs. Flannigan is here," she hissed.

Mima's eyes widened. "What?"

She spun in her seat to see where Edie was looking, then faced the front with a wrinkled nose. "Ugh. Do you think she can make me write lines if we're not in school?"

Edie chuckled. "You do write a lot of lines, that's for sure."

"She finds some excuse to get me to write lines every single day. And it's really for nothing at all. Sure, I talk... a little bit. But everyone talks. That's why we have mouths. So we can talk." Her voice grew louder with each word.

Mother glared at her, then raised a finger to her lips. When she faced the stage again, Mima rolled her eyes.

"I think we have mouths for eating and breathing, not only for talking," said Edie with a giggle.

"Oh yeah, those things too." Mima laughed. "But talking is way more important than any of that."

Edie looked over the crowd again, noting that everyone had taken a seat now. The chatter died down and people waited expectantly for the first performer to take the stage. Just then, her gaze landed on a familiar face. It was Charlie Jackson, Bobby's friend. The one who stopped by their house on his bicycle whenever the two of them wanted to go shooting, or swimming in the river, or any of the number of things they got to do together.

It wasn't fair how much freedom boys had compared to girls. She'd pointed that out to Mother once and had received the same old speech she always did about how life wasn't fair, and she shouldn't expect it to be. It still didn't explain why Bobby got to do what he liked, and she didn't.

Charlie's eyes connected with hers in that moment, and she got a funny feeling in her stomach. Her heart skipped a beat, and she tried to look away but found she couldn't.

He smiled and tipped his head in her direction. He was sixteen years old now and had shot up in the last year. She wouldn't be surprised if he was taller than Father already.

She offered a shy smile in return, then spun in her seat to face the front, her heart hammering. His blue eyes and dimpled cheeks gave him a mischievous look, and there was something about the way he stared at her that made her feel as though he could see right through her.

"What's wrong?" asked Mima, her forehead creased with concern.

"Nothing," Edie replied. She glanced back over her shoulder again and found him still watching her. He smirked and she jerked back to face the stage, her cheeks blazing.

Mima shot her a suspicious look. "What is going on with you?"

"Just anxious for the music to start," sputtered Edie.

She'd seen and talked to Charlie Jackson dozens of times in her life. Still, something about him had changed. And the way he'd looked at her... the memory of it dragged a shy smile across her lips.

TWO VOCAL DUETS, A PIANOFORTE PERFORMANCE, AND A sestetto later, Edie was finding it difficult to pay the recital her full attention. She loved listening to music, but people watching was far more fun. She'd spied the mayor's wife, sporting a signature silk gown, this time in a pale green. She wore a fur stole around her neck, and her hair shone under the chandelier's golden light as though it had been doused in lanolin or some kind of oil.

Next, she'd watched as old Mrs. Peterson flirted with one of the young men in the row behind her, her hat tipping dangerously to one side with each attempt. The man's cheeks from where Edie sat, seemed to have taken on a permanently red hue, which tickled her funny bone. No one but the man seemed to mind, since it was common knowledge that Mrs. Peterson had lost her marbles years earlier.

Even as Edie let her attention slide from person to person in the rows ahead of her, she resisted the urge to look back over her shoulder again, to see what Charlie was up to. Was he engrossed in the recital, or watching the people in front of him like she was? Watching her, perhaps.

Her stomach twisted into a knot, and she wriggled in place. Mima shot her a curious look, then peered back down the aisle as though hoping to spot whatever it was that was making Edie so uncomfortable.

Edie leaned toward Mima, to whisper into her ear, one hand cupped to the side of her friend's head. "Don't you think Charles Jackson is looking more handsome than usual?"

Mima's mouth curled into a grin. "Ah, that's who you're looking at. I was wondering what had you all hot and bothered. And yes, he's always been attractive, but getting more so every day, I'd say."

"Really? *Has* he always been attractive?" Edie frowned.

Mima laughed. "You must be the only girl in Bathurst who hasn't noticed." Then she hugged Edie's arm tight. "That's one of the things I love about you."

A woman on stage began an elocution performance, her lips forming round sounds with wide exaggeration and tempting Edie and Mima to giggle uncontrollably which they hid by burrowing their heads together with mouths covered, when the evening's compere, a rotund man with a bald pate and round spectacles balanced on the bridge of his bulbous nose, paced to the centre of the stage. He took hold of the microphone and tapped it with the end of his finger, interrupting the performance with a nod of his head.

"Good evening, ladies and gentlemen, the time is ten past nine, and though we only have a few minutes to go until the end of our programme, I'm afraid I must interrupt."

He cleared his throat as two women, dressed in smart, grey suits, carried a small table holding a wireless radio onto the stage. Edie straightened in her seat and sat as high as she could to peer over the audience members in front of her. She glanced at Mother, who looked at her with a frown, then shook her head as if to say she had no more idea of what was going on than Edie.

The man continued. "In approximately four minutes' time, the Prime Minister of Australia is to make an important announcement. It is my belief that each of you present tonight would wish to hear this broadcast, and so I have arranged for it to be transmitted through this microphone."

The crowd stirred and a murmur rose up, growing louder by the moment. One man from the crowd yelled over the group. "What is it? What's happened?"

The compere shushed everyone with a few waves of his hands and shook his head. "Please, everyone, settle down. The broadcast is about to begin, and we don't want anyone to miss it."

He held the microphone down to the radio's speakers, and the familiar crackle of a radio transmission filled the ballroom. The sound of a radio announcer's voice crooned in the background. One of the women twisted a knob on the front of the device, and the voice boomed out.

"Here is the Prime Minister of Australia, the Right Honourable, RG Menzies."

EDIE INCHED FARTHER FORWARD UNTIL SHE SAT PERCHED on the lip of her chair, her eyes and ears trained on the radio. She loved hearing the Prime Minister speak. His voice always sent a thrill down her spine and gave her arms goose pimples.

"Fellow Australians, it is my melancholy duty to inform you, officially, that in consequence of a persistence by Germany in her invasion of Poland, Great Britain has declared war upon her, and that as a result, Australia is also at war.

No harder task can fall to the lot of a democratic leader than to make such an announcement.

Great Britain and France with the cooperation of the British dominions, have struggled to avoid this tragedy. They have, as I firmly believe, been patient. They have kept the door of negotiation open. They have given no cause of aggression. But in the result, their efforts have failed. And we are therefore as a great family of nations, involved in a struggle that we must at all costs win, and that we believe we will win."

THE ENTIRE AUDITORIUM HELD ITS COLLECTIVE BREATH AS the sombre voice continued, explaining the events of the past few weeks and how there was no other option than the declaration of war.

By the time Menzies had finished, Edie could hear sobbing in some quarters of the room. A few men stood and paced back and forth, up and down the centre aisle, their hands on their hips, waistcoats showing. Then, as the broadcast came to a close, suddenly everyone was on their feet and making their way toward the exit.

Edie reached back for Mima's hand but was disappointed to find she could no longer see her friend.

Buoyed along by the crowd, she figured resistance would get her nowhere, and let herself be half carried, half pushed along the aisle and out through the doorway. She stumbled and almost fell but clutched onto the back of someone's jacket to steady herself. She sobbed as panic churned in her gut. She couldn't lose her balance, she'd be crushed. As she stepped over the threshold and out into the cool night air, she found herself looking into Charlie Jackson's wide blue eyes. He reached for her hand, covered it with his own and led her away to one side of the group and out of the crowd, pushing ahead of her to clear a path.

When they reached the café's stout brick wall she fell against his chest, sorrow sweeping over her.

"You're all right now," he said, patting her back. "We'll find your mother in a moment."

She stared up at his face through a mist of unshed tears. In response, a half grin split his lips and dimples danced in each cheek.

"Thank you," she whispered.

He gave her a nod. "Can't have you crushed underfoot, can we? Bobby would never let me hear the end of it."

She laughed softly and wiped her eyes with the handkerchief she kept in her skirt pocket. "Can you believe it?"

His smile faded. "What... war?"

She nodded, still dabbing at her eyes.

"I guess it was coming," he said.

"I guess so."

"It's too bad I'm only sixteen, they won't let me enlist." A muscle in his jaw clenched. "But if I could go, I'd sure let that Hitler know what we think of people like him."

She pushed the handkerchief back into her pocket. "Well, I'm glad you're too young. I wouldn't want you to go."

"You wouldn't?" he asked, his eyes gleaming.

She shook her head, her cheeks warming even as she shivered.

He smiled, removed his jacket, and slipped it around her shoulders. "I hope we'll be able to see each other again soon."

Her heart thudded as blood rushed to her face. "I'd like that."

10

AUGUST 1995

CABARITA BEACH

It rained all morning long on the day of the funeral. Big fat raindrops pelted against the inn's tin roof like a drumroll before an announcement. Kate stood on the verandah and stared out through the wattle bushes toward the beach. The cove was hidden from view, but when the rain stopped, she knew she'd be able to hear the steady roar and crash of the waves against the shore, as always.

The waves were reliable, constant, never ceasing. They remained unchanging through joy and sorrow, heartache, grief, and celebration, kept on crashing against the sand no matter what state her heart was in.

"Not a great day for a beach funeral service," muttered Reeda, coming up beside her with two mugs of coffee. She handed one to Kate.

"Thanks."

Kate took the cup and held it to her lips, then sipped. The heat of it burned the tip of her tongue, then warmed a trail down her throat and into her stomach.

Bindi joined them. "I thought I might go for a run this morning," she said.

Kate's nose wrinkled. "Uh huh."

"You may have to wade back." Reeda chuckled before gulping a mouthful of coffee. "Ouch! Hot!" she sputtered, wiping drips of coffee from her T-shirt.

"I don't know, it might be a good idea. We could work off some of our frustrations," replied Kate.

"What frustrations could you possibly have?" grumbled Reeda, still dabbing at the stain on her shirt. "Perfect fiancé, fancy chef position at an amazing restaurant, and the same athletic figure you had when you were eighteen years old without having to work for it."

Think again.

Was that really how Reeda saw her? All these years she'd felt as though she'd never measure up to Reeda's impossible standards of perfection. It was why she never told her sister when things went wrong in her life, or if she was feeling low. It would've been another flaw to reveal how imperfect she was, how she'd never be like Reeda.

"Ha! My life perfect? Hardly. You're the one who looks like a super model, with all your designer outfits and shiny hair that hangs perfectly straight down your toned back."

Bindi shook her head. "You two were always so competitive. How about you both accept that each of you is amazing, beautiful, and talented, and that life isn't a competition but a journey we take together. Huh? Do you think you can do that? At least for today..." Her voice broke and she set her coffee cup down on the floor by her feet, then laced an arm around each of her sisters, hugging them to her sides.

Kate couldn't speak. Tears pricked her eyes. Her heart hurt to think that Reeda had so misunderstood her all these years. Perhaps she'd done the same to her sister.

"Okay, I can agree to that," replied Reeda with a quiet nod.

"Good, let's go for that run together," Bindi said. "Then, we'll just have time for a shower before the funeral."

Kate cleared her throat. "Do we know how many people are coming?"

Bindi's lips pursed. "I have no idea. I asked Mima about it, and she shrugged. Could be just us, or maybe some friends from town... it's hard to say. It's Monday after all, so most people are probably at work."

They all changed into bike shorts, T-shirts, and joggers and headed out into the rain. The run was good for Kate. It'd been so long since she'd done much in the way of exercise, other than climbing the stairs to her unit when the lift was broken, she had to ask the others to stop three times while she caught her breath.

Still, it felt good to stretch out her legs and push her body to perform. By the time they got back, she'd made a resolution to do it more often. Or maybe take her bike out of the storage cage in the building's shared garage, and ride the bike trails from Kangaroo Point, through Southbank and South Brisbane. She'd ridden them often enough when she first moved to Brisbane, but the busyness of her life had gotten in the way since. Maybe it was time to get back into some of her old habits.

She headed for the communal bathroom on the second floor and jumped into the shower ahead of Reeda, who complained loudly all the way up the stairs to the third-floor bathroom that it wasn't fair since she'd called first dibs. The heat of the water thawed the cold of the rainy outdoors that'd seeped into her bones despite the exertion.

By the time she'd donned a long, black dress and combed her hair into a neat bun, she'd let her thoughts wander to Nan, and saying goodbye. As she finished applying makeup, she noticed red splotches on her neck. The rain had tempered the cool of the day, but there was still a chill wind and they'd likely get wet during the service. She threw on a black cardigan over the top of her dress, and a long, blue scarf that she wound around her neck.

Downstairs, people were already starting to arrive for the funeral. A fire roared in the hearth, pushing the cold, wet, weather back onto the verandahs. Some of the mourners dried themselves by its warmth, hands outstretched toward the leaping flames hidden behind a black grate. Many had brought casserole dishes, warm from the oven, or bunches of flowers. Kate, Reeda, and Bindi all warmed their faces with smiles and moved to greet each person as they walked through the inn's front door, leaving umbrellas to drip dry on the verandah, propped up against the wall and railings.

The service was set to start at eleven. By ten forty-five the sitting room at the inn was full of mourners and the rain had stopped. Beams of sunlight peeked out from behind a black, voluminous cloud and crept over the dripping landscape. They hadn't known how many to expect, but none of them were prepared for the dozens of faces that peered at them over cups of coffee and shot glances their way above plates piled high with the Anzac biscuits, slices of apple tea cake, and scones with jam and cream Mima and Kate had baked together the previous day.

"I hope I'm not late," said a voice, startling her out of her worrying over whether they'd made enough food for the rapidly expanding group of mourners.

Kate looked up into Alex's hazel eyes. He held a bouquet of waratah flowers toward her. They were bright red with soft greenery, and nothing holding them together but a piece of white string.

She smiled and took the flowers. "Wow, thank you. Where did you get these?"

He cocked his head to one side. "I have a greenhouse. It's no big deal."

"You have a greenhouse?"

He was full of surprises.

"I knew these were her favourites, since she gave me the seedlings when I first started working here. I hope you like them." He was awkward, shifting from one foot to the other. His hair was combed to one side, slicked into place. He wore a black, button-down shirt with a pair of blue jeans and black leather boots that looked better suited to riding a Harley Davidson Hog than a horse.

"This is perfect. Thank you." Kate's throat closed over and she willed herself not to cry.

He nodded then manoeuvred his way through the crowd. She watched him go. The flowers were a simple gesture, but it'd touched her in a way she hadn't expected.

When she turned away, she came face to face with a group of her own friends from Brisbane. She embraced them each with tears in her eyes. It felt good to have a little piece of home there with her for the day. They offered her their sympathies and several bunches of flowers which she added to the display.

The service began at eleven as planned. The pastor of the local Baptist church, where Nan had attended since they first moved to Cabarita, officiated. He was an older man and seemed to know Nan well, sharing some heartfelt stories that made all three of the girls cry.

When it came time to give the eulogy, Reeda spoke first, then Kate and finally Bindi. Kate held back the tears until her turn was finished, then sobbed while Bindi spoke. By the time they'd all eaten and told everyone goodbye, each of their faces was red and streaked with tears and mascara. The inn looked as though it'd survived a cyclone, with the remaining food in scattered piles throughout the kitchen, on benches and tables. There were a few half-empty casserole dishes left on the floor.

Mima dabbed at her eyes with a handkerchief and lowered herself into a chair at the end of the long, ageing dining table with a grunt. "Well, that was beautiful. Edie would've loved it. The way you girls spoke was the sweetest thing, and then all three of you holding the urn and scattering her ashes... well, there wasn't a dry eye anywhere on that beach."

"I'm glad the rain stopped long enough for the service," replied Kate, peering out through the windows. As soon as the service ended the downpour had resumed. Rain lashed against one side of the inn, thoroughly wetting the verandahs and windows, and pummelling the roof in a loud and steady rhythm.

"We don't often get rain like this in August," said Jack, breaking the silence he'd kept for most of the day. "All I can think is that the world is crying with us." His silver hair was combed neatly to one side, missing his signature hat and the permanent impression it generally left on his head.

Kate's throat ached and tears filled her eyes again. She'd thought they'd run dry by now. She patted Jack's arm, while his reddened eyes stayed trained on the ground ahead of him.

Jack cleared his throat. "Well, I'd help you ladies clean up, but I've got to get the chores done. The animals will want to eat, rain or not."

He found his hat on the coat rack, pushed it onto his head, waved quickly and stepped outside, tugging the collar of his knee-length oilskin coat up high around his ears.

"Emotions make him uncomfortable," said Mima with a smile. "Well, not all emotions, but today — this is hard for him."

"For all of us," agreed Reeda, wiping her own eyes with a tissue.

"Let's clean up, then go sit on the verandah and watch the rain," suggested Bindi.

They got to work, tidying and cleaning until the place gleamed. Then they wandered out to the verandah with a pot of tea.

Kate slumped into a wicker chair, setting her feet on a footrest with a sigh. Her feet ached, her legs were tired, her head throbbed, and her hands were wrinkled by dish water.

She squeezed her eyes shut and let her head loll back. "I feel as though I've been run over by a truck."

Bindi laughed. "Me too." Then her face fell. "Does anyone else feel bad when they catch themselves laughing?"

Mima shook her head. "Oh pshaw, don't worry about that. Your Nan loved to laugh more than anyone. She wanted you girls to be happy. I know that because she talked my ear off about it more times than I care to remember."

Kate exchanged a smile with Reeda.

"Where was Davis today?" asked Reeda.

Kate inhaled a sharp breath as a pang went through her gut. She'd tried not to focus on the fact that her fiancé hadn't made it to the funeral. She hadn't heard the phone ring, although it was possible he'd tried to call, and she'd missed it with everything that was going on.

"I don't know," she said. "I'm going to call him in a little while. Maybe he got caught up with work, or something."

"I'm sure he wanted to be here," said Bindi, reaching out to rest a hand on Kate's arm.

"Well, forget him. And forget Duncan too," Reeda said. "He had surgeries scheduled that he couldn't move, he said. I told him it was important to me, and he reminded me that his patients sometimes wait six months to see him, so it wouldn't be fair to them."

"What a selfish jerk he is," quipped Bindi, winking an eye in Reeda's direction.

Reeda laughed. "I know. Isn't he?"

Kate thought Reeda's laugh sounded forced and that her smile faded a little faster than it usually did. Or maybe she was imagining things.

"Well, let's forget all about them, and talk about something else," Kate suggested.

"Hear, hear," replied Bindi, straightening in her chair, and crossing her legs in front of her on the seat.

"How long are you planning on sticking around?" Kate asked, her gaze travelling from Bindi's face to Reeda's and back again.

Bindi shifted in her seat. "I thought I might stay awhile. We still haven't found Nan's will, or figured out what to do with the inn..."

"Yeah, I'm not ready to go back to Sydney yet," agreed Reeda. She swallowed. "Maybe after we find the will. If we sell, I might stick around to help get the place ready for buyers... either way, I'm needed here. What about you?"

Kate shrugged. "I thought I'd head home in a few days. But maybe you're right. We should find the will first and make our decisions while we're together. It's hard to work things out over the phone. Face to face is better."

Bindi's shoulders relaxed and Reeda's lips pulled tight. Kate was surprised both her sisters wanted to stay at the Waratah longer. Whenever they met up for Christmas or holidays at the inn, Reeda usually flew back to Sydney the first chance she got. She didn't seem to be able to unplug from her business. For some reason, things were different now. Perhaps it was because Nan's death had been so sudden, all of them needed time to mourn.

"I remember when your Nan was only fifteen years old and the two of us decided we were going to sneak out to meet up in the middle of the night." Mima shared her thoughts, as she reached into the basket by her feet and picked up her knitting needles and yarn. Soon, the needles clacked between her fingers.

Kate leaned forward, a smile tugging at the corners of her mouth. "Really? I can't imagine Nan doing anything like that."

Mima laughed. "Oh, we got up to plenty of mischief, don't you mind about that. Still, you're right, it wasn't like her. Edie was a good girl. She had strict parents, who brought her up to mind her manners, respect her elders and do what she was told. But then something happened in her teenage years that lit a fire in her gut. When I suggested to some of our friends we meet for a moonlit get together, I never imagined Edie would agree to come with us."

Reeda's eyes flashed and she rested her chin in one hand. "Nan the rebel."

Mima nodded, her eyes on her knitting. "And you have to remember, Nan didn't live in town like we did. Oh no, she lived two miles outside of town. Which meant, she'd have to ride, alone, through the countryside in the dead of night, all the way into Bathurst."

Bindi shivered, and hugged herself, wrapping her arms around her jumper-clad body.

"That seems a bit crazy, even in this day and age," said Kate. "I'm not sure I would've done that, and I didn't have the strict parents she did."

"She was so determined. If she decided she was gonna do something, there wasn't anything or anyone who could convince her not to. Well, except maybe one, but that's a different story for another time."

Before Kate could interrupt, Mima went on. "She snuck out of the house after she was certain everyone else was asleep. She had a horse that she rode, and she competed in hack, show jumping, dressage, you name it. She was a keen horsewoman and loved that horse of hers. So, she saddled up and rode to town. And we had a great old time. We laid out on a picnic rug, about six of us, and gazed at the stars. We counted how many falling stars we could see, and we joked and laughed and talked about the future." Mima sighed, her fingers stopped their hurried movements, and she stared off into the distance. "It was a wonderful night."

"Were there any boys in this group?" asked Reeda with a smirk.

Mima grinned. "I'll never tell."

Kate giggled. "Oh... Mima, now we're interested. You have to tell. Did Nan have a boyfriend?" Her thoughts wandered to the diary entry about Charlie Jackson. Could it have been him?

Mima's eyes glazed over. "She always had one or two of the boys interested in her. She was a beautiful girl, our Edie. When it came time for her to go home, one of the boys decided it would be gallant of him to walk home with her. But she said no, it'd be much quicker with her riding on her own, and besides she'd suddenly realised how late it was. Her father was a farmer and she knew he'd be up before the sun. If she didn't get moving, he'd catch her out of her bed, and then there'd be hell to pay."

Mima stopped talking, her attention returned to her knitting, brow furrowed.

Kate exchanged a glance with Reeda. "So, what happened?"

Mima startled, as though her thoughts had been interrupted. "Oh my, I was in the middle of something... where was I?"

Kate and Reeda's gazes met. How often was Mima forgetful? None of them knew since they weren't around often enough. Maybe it was the stress of the day.

"You were talking about how Nan rode home alone in the dark, after a night out with friends," replied Kate.

"Ah, yes. Well, she rode home as fast as that horse would carry her. Of course, I didn't find out until the next week what'd happened, because we didn't see each other. But she said she could see the sun rising behind her because it lit up the plains around her with a golden light that set her heart racing. She knew what she'd find when she got home, but she couldn't stop. She had to keep going and hope against hope she'd be able to sneak by her father. Although with the horse to put away, she couldn't say how that would happen."

Bindi chewed on the end of one fingernail, her eyes wide. Kate imagined Nan galloping along the edge of a narrow, deserted road through seemingly endless fields of still, gold-tinged grasses.

"When she got home, she slipped off the animal's back and crept around the outside of the house. She put the horse away in the stable, rubbed her down as quick as can be, stowed away the tack, and then tiptoed through the yard. She was almost there when she heard her father's voice behind her, say, 'Where have you been, my girl?'"

Kate's breath caught in her throat. "Was she in trouble?"

"Oh, you better believe it," Mima chuckled. "She was whipped, and only allowed out of the house for church on Sundays and to attend school. They didn't believe it when she told them she'd gotten up early to go for a ride, since she was wearing a dress and coat. She'd borrowed her mother's lipstick if I recall. So, there wasn't much chance of her getting away with that lie. Still, she never broke when they grilled her about who she was with. She stuck to her story and refused to admit she'd met up with any of us. So, we were never found out, though of course her parents suspected I was involved. They never much cared for me." Mima sighed and rested her hands in her lap. "That was your Nan, always loyal to the ones she loved, no matter the cost." Her eyes clouded over and a single tear escaped from one watery corner. She ignored it and let it find its way down her lined cheek.

A lump worked its way up into Kate's throat. Inside the inn she could hear the soft keening of the kitchen telephone. She jumped to her feet and bolted for the door, letting it slap shut behind her. "It's the phone," she yelled over her shoulder.

❧

"I'M SORRY, KATE. I WANTED TO BE THERE." DAVIS'S VOICE was soft, with a slight hoarseness to it, as though he'd just woken up.

"Are you at your place?" asked Kate.

"Nope. I'm at work. There was an emergency with one of our clients. I couldn't get away. I feel really bad about it."

She sighed. "It's fine, I understand. I wish you could've been here. It was really beautiful. Sad, but lovely."

"Are you okay?"

She swallowed to dampen the surge of tears that threatened to overwhelm her. "I'm fine. It's hard to say goodbye, but I've got Mima, Jack, Reeda, and Bindi here with me. So, we're all taking care of each other. I think I'm going to stay here a while longer, until we figure out what to do with the inn."

"That's good," he replied with a yawn. "It'll give you some time to think about things, you know? To reassess."

She frowned. "What? What things?"

"Life, direction, purpose..."

What was he saying? "I suppose... although I'm not really sure what you're talking about. Do you think I need to reassess?"

He exhaled slowly before responding. "You're not happy, Katie. Your light has gone out. It went out a long time ago, and you've been treading water ever since. I don't know what it is, I've tried to make you happy, but..."

Her eyes widened, then filled with tears. "Do you really mean that?"

He didn't reply, instead he sighed.

There was an ache in her chest that grew with each passing moment, each breath added more tension, each word seemed to choke the breath from her body.

"Okay. I didn't realise you felt that way."

"I want you to be happy. You know that."

"I know." She covered her mouth with one hand. She didn't want to cry. All she wanted was to run upstairs to her room and bury her head in a pillow.

"I'd like to see you of course, but you should take your time in coming back. This is your chance to have a break from it all, rebuild your family, try to figure out what it is you want in life... because I don't know if it's..." He sighed. "Well, anyway, call me."

She nodded, unable to speak.

"I'll talk to you later, okay?"

"Okay, bye," she whispered.

Kate set the phone back in its cradle and covered her face with both hands, sobbing softly. Was Davis right? Had her light gone out? Whatever that meant. She'd felt a bit low lately, that was true. And she'd skipped a lot of parties and events, the ones she didn't absolutely have to attend. But that was because she was tired, she worked hard and going out after a long evening slaving over a stove was the last thing she wanted to do late at night.

Still, Davis didn't seem to understand. She knew it frustrated him but hadn't stopped to wonder what was behind her desire to spend lazy nights in her pjs watching *Friends* reruns rather than going out on the town with her fiancé. Maybe she was more than a little bit low, after all.

She wiped her face dry with a sleeve, then headed for the stairs. So what if she wasn't completely happy? Was anyone truly happy? That was life. Wasn't it?

Being an adult wasn't all sunshine and roses. There was work to be done, responsibilities to manage, relationships to navigate. And it was hard. Hard to do it all alone. She missed her family. Missed her parents, missed Nan. She climbed the stairs with slow deliberation, then lay down on her bed, curling her legs up to her chest and sliding her hands beneath her cheek. Things would get better. They had to.

11

BATHURST

Eddie squinted at the bright sunlight that filtered through the tree branches overhead. She ducked behind a red brick wall that lined one end of the quadrangle, one hand holding tight to the strap of her leather satchel.

Where was he?

She glanced back over her shoulder, her heart pounding. Then she walked quickly and with as much confidence as she could muster through the quadrangle and out of the school grounds. One last look back at the tall, red brick building sent adrenaline coursing through her veins.

The words *Bathurst High School 1926* stood out dark against the cream-coloured verandah that wrapped around the building's second storey. An Australian flag flapped on a silver flagpole in front of the building. She watched the front steps. No one was there. No sign of anyone coming after her. She hurried down the street, then stepped behind a tall fir tree, breath inhaled in ragged gulps.

She'd done it. Classes were underway and she wasn't there. She was wagging, something she'd never dared to do until today, and if her father found out she'd be in more trouble than ever. The grounding they'd given her for sneaking out a year earlier would be nothing compared to how he'd react to finding she'd skipped class to spend time with her boyfriend.

Not that Daddy knew about Charlie. He and Mother suspected that she and Charlie liked one another, her mother had mentioned something to her about guarding her reputation a time or two, whenever Charlie came to visit her brother, but they had no idea how much time the two of them spent together. Especially since she was barely allowed to leave the farm these days unless she was going to church or school. She hardly got to see Mima, let alone spend time with Charlie.

Still, somehow, they managed it. They saw each other around the school on occasion, and sometimes he'd ride his bike out to the Watson farm and they'd meet up on the creek bank. She'd ride her horse, Eliza, beside the creek until she saw him, seated in the grass, the bike on its side next to him. He'd grin when he saw her, then she'd slide down and run to him, throwing her arms around him. He'd twirl her until she thought the two of them would spin right off the face of the earth, then he'd set her feet on the ground and kiss her, his lips soft and urgent against hers.

Edie chewed on the end of a fingernail while she waited, her heart still thudding loud in her ears.

"There you are!" Charlie's voice behind her made her almost jump out of her skin.

She turned to him with wide eyes, then slid her arms around his neck. "You scared me."

"Sorry," he grinned. He pressed his lips to hers and she breathed him in, surrendering to the pressure of his strong arms closing around her and pulling her body to his. "We don't have long."

He lifted his head and gazed into her eyes. His own hazel eyes sparkled with mischief, the way they always did when he had a plan.

"Let's go," he said. He took her hand in his and together they walked along the side of the road, her satchel bumping against her back with each step.

It was important to look as though they knew where they were headed, he said, otherwise someone was bound to spot them and turn them in. So, they walked hand-in-hand, with long, confident strides. They found their way to the outskirts of town soon enough, heads held high. Peel Street took them all the way to the banks of the Macquarie River. Edie followed Charlie down the narrow, dusty trail that led to the winding, mud-coloured river.

Charlie released Edie's hand and bent to select three round stones. He straightened, strode to the water's edge, and skipped the stones, one by one, over the glassy surface. Then, faced her with a half-smile.

"Do you think they know we're gone?" she asked, worry edging her voice.

He laughed. "What does it matter if they do?"

Her lips pursed. "But if Daddy finds out..."

"What? He'll ground you?" Charlie huffed, then reached for another stone.

She chewed on her lip. He had a point. She lived in a constant state of grounding as far as she was concerned. Her parents didn't trust her, not after Daddy found her riding home at five o'clock in the morning the one and only time she'd snuck out of the house to meet friends. She wouldn't have done it either, only she'd known Charlie would be there. That was the night of their first kiss. Her heart warmed at the memory.

She walked to his side, then slipped her hand into his. He faced her with a wide smile. She could always tell what he was thinking, by the look on his face. He was so open, unassuming, and free. His strength inspired her to be strong. His love stirred her heart to open in ways she'd never expected. He was everything she never knew she needed, but now couldn't imagine living without.

He cupped both cheeks with his hands and let his lips linger softly over hers.

"Marry me," he whispered.

She giggled, her cheeks warming at his touch. "I'm only fifteen years old, I haven't finished school yet."

He whistled, a short, sharp note. "Well, I'm almost finished, and I've been working over at the news agency after school for six whole months. I've got some money saved. Anyway, we're going to get married one day, it's only a matter of time."

"Ask me then. And do it proper," she replied.

He stepped away, finding a large, flat stone and fingering its edges, brushing away the dust and dirt. "Fine, I'll ask you then. But so you know, I'm gonna marry you."

She laughed. "And I'm gonna marry you."

He smiled at her, the dimples in his cheeks flashing. Her heart skipped a beat. "When I graduate, I'm going to Sydney to study engineering at uni. I've already talked to Dad about it. He said he'll pay my way. And when I get a job, I'll ask you to marry me. We'll be married and we'll buy ourselves a nice little house here in town. We'll have children, and I'll save up to buy us a car, if you like."

She smiled, shading her eyes from the morning sun with one hand held to her forehead. "I'm going to be a scientist," she said. "I'll discover the cure to a disease of some kind, and when we marry, I want to have land. Not a lot of land, but enough for horses."

He faced her, shoving his hands deep into the grey pockets of his pants. He'd loosened the tie that hung around his neck and undone the top two buttons of his pressed white shirt. "A scientist?"

She nodded, a grin curling up the corners of her lips. "Uh huh. I love science. There are so many things to discover. It's like there's a whole world waiting for me." She linked her fingers together in front of the navy school tunic, studying his face as he watched her closely.

"But what about children?"

She laughed. "What about them?"

"You can't be a scientist; you'll be raising our children. How will that work?"

Her brow furrowed and irritation squirmed in her gut. "I guess they'll come later, I don't know. I know I want to cure something. I don't want to sit in the background all my life. I want to do something, achieve something, make a difference."

"Well, so do I."

She cocked her head to one side. "Good, so we're agreed?"

"No, you're gonna be my wife..."

"Yes, and you're gonna be my husband, and that means you're supposed to love me, and everything about me." She crossed her arms over her chest, her eyes narrowing.

He closed the gap between them, then took her hands in his, kissing the back of each one at a time. "Fine, you can be a scientist."

"I don't need your permission," she sniffed.

He laughed. "Okay, okay. Promise me one thing."

"What's that?" she asked.

"Don't ever leave me."

He leaned forward to kiss her, and she smiled against his lips.

"I promise. Let's swim," she said.

He grinned, then shucked off his shoes. Hers came next,

and soon they were clothed only in their white, cotton underwear. He studied her, with one sweeping gaze, then ran for the water.

"Last one in's a rotten egg!" he called as he plunged into the river, then dove beneath the surface.

She followed him in at a more sedate pace and lowered herself into the cold water with a low gasp. He found her then, and threaded his arms around her, drops of water slipping down his tanned face.

"You're a frustrating one, Miss Edith Watson," he said.

She grinned. "But I'm worth it."

"Definitely worth it," he replied, then kissed her again.

❦ 12 ❦

SEPTEMBER 1995

CABARITA BEACH

When she couldn't read any more, Kate closed Nan's journal and crawled up onto the bed. Her back ached, her legs needed stretching and part of her rear end had lost all feeling. She curled onto her side and set her hands beneath her cheek, feeling the wetness of her tears as they adjusted course and slid sideways toward the quilt.

She didn't know why she was crying. Only that she hadn't expected to find what she did — an epistle of Nan's life, in her own words. It was breathtaking, enthralling, and made her feel a little like she'd snuck into Nan's room and surprised her while she was taking a bath.

Who was Charlie Jackson, the boy who'd stolen Nan's heart when she was only fourteen years old? His presence wove a measure of intrigue throughout the journal's pages, and the mystery whispered questions to her as she read.

She'd believed Pop was Nan's first and only love. They'd met while she was so young, she couldn't remember exactly how old. Sometime during the second world war Pop had turned up at the hospital where Nan worked, a member of the United States Navy. He'd been recovering from an injury. Kate remembered that much. It was how her grandparents had met. She'd heard the story a time or two, though Nan never seemed to want to tell it. It was always Pop who spilled their secrets. Nan held hers close to her chest.

Kate wiped the tears from her cheeks with one hand and stared absently through the window to the tops of the gum trees in the distance.

How could Nan have loved this boy Charlie so much that they planned on getting married soon after she finished high school, and then go on to marry Pop instead? What'd happened to Charlie? Where was he? Who was he? She didn't remember ever hearing his name before, not that her seventy-year-old grandmother was likely to talk to her granddaughters about a boy she'd known all those years ago. Although she hadn't only known him, she'd loved him. And loved him with the kind of passion Kate couldn't say, in all honesty, she'd ever felt for anyone.

The tears started up again and she hugged her bent legs to her chest.

When her tears finally dried, she brushed her hair, and wiped her face. Then she walked downstairs for lunch. She wouldn't say anything to the others about the journals yet. She wanted to keep them to herself for a little while longer. To find out more about Nan, and the boy she'd loved so long ago. She'd tell them eventually, Reeda and Bindi were Nan's granddaughters too, and they deserved to get the chance to read about her life. But what would they say? Would they tell her not to pry, that the journals were private? She shuddered and tugged her cardigan more tightly around her body. Private or not, she couldn't shake the longing to spend more time reading the words Nan had scrawled onto those fragile pages when she was a girl. And to find out what'd happened to Charlie Jackson.

๛

KATE ROLLED ONTO HER BACK AND STARED UP AT THE ceiling. Another night of restless sleep as the outlaw possum held a dance party in the roof cavity over her head. Her thoughts fixated on Davis, Nan, and her sisters and spun into dreams she couldn't escape from and problems she couldn't resolve.

In one part of her dream she'd found herself running along a beach, with Davis behind her, calling out that she should wait for him. She'd been frightened, lonely, and desperate, blowing harder with each step she took as her lungs begged for air.

Her sisters were up ahead. She tried to call out to them, but they ignored her, talking and laughing, just out of reach, until finally, she tripped over her own exhausted feet and fell onto the wet sand. A wave rushed up and crashed over her, and she was drowning, bathed in sweat, and sucking in great mouthfuls of air when she woke, as the mournful screams of curlews echoed in the still night.

She'd lain on her back, unable to fall back to sleep, ever since.

The sun had risen, and birdsong marked a new morning. Kookaburras had been the first to sound, their laughter shaking the coast to wakefulness. Then, the warble of magpies, the haunting call of seagulls, the chirrup of swallows and the screech of plovers chasing an intruder from their grassy nests, all swelled and built as the sun rose in the sky.

She reached for the journal she'd stuffed beneath her pillow the previous night, turned the pages to where the bookmark peeked out, and rubbed bleary eyes with the back of her hand.

The more she read, the more she realised how much Charlie had meant to Nan, and her wonder at why she'd never heard of him grew. Maybe it wasn't the kind of thing a grandmother talked to her grandchildren about, a love affair in her teenage years, but their relationship had the distinct ring of something more than that. More than a crush, greater than a first love, it resounded with a depth that gave her heart an ache of melancholy mixed with nostalgia, and a whiff of envy.

If only Nan were still here, she could ask her about it. Ask her who this boy was who'd stolen her heart, and why they weren't married the way they'd obviously planned to be.

What had stopped them?

She slapped the diary shut and put it back where she'd found it, then dressed to go downstairs to breakfast. Reeda, Bindi, and Mima were already seated at the breakfast table. Through the back screen door Kate saw a black cat with white socks and a white nose crouched at a bowl of food, eating.

Jack was wiping his boots off at the back door. He met her with a quiet smile, then took his place at the head of the table. There was something peaceful about his presence. It offered her a sense of safety, security. He didn't say much, but he brought so much to the room. She smiled in response and picked the seat beside Bindi. The table held plates of bacon, scrambled eggs, buttered toast, and a tub of creamy mango yoghurt.

"I don't know, I think I'll take some time off to travel or something." Bindi finished her sentence as Kate joined the group. She glanced at Kate with a half-smile, her eyes full of emotion.

"You're going to travel?" asked Kate, as she reached for the plate of scrambled eggs.

Bindi nodded as she pushed a spoonful of yoghurt into her mouth.

She swallowed. "Maybe. I feel like I missed out when I was younger. I wanted to be a journalist, so as soon as I finished school, I went off to uni to study. Then, all the good positions were being snapped up at the major newspapers and television stations in my final year, so I jumped on the band-wagon. I didn't think about taking time off to do something as luxurious as travel, to see the world. My only focus was my career, getting that perfect job, the one that would catapult me into journalistic stardom." She let out a sarcastic "ha," then shook her head. "How ridiculous."

Kate chewed a mouthful of eggs with a frown. "That wasn't ridiculous. You dreamed of becoming a journalist and you went after it. I've always admired the way you did that — and now you're one of the top television journalists in Australia. I see you on TV all the time, whenever the Bris-bane news broadcasts a national story, there you are, reporting live from Canberra, or Melbourne, Singapore, or Tokyo. You've travelled a lot."

"Yeah. But not for fun." Bindi kept her head down, eyes fixed on the bowl in front of her. "So, how's the chef life treating you?"

Kate sensed her sister was changing the subject on purpose, but she could also tell Bindi wasn't ready to talk about whatever it was that was eating at her. Bindi always came around, she only needed time and a little space. At least, that was how she'd been when they were girls, and maybe things hadn't changed as much as she'd thought.

Kate drew in a deep breath. "It's been great... well, it was, until I came here for Nan's funeral. Now, I'm not so sure."

"What do you mean?" asked Reeda, around a mouthful of toast.

Kate pursed her lips. "I was about to launch the new

menu that I've been working on for months, and that Marco took his sweet time approving. He's a complete control freak and hates to try anything new at the restaurant. So, it was a huge deal that he approved it, and it was all set to happen, but I had to come here. I'm not complaining, of course I'm not, but that meant my staff had to try to launch the menu without me, and apparently it was a disaster."

Reeda shook her head. "I'm sorry, Kate. That's rough."

"I'm sure he'll give you another chance. You'll be back in Brisbane before you know it, and you can try again," encouraged Bindi with a half-smile on her lips.

"I don't know... the longer I stay in Cabarita, the more I think he's looking for a permanent replacement."

"But you've been there forever," said Reeda, her brows drawn together. "Haven't you?"

"Five years. But Marco isn't exactly loyal. He's... more concerned about his business than his staff."

"Well, if that's true then good riddance," said Mima with a sniff. "You can work here. We need a good chef in the kitchen."

"But you're the cook at the Waratah," objected Kate.

Mima sighed. "I know, but I won't be here forever. You girls need to think about the future, what you want to do with this place. And you'll have to think about what you'll do without me and Jack someday. We're both getting a bit long in the tooth."

Jack looked up from his plate of bacon and eggs with a frown. "Hey, speak for yourself."

Mima chuckled. "Yes, you are getting old, Jack, my friend. Even you."

LATER, WHEN KATE AND BINDI HAD CLEANED UP THE breakfast things, and Mima was sitting in the breakfast nook with Reeda, talking knitting patterns and the best kinds of yarn, Kate felt the pull of the diary hidden beneath her pillow.

She shook her head. It wouldn't be right to spend the day tucked up in bed reading. Not when there was so much to get done. It'd do her good to get out and about, breathe some fresh air, maybe go for a run.

Suddenly she knew what she wanted to do. She dressed in her yellow bikini, then covered it up with tracksuit pants and a jumper, and threw on a rain jacket as a last-minute addition, just in case. Her car was still parked in the empty lot at the front of the inn. She turned the key, and it idled a moment before roaring to life in the cold morning air.

The car tyres crackled on the gravel driveway as she pulled the car around the outside of the inn to where the garden shed sat, squat, dark, and leaning slightly to the left. Leaving the car idling, she jogged into the shed and reached for the surfboard that lay against the wall in one corner of the shed.

Covered in a fine layer of dust, the surfboard was badly in need of a wax, but she didn't have time. Buoyed by excitement and a desire to keep moving, she fixed the board to her car's roof rack, then slid into the driver's seat.

The track she followed, slow and steady with the car in second gear, was as familiar to her as the inn itself. The small, private beach was part of the inn's property, and was Nan's favourite place to go to get away from it all, as she'd said. Though now she thought about it, Kate couldn't imagine what Nan was getting away from in this sleepy and idyllic paradise.

Nothing had changed when she pulled the car to a stop in their usual spot. There was perhaps a little more undergrowth than she remembered, but the narrow path that led down to the sheltered beach was just the same.

She climbed out of the car and stood with her hands on her hips, sniffing the salt infused air. She smiled and reached for her wetsuit. By the time she was dressed, she was shivering from top to bottom so that her teeth tapped against each other like they were sending a message in Morse code.

With the surfboard firmly tucked beneath her arm, she jogged through the cold sand, along the path and down to the beach. Memories rose to the surface — Nan, pacing along the shore, or swimming at the water's edge when the waves died down until the ocean wasn't much more than an azure coloured lake. She'd laid on her back, hands fanning at her sides, and slid up and down the smooth rising and sagging of the waves' gentle humps, her gaze fixed on the blue sky overhead.

Nan wouldn't have gone for a swim today though. The wind tugged at the top of the water, sending sprays of whitewash skyward. Waves dumped on the sodden, sandy shore, and seagulls huddled in clumps behind dark, forlorn rocks that were scattered along the beach like the bony backs of sleeping cattle. Overhead, grey clouds surfed across the sky at a brisk pace, colliding and reshaping as moisture filled their bellies.

Kate hesitated on the shore, taking it all in with eager eyes. This is what she'd missed. The wild abandon of the ocean, the beauty of nature, the mystery of the unknown adventure that lay ahead. It gave her spirit a surge of hope, as anticipation of standing tall on those waves pumped through her veins.

Then, she was in the water. She ran through the last vestiges of a wave as it pulled back into the depths beyond the breakers with a hiss and a sigh. The first wave came at her and she launched the surfboard forward, landing on it with a grunt as her stomach took the impact. Then, when the next wave reached her, she duck-dived beneath it, pushing the front of the board down under the thunder of saltwater that crashed over her.

By the time she'd caught three waves, she needed a rest. She sat on her board, out beyond the break, to catch her breath. A blanket of rain pattered over the water toward her, catching her in a heavy downpour. She rubbed the droplets from her eyes and smoothed her hair back, letting the frigid rain pummel her face.

A fisherman stood on an outcropping of rocks at the end of the beach. Clothed in a black raincoat, a hat pulled low over his eyes, he stood immobile, his fishing line stretching long into the restless water. She waved a hand over her head, wondering if he could see her. It was a private beach, after all, and perhaps she knew him. He waved back, a brief tap of fingertips to the edge of his hat.

As she sat there, watching wave after wave roll and fizz against the shore, her thoughts returned to Nan's diary. The way Nan described her life, it seemed as though she was talking about someone else, someone Kate had never met. Who was this girl rebelling against strict parents, living on a farm, in love with a boy she planned to marry? Kate didn't recognise in her the carefree, warm, determined woman who'd been her grandmother, who'd raised her after she lost her own parents.

She shivered in her wetsuit with her lips pressed together. Would she ever find the kind of love Nan described? Could she love Davis that way, or should she want that? The relationship she and Davis shared wasn't the heady crush of two adolescents. It didn't carry with it the sweet scent of rebellion against overly strict parents. It was a mature decision, a choice to be together, made by two adults. How could she compare it to what Nan shared with Charlie?

Still, something inside her craved it.

She tried to imagine what Mum and Dad would think of

Davis. Would they approve? Her heart constricted, bringing an ache into her chest. They'd never get the chance to meet him, so she had no way of knowing. Each year that passed, her memories of them faded until she wasn't sure which of the pictures in her mind were real and which she'd conjured out of her own longing.

Kate scrubbed her face with both hands. It wasn't fair to lose them so young, but for some reason it almost seemed worse to realise the memories she had of them were weakening. Would they disappear entirely one day, and she'd wake up wondering who they'd been after all?

White caps surrounded her, so when the humpback whale breached only ten metres away from her, she had to swallow down a scream. It startled her, and she clung to her surfboard as its black back curved through the dark water, its blowhole shooting air and water toward the sky with one, sharp exhale.

When she'd regained her senses, she hooted loudly, yelling in delight, her heart thundering against her ribs.

"Woohoo!" she cried.

Two more whales broke the water's surface a short distance away, and her broad smile widened further still.

"Amazing," she whispered, her wide eyes fixed on the place where the creatures had disappeared.

She lay down on the surfboard and paddled after them. They continued surfacing every thirty seconds or so, breathing hard and rolling through the water with unhurried ease. She followed them, breathless, unwilling to say goodbye. They were magnificent, beautiful, awe-inspiring.

When she neared the rocks that marked the end of the beach, she pulled up and sat on her board to watch them go. She didn't want to travel too far, her car was parked at this beach and she could feel the tug of a rip beneath her, pulling her out into the wide, harried ocean.

She watched for several long minutes as the whales

continued their way northward, heading toward the main beach at Cabarita, and on to their final destination. Her pulse returned to its normal rate, and she squeezed her eyes shut. It was a sign. There was so much beauty in the world, sometimes it was difficult to see, but it was there.

With a deep breath, she paddled onto a wave. She stood to her feet and followed the wave toward the shore. Too late, she realised she'd caught the wave spine-tinglingly close to the rocks. She turned at the last moment, hoping to follow the break in the other direction, but lost her balance. As she tumbled from the board and into the water, pain burst out over one thigh. The rocks scratched her flesh and tore through her wetsuit, cutting into her skin as she rolled over and over.

Instinctively, she covered her head with both arms, and when the wave passed over her, she found her footing and climbed the rocks as quickly as she could. She tugged the surfboard behind her, grabbing it up beneath her arm as soon as she was able, then scrambled higher up the pile of sharp, black rocks as the next wave hit them.

Kate hunkered down against the rocks as sea spray showered her from behind, then stood again to hurry forward.

"Are you okay?" The fisherman strode toward her across the sand. He wore a hat, black with rain, pulled low over his eyes. A blue raincoat was zipped beneath his chin, waders covered his jean clad legs and became a pair of charcoal gumboots. He stopped a moment to push his fishing pole into the sand, then climbed the rocky outcropping, closing the space between them in a few strides.

When he drew close, she recognised him, and relief flooded over her. It was Alex, his eyes crinkled with worry.

She nodded. "I think so," then, glanced down at her legs and examined her arms. Rivulets of blood wound their way from several places, but none of the wounds looked deep. Not that she could see, anyway.

He took her hand and wrapped her arm around his shoulders. "Here, lean on me. Leave the board, I'll come back for it."

She nodded and slipped off her ankle strap. Then, leaning her weight on him, she hobbled over the rocks and down the other side, grateful for the respite of the cool sand on the soles of her feet.

When they reached the beach, he scooped her up into his arms and carried her easily back to her car and set her feet in the gravel.

"What were you thinking?" he asked, irritation darkening his features.

Her lips pursed, and she inhaled a sharp breath. "What do you mean? I caught the wave a little close to the rocks, that's all. It was an accident."

His hazel eyes flashed. "Well, you shouldn't be surfing on a day like today if you can't tell where to drop in and where not to."

Her throat tightened. A lecture was the last thing she needed. Her legs were bruised, and likely her arms as well. What she needed was first aid. She blinked.

His voice softened. "I'm sorry, I was worried. I thought you might really be injured when I saw you fall."

"There were whales," she whispered.

His lips broke into a half-smile. "Ah yes, the whale pod, I saw them too. Pretty amazing. I usually see whales out here at this time of year, that's why I like to come to this spot. It's great for whale watching... and for time to myself."

She hugged herself, her teeth chattering. "I'm sorry to interrupt."

He shrugged. "You didn't, and anyway, it's your land. I'm the one interrupting."

"I used to love coming here. It was Nan's favourite beach." She stared back toward the water.

"I know, she and I used to fish here together sometimes." His voice was soft.

Kate studied him, his black oilskin coat, brown jumper poking through, sodden Akubra hat pulled low over his brow, and gumboots pulled high over rain-soaked jeans. Nan had come here, to her favourite beach, to fish with this man? A man she'd never heard of until two weeks ago when she ran into him at the stables. She must've liked him.

"I'll go and get your board before it's washed away."

He disappeared up the trail, and Kate quickly dried off and changed back into her warm tracksuit. She glanced at her reflection in the rearview mirror, and was startled by the paleness of her skin, the way her freckles stood out against her thin nose, and the dark blue tinge to her lips.

"Here you go," said Alex, pushing the board onto her roof racks.

He secured the board in place, then stood in front of her with his hands pressed to his hips. "You okay to drive back?"

She gave one quick nod. "Fine, thanks. And thank you for your help."

He smiled. "No worries."

Kate climbed into her car and started the engine. Alex stepped forward and leaned down to look through her open window.

"Hey, I was thinking about what we discussed... you know, about the stables."

Her mind scrambled to recover their conversation. So much had happened since then, it felt like a lifetime ago.

"I've got a few bits and pieces of timber and whatnot hanging around at home that my carpenter mate gave me. I thought I might go ahead and get started rebuilding the stables."

She smiled. "That sounds great. Thank you."

He shrugged. "No worries. I know you've got a lot on your plate at the moment. I'm happy to help."

As she drove back to the inn, she couldn't dislodge the image of him in her rearview mirror, standing with his arms crossed over his thick chest as he watched her drive away. She'd misjudged him during their first encounter. The way he'd helped her over the rocks, then carried her up the beach, it quickened her pulse and warmed her face.

She parked the car in the lot, then hobbled inside, already feeling her body stiffening. Mima exclaimed over her and bustled off to get the first aid kit. By the time she was patched up, she was yawning in the warmth of the kitchen. She hauled herself up the staircase, grimacing with each painful step, then fell into her bed. Her eyes felt leaden, and her body exhausted. And within a few moments, she was fast asleep.

❦

WHEN KATE WOKE, THERE WAS A NOTE SLIPPED UNDER THE door.

Marco called.

She rubbed the sleep from her eyes, pulled on a dressing gown, and padded down the stairs, still yawning.

What could her boss want? They must need her feedback on something, or more likely he was calling to order her to come back to Brisbane. She was already planning her return, but she hadn't had the heart to tell Bindi or Reeda yet.

For some reason, Reeda didn't seem to be in a hurry to go back to Sydney, like she usually would, something neither Kate nor Bindi had thought she'd do. They'd both discussed it — she wasn't one to open up about her feelings, so maybe she needed them. They should both try to be there for her, she'd always done the same for them when they were younger. She'd been like a mother to them when they'd lost their own.

In the office, Kate slumped into the desk chair and dialled Marco's number. He answered right away, which was unlike him and took her by surprise.

"Oh, Marco — it's Kate. I'm returning your call. How are you?"

"Kate, good to hear from you. Thanks for calling me back. I wanted you to hear it first from me before the grapevine got back to you somehow — I've hired a head chef for the restaurant."

Her stomach clenched. "Okay. You mean, a temporary head chef?"

"No, I'm sorry Kate. This guy is amazing, and he was looking for a position. I had to snap him up while I had the chance. And you're busy, down south, doing family things. It'll be good for both of us — you get some time off and I get someone to run my kitchen."

She shook her head, dispelling any sleepiness that remained. "You've replaced me already?"

"Things move fast in the restaurant business, Kate. If you don't act, you miss out. I've wanted this guy for years, but he was tied up in another contract. Now's my chance to bring him in and I'm not going to miss it. I'm sorry, but I know you'll find something great."

She grunted. There were no words.

"Anyway, I've got a ton of work to do, so I'll have to talk to you some other time. All the best, Kate. Bye."

She hung up the phone, then sat staring at it for a full minute before she moved.

Marco had always been a callous boss, but this took it to a new level. Her grandmother had died, and he'd replaced her before she even got back from the funeral. It didn't seem possible he could've topped the time he called her back from a vacation to fill in for him so he could get plastic surgery *for the little crinkles around his eyes that made him look like an old fogey* — in his own words. She hadn't believed he could be more thoughtless than that, but he'd proven her wrong.

She hugged herself as she stood, still coming to terms with the fact that she was now officially unemployed.

Well, one thing he'd said was right — this would give her the chance to spend more time with family. She could stay longer at the Waratah now, get to know her sisters again, rest and relax. She hadn't done that in a long time, she needed the break. And it was true, she'd be able to land another job without too much trouble — restaurants contacted her regularly, offering her signing bonuses and higher salaries to ditch Marco and come work for them. Well, now she could take up one of those offers, and she could leave that heartless jerk in her dust.

❧ 13 ❧

CABARITA

The pancake sizzled in the butter. Kate slid a spatula beneath it and flipped it over, revealing a golden-brown underside. Her stomach grumbled and she patted it with her free hand, wondering when it'd gotten so soft. She must've gained weight since she arrived at the inn three weeks earlier. If she had, she wasn't surprised. Mima fed them all like they were starving and destitute, in need of fattening up.

"That looks delicious," said Mima, peering over her shoulder.

"I'm so hungry, although I shouldn't be after the braised lamb shanks and mash you fed us last night. That was amazing by the way. I could've eaten thirds, except my stomach would've burst," said Kate.

"Glad you enjoyed it, love. For a chef, it seems to me, you don't eat well enough. You're all skin and bones, and no one trusts a skinny chef." Mima laughed at her own joke as she whipped a bowl of eggs with a whisk.

Reeda wandered into the room, her slippers sliding against the floor with each dragging footstep. She yawned and fell into a chair at the dining table.

"Good morning," she said, with another wide yawn.

Her brown hair was piled on top of her head in a messy bun, and one side of her face held the imprint of a wrinkled sheet.

Kate grinned as she flipped another pancake. "Good morning, sunshine. You had a nice sleep in."

"What are you doing up so early, and so... chipper?" asked Reeda with a groan.

"I slept the sleep of the dead last night. In fact, I think I slept the entire afternoon and all night long. And I barely moved. Of course, my entire body is stiff and sore from surfing yesterday. Did I tell you I crashed into the rocks at Nan's beach?"

Reeda's eyes widened. "What? Are you hurt?"

"Just a few scrapes and bruises. Thankfully, Alex was there to help."

"Was he just?" Reeda winked, her lips pulling into a grin.

"Nothing like that," objected Kate, her cheeks already flushing with warmth. "He was kind and considerate and helped me back to my car."

"I'm sure he did." Reeda's voice dripped with innuendo.

"Oh, and my boss called me early this morning to fire me... so there's that as well."

Reeda's mouth fell open. "What?"

"Yep. He's a real treat, that Marco." Kate shook her head. "Anyway, I'm over it. I'm not going to get worked up over a job that... let's face it... I secretly hated. He never appreciated me or gave me opportunities to grow. It was a dead end, and I can't believe it took me this long to realise that. I wasted so many years on his stupid restaurant..."

"Not wasted," replied Reeda. "The way I see it, it was a learning experience."

"Well, I sure learned a lot," smirked Kate.

Reeda chuckled. "Good for you. On to bigger and better things then. Eh?"

"So, what are your plans for the day?" asked Kate, ready to change the subject.

"I meant to tell you last night, but you were already in bed — I found Nan's solicitor."

Kate slid a pancake onto a plate that held a stack of the golden discs.

"Really? That's great news."

"So, the three of us have an appointment to see him later today."

"Great." Kate's gut twisted with nerves. What if things didn't go the way they hoped? What if Nan had decided to gift the inn to a charity, or a nursing home? Knowing Nan, anything was possible. The idea of seeing the solicitor and hearing Nan's final wishes meant that soon everything would be finished, done. She could return to Brisbane, pick up her life where she'd left it, and everything would go back to normal. Only, she wasn't sure that's what she wanted any longer. She didn't know what she wanted, all she knew was that she felt better than she had in a long time, and she didn't want to say goodbye, to the inn, to Mima and Jack, to her sisters, or to Nan.

THE RECEPTIONIST SHOT THEM A SMILE, THEN RETURNED her attention to the computer screen in front of her. The phone rang, and she answered it in a sing-song voice.

"Daley, Johns, and Hathaway Solicitors, how can I help you?"

Kate exchanged a glance with Bindi, who was fidgeting with the hem of her skirt.

"You don't think Nan would've done something crazy, like give the inn away to someone else, do you?" asked Bindi in a whisper.

Kate shook her head. "No, of course not." She wasn't sure about that, but didn't want to worry Bindi, who looked as though she might throw up at any moment.

"Is there something bothering you? Everything okay?" asked Kate.

Bindi shrugged, her eyes wide. "Nothing I can't handle."

Kate was about to ask another question when a man stepped into the reception area, wearing a blue button-down shirt and navy pinstripe slacks.

"Reeda Houston?" he asked.

Reeda raised her hand.

He shook her hand. "Pleased to meet you."

"These are my sisters, Kate and Bindi Summer," said Reeda, waving her hand in their direction.

They each shook hands with the solicitor, who introduced himself as Bill Daley. He led them into his office and offered them seats opposite him.

"Thank you for coming in, ladies. I was sorry to hear that Edith passed. She was a wonderful woman and made me a batch of delicious scones the last time we met."

Kate smiled, then scanned the room, taking in the plaques and certificates hung on the wall, photographs of Bill and various other people she didn't recognise.

Nerves squirmed in her gut. What would they do if Nan didn't leave them the Waratah? What would they do if she did? Kate didn't have the money to invest into fixing the place up, and likely they wouldn't get much for it if they sold it as it was. And what would Jack and Mima do then?

"So, let's get started." Bill rifled through a pile of papers on his desk and set a pair of half-moon reading glasses on the end of his round nose. "It won't take long, since Edith's final wishes are relatively straightforward." Bill cleared his throat. "We're here to read Edith Summer's final will and testament. Reading of the will is not standard practice, but I'm happy to do it when requested. And in this case, I received a call from Nyreeda Houston, asking that the will be shared with the three of you, so you could learn its contents at the same time." He cleared his throat with a cough.

Kate nodded. Bindi tugged at the hem of her skirt and Reeda chewed on her lower lip. They looked even more nervous than she felt.

The list of Nan's assets began with the small items around the inn, including the contents of a storage locker to be found somewhere beneath the building that apparently contained stamp and coin collections gathered by Pop over the years. Nan bequeathed a few pieces of art to Mima, along with some of her handmade quilts and cookbooks. To Jack, she left his cottage, along with the acre of land around it, which she'd apparently already transferred into his name through the official council channels.

Kate remembered her curiosity over the place. Now it belonged to Jack, perhaps she could suggest they meet for a cup of tea and she could finally discover where it was on the heavily overgrown ten-acre property.

Her mind wandered back to the day her parents died and Nan became both father and mother to her. She was fifteen years old, and they'd flown up from Sydney to allow Reeda to attend a dance eisteddfod in Brisbane. It wasn't as big an event or as prestigious as the competitions in Sydney or Melbourne, but some of her friends had signed up to go and she'd begged their parents to let her as well. Finally, they'd agreed, and decided the family could all stay at the inn and turn the trip into a holiday, a visit with Nan.

Kate had wanted to go to the eisteddfod as well, but Bindi wasn't feeling well and had cried, asking for Kate to stay back at the inn with her and watch a video instead. With a roll of her eyes, Kate had agreed. And besides, her parents had reminded her, the competition would run late, and with the three-hour drive south afterward, it'd be a very late night for her. She should stay back with Bindi, they could spend some time with Nan and Mima, and get to bed early so they could all enjoy themselves together at the beach the next day.

She'd agreed with a huff, never able to say no to her younger sister, especially when her eyes glimmered with tears. So, it was set, that Mum, Dad, and Reeda would go to Brisbane in the hire car and be back around midnight.

She, Nan, and Bindi had gone fishing together in the cove, then cooked the fish with plenty of lemon, salt, and laughter before sitting around a fire pit and sharing scary stories as the sun set over the horizon. When she and Bindi went to bed at ten o'clock, she'd stared out the front window of the inn, hoping to see their car, to find that they'd returned early, but there was nothing there.

It wasn't until three a.m., when she was woken by blue flashing lights that illuminated the entire inn and pulsed across the bedroom wall, that she knew something was wrong. She stumbled down the stairs, bleary eyed, to find Nan crumpled on the floor by the front door, a policewoman, in uniform, kneeling beside her, one hand on Nan's back.

Her throat had constricted then, Nan never fell apart. Not when Pop died of a heart attack in his armchair while he was taking an afternoon nap. Whatever had happened, it must've been bad.

The sound of her name pulled her back from her reverie and she blinked away the tears that'd filled her eyes.

"... Reeda, Kate, and Bindi I leave the Waratah Inn, and everything contained within the building and the property, other than those items that have already been named. I also leave to my granddaughters the contents of my bank accounts, retirement account and investment account. The money can be used however they see fit, whether to invest into the inn, or to add to their own investment holdings. I will leave to their discretion what they wish to do with any of the assets bequeathed to them. All I ask is that they do not sell or make changes to the inn, or the running of the inn, unless the three of them agree."

Bill hesitated, peering over the top of his spectacles eyeing the three girls, one by one. "Any questions so far?"

Kate found she'd been holding her breath, so exhaled before responding. "No, not really. That seems pretty clear."

"We all have to agree?" asked Reeda.

He nodded. "That's what she wanted. Of course, you can do as you wish, it's only a request — nothing legally binding about it."

He set the paper back on his desk, then tugged open the top drawer. His hand soon re-emerged, holding fast to three, white envelopes. He handed one to each of the women.

Kate turned hers over, noting the front was marked with her name in Nan's distinctive scrawl, and the back held a wax seal she recognised as the one Nan often used on letters and cards. Nan had loved that she could press her initials, *ES*, into the wax. *It's the personal touch that matters*, she'd say with a grin as she blew on the wax to cool it.

"What are these for?" asked Bindi. "Can we open them now?"

Bill nodded with a smile. "You can open those whenever you like. As to what they say, I can only guess. But for now, I have another appointment, so I wish you ladies all the best."

"That's all?" asked Reeda.

He chuckled. "Yep. That about sums it up. I've sent copies of everything I just read out loud to each of the beneficiaries, as well as the executor, which as we discussed, is yourself, Reeda."

She nodded. "Well, okay — thanks."

They each thanked him, then wandered back to the car in silence. Kate's head pounded with the beginnings of a headache, and her mind couldn't fix on a single thought for more than a moment. The inn was theirs, as they'd thought it'd be — so why did she feel so off kilter?

"It's so surreal," said Bindi, summing up exactly what Kate couldn't express.

"I know. The inn is ours. We should've asked how much money is in the accounts — is it enough to renovate the old place?" Kate waited for Reeda to unlock the car.

Reeda sighed. "I've got all the information here with me. There's plenty of money, more than enough actually, when you take into account her investments and retirement account. We could renovate the inn and run it in the red for a year before we'd have to look at cutting back."

"Wow, really? Who knew Nan was sitting on so much money? I wonder why she didn't fix up the Waratah herself?" exclaimed Kate.

"I think she was happy living her life the way it was," suggested Bindi with a hitch in her voice.

"Should we read these?" asked Kate, holding her envelope high.

"I'm going to wait until later," said Bindi. "I'm not up for it yet."

"Me too," agreed Reeda, her voice soft.

The drive home was quiet, with each of the women lost in their own thoughts. When they got home, Jack and Mima were waiting for them. They explained what they'd learned, and both Jack and Mima nodded in agreement.

"It's what she wanted," said Jack.

"I'm glad she thought of me for her quilts," added Mima,

crossing her arms over her chest. "She knew how much I loved those things, and they remind me of her." She bit down on her lip.

"Have you decided what you're going to do with the inn yet?" asked Jack, looking more tired than Kate had ever seen him look before.

Kate exchanged glances with her sisters, then shook her head. "Not yet."

"Well, make sure and tell us when you figure it out," responded Mima. "I'll have to make plans if you're selling the place."

"We'll give you plenty of notice." Reeda's eyes were misty, and the end of her nose glowed red as she patted Mima's arm.

Bindi boiled the kettle and filled a teapot, and the three of them carried it along, with three cups, out to the breakfast nook. They took their seats, gazed out over the inn's lawn toward the sound of the waves rolling into the cove. Seagulls cried, and somewhere a crow cawed to a steady beat.

"So, what do you think we should do?" asked Reeda, looping her legs over one arm of the chair.

Kate sipped her tea, cupping both hands around to feel its warmth. "I think we should sell."

"Yeah, I think so too," replied Reeda. "I mean, I have to get back to Sydney. I've been gone too long already; my clients have probably forgotten my name by now."

Kate chuckled. "My boss has definitely forgotten me, or at least wishes he could. Without a job to go to, it's time to head home. I feel so out of touch here. Some of my friends called me a few times after I first arrived, and they came to Nan's funeral, but now several weeks have passed, I'm not hearing from anyone anymore. And Davis..." She couldn't finish the thought. Davis hadn't called in days and she hadn't been able to reach him either.

"I don't want to sell," said Bindi, her voice so quiet Kate wasn't sure she heard her.

"Sorry?" questioned Reeda.

"I think we should keep the inn. It was Nan and Pop's, it's where we lived when we were teenagers. It was my home for almost five years. It's home to me now. I don't want to lose my home; we've already lost so much..." She fell quiet, one finger trailing along the arm of her chair, her eyes following its path.

"But we can't run the place — not with all three of us living in different cities. Mima and Jack are too old to do it alone, and we're all scattered... how would we keep it?" asked Kate, her stomach twisting into a knot.

What was Bindi thinking? It didn't make any sense. All of them knew they'd have to sell, even Jack and Mima knew it. No one was saying it, but everyone understood — the three of them couldn't do it. They couldn't manage an inn from three different parts of the country. And if they could, none of them knew how to do it. The idea of leaving Mima and Jack to cope with it seemed wrong. Mima had already hinted at leaving, that she and Jack were too old to keep things running alone.

"That's crazy, Bindi," said Reeda, exasperation flashing across her face. She pushed her straight, brown hair behind one shoulder, her deep brown eyes flashing. "How would that work? We'd have to hire someone to manage the place, and who knows how many other staff. From what I've seen, it'd take months to refurbish the place, and then we'd have to advertise... running an inn, it's a lot of work."

Bindi's jaw set in a stubborn line and her nostrils flared. "I know it's a lot of work, that's why I'm putting my hand up to do it."

"What?" exclaimed Kate, straightening in her chair. "What do you mean, you're going to do it? You live in

Melbourne, you have a great job, and a successful career, you have a boyfriend you love... you can't uproot your entire life for this. It doesn't make sense. I don't think Nan would want you to make that kind of sacrifice, I know I don't want you to."

Bindi shrugged. "I want to do it. For Nan, Pop, Dad, Mum, for the two of you. You don't realise yet what you'd be giving up, but one day you'd regret selling the place. It's important to us, all of us. It's a part of who we are. We have to keep it, and I'm going to stay here. I'm not going back to Melbourne."

Reeda and Kate stared at each other, open-mouthed. Kate couldn't understand what was wrong with Bindi. She was usually the quiet one, the compliant peacemaker who went along with whatever Kate and Reeda agreed to do. But not this time. She could see by the tilt of her sister's head that she wasn't going to back down.

"I can't believe you want to give up everything to keep this place," said Reeda, her voice low.

"I'm not giving anything up, I have nothing else. Nothing left. This is my home and I only wish I'd come back here sooner." Bindi's voice broke, and with a sob she leapt to her feet and ran from the room.

Her footsteps pounded up the staircase and her bedroom door slammed shut behind her. Kate stared after her, eyes wide and throat aching.

"What was that all about?" asked Reeda with a shake of her head.

"I have no idea. Has she said anything to you about what's going on?"

Reeda shrugged. "Nothing. I mean, I knew she was getting some flack at work over a piece she reported on a while ago, but I didn't think it was anything serious."

"Has she broken up with Brendan, do you think?" Kate

couldn't wrap her head around what Bindi had said. How could her sister be at a place in her life where she felt she had nothing left other than the inn? And without a word to her sisters?

Guilt flooded through Kate and her stomach roiled. She hadn't been there for Bindi. She had no idea what her sister was going through, and it was her own fault. She should've called, checked in on her more, asked her how she was. She'd been too caught up in her own life.

"I'm going after her," she said, jumping up suddenly.

Reeda lay a hand on her arm. "Give her some time. She'll open up eventually, she always does."

❄ 14 ❄

CABARITA BEACH

A week later, Kate sat at the dressing table in her room and studied her reflection in the chipped mirror. She slid a pale, pink lipstick across her lips and sighed.

It'd been so long since she'd made any effort to do her hair or wear makeup, she'd almost forgotten how to. Although, in Cabarita there weren't many reasons to get dressed up. The only time she'd worn something other than tracksuit pants, pyjamas or her wetsuit in the past week was when she'd donned some jeans to go grocery shopping with Mima in Tweed Heads. The sleepy coastal city seemed like a booming metropolis after weeks at the inn with no one to talk to but Mima, Jack, her sisters, and the occasional run in with the tight-lipped Alex.

Nan's old wooden box sat on one side of the dressing table and she glanced at it. She'd tucked Nan's letter into the small space left in the box, on top of the journals.

Outside, she studied the sky. It appeared the rainy weather had finally passed. The sky was a blanket of brilliant blue and the bright sun made her blink. Tree branches rustled in the cool breeze that blew in from the beach and leaves scattered and rolled over the patches of grass that struggled to grow in the sandy soil.

She grabbed two cups of fresh coffee from the kitchen and found Alex in the stables. It was Saturday, his day to spend guiding guests around the property on horseback. Although, now that there were no guests, he was going to use that time to rebuild the stables.

She'd taken to visiting the horses every morning either for a ride or to pat them and talk to them about whatever it was that was on her mind. It calmed her nerves to face the day ahead, although she'd already found the nervous energy she'd lived off in Brisbane had faded to occasional bursts of adrenaline whenever she thought about her job, Marco, Davis or driving back up the two-lane highway and home. Going home was less appealing with each passing day. But what option did she have? Soon they'd sell the inn and she'd return to her old life. That is, if they all agreed selling was the right thing to do.

"Morning," said Alex, glancing her way for a brief moment, before he turned back to hammering whatever it was he was working on.

He'd begun tearing the stables apart the evening before, leaving old timber in neat stacks around the outside of the yard, beside piles of new, light-coloured timber.

"Good morning. I brought coffee," she said, holding one of the cups toward him.

He straightened with a smile and took the cup. "Thanks."

"How's it looking?" she asked.

He shrugged. "About what I thought — termite damage,

timber falling apart, holes in the roof — but the concrete foundation's good."

"Well, that's something." She forced a smile. They still hadn't received the paperwork to be able to access Nan's bank account, so she'd be dipping into her own meagre savings account to fund the work on the stables. Although, their solicitor assured her the money would be available soon.

"Thanks for doing this," she said, as they each sipped the steaming coffee.

He nodded. "Gives me something to do."

He'd taken off his jacket and hung it on one of the pieces of new timber. His truck was parked nearby, the back full of tools and sheets of Colourbond roofing.

"Well, I appreciate it."

He seemed to be studying her, as though she were an insect or a class project. Inwardly she grimaced. Was he always so taciturn? He couldn't scrounge up a "you're welcome," or "happy to do it"? Although, why did she care? It made no difference to her. He was an employee, and she was his boss, or at least, one of them. He didn't owe her anything other than the work she was paying him to do.

He emptied his cup and handed it back to her. She pursed her lips. "So, I thought I could help you today."

He dipped his head as he reached for the hammer. "Fine by me."

Alex returned to his hammering and Kate watched as the tanned muscles in his arm flexed with each downward stroke. He paused and caught her staring. Her face flamed.

"Uh, I'll take these back inside and then I'm all yours," she stammered.

He arched an eyebrow, and Kate scurried for the kitchen, her heart racing. What was wrong with her? She was an engaged woman, happily betrothed to the man she'd marry and spend the rest of her life with. Yet a few muscles and a bit of sweat had sent her heart racing. She'd need to spend five minutes hovering in front of a pedestal fan if she stayed out there much longer.

Perhaps she'd been away from Davis too long, although she didn't remember ever having that reaction to him. He was a good-looking man, but he'd never built anything with his hands as far as she was aware. Never wielded a hammer, never ridden a horse. He was too busy dealing with server melt-downs, or something like that. She wasn't exactly sure what he did, but it sounded very important whenever he described it to someone. She couldn't ever seem to sum it up any better than, *he works in operations*. What did that mean?

In the kitchen, she found herself alone and leaned against the bench to catch her breath. She rinsed the cups, set them in the dishwasher, then hurried back out to the stables, deter-mined to be more mature and professional when she faced Alex again.

They spent the morning working together and by lunch they had a sturdy frame in place for the main part of the stables. Every part of Kate's body ached, and she was bathed in sweat, her jumper tied in a knot around her waist. Still, she was satisfied in a way she hadn't felt in a long time. They'd started with nothing, just a pile of old timber and a rickety frame. Alex had torn that down and she'd helped him build something — something solid. They'd done it with their own hands. Granted, she hadn't done much but hold this and carry that, but what they'd built would last for years to come. She liked it. Building something, being part of something bigger than herself. Life at the inn was growing on her in ways she hadn't expected.

She stood puffing, her hands on her hips, surveying the frame.

"It looks great."

Alex sat on the tailgate of his truck and swigged water from a bottle. "It'll do the job."

She frowned. "You're a glass is half empty kind of guy, huh?"

He huffed. "Guess so."

"Well, life might surprise you, Alex."

He shrugged. "Life's thrown me all kinds of surprises. Can't say I've enjoyed them. I prefer to keep things simple these days — no surprises, no disappointment, no pain."

She held back the questions she wanted to ask. What'd happened in his life to give him that outlook? He'd hinted at something dark or tragic, but she'd be crossing a line to ask him about it. She was his boss; she hardly knew him. If he wanted to open up and tell her about his life, he would. And she had a very strong feeling that wasn't likely to happen in her lifetime.

He stared off toward the sound of waves as they crashed and sighed against the shore, his look wistful.

"The surf's up today," she offered.

He inhaled a slow breath. "Yep."

"You should go... take out the surfboard."

He shook his head. "I don't surf. Not anymore."

"Go fishing then... do something you love. It's Saturday and you've probably got work the rest of the week. Sorry, I didn't ask you what it is you do with your time when you're not here." She offered an awkward laugh.

He swallowed another mouthful of water. "I'm a teacher at the high school in Kingscliff."

"Really?" That wasn't what she'd expected to hear. Maybe a carpenter, or a labourer, or a mechanic, but not a teacher. Teachers were usually a little more... talkative. "What do you teach?"

"Maths," he said.

Her eyes widened.

"Kate!" called Reeda from the direction of the inn.

Kate spun toward the sound, lifting a hand to block the glare of the sun. Her sister stood on the step, waving her over. There was a truck parked beside the inn and a man stood next to Reeda, a clipboard in his hands.

She remembered with a groan the meetings she'd lined up with prospective contractors to renovate the inn. The three sisters had all agreed to look into renovating the inn, even though Reeda was fighting to sell the place.

They all had to agree on a course of action, and so they were spending the afternoon interviewing contractors. According to Reeda, the only thing that made sense was for them to keep the inn closed to guests while they renovated, since whether they'd sell or reopen the place after they were done was still open to discussion. Kate and Bindi had agreed, because it made sense and to give Reeda a concession.

"Sorry, got to go," she said.

He nodded, gulping down the last of his water.

Kate hurried toward the inn, wishing she'd had a chance to shower before the meetings.

She held out her hand to the man, dressed in jeans and a collared shirt. "Hi, I'm Kate Summer, pleased to meet you."

"Bruno Moore," he replied, shoving a pencil behind his ear to shake her hand. "Pleasure."

⚜

THE SPRAY FROM THE SHOWER HEAD MASSAGED KATE'S tired shoulders. She leaned her hands against the shower wall and ducked her head, letting the full power of the spray pummel her aching muscles. By the time she'd dried off and dressed in her pyjamas for tea, she was so tired she could've dropped right to sleep without eating a thing. And if her stomach hadn't been clenched with hunger, she would've.

The delicious scent of roasted meat wafted up the staircase to greet her and her stomach growled. She was enjoying living at the inn. It'd revealed to her how lonely her life in the city was. She lived alone, woke up alone, worked at a busy restaurant until late most nights, which made her feel lonelier than anything, then back to her empty unit. Alone. It was nice to be around people again, people who cared about her, even seemed to like her.

"That smells so divine; what are you making?" she asked Mima, as she slid into a seat at the kitchen table.

Mima grinned, stirring something in a saucepan on the stovetop. "Roast beef, with vegetables and gravy."

"Wow, I'm starving, I think I could eat the whole thing."

"Physical work will do that to you," replied Mima. "Looks like you and Alex got a lot done today."

Kate nodded. "We did the entire frame. I'm pretty chuffed actually — didn't think we had it in us. Well, I was certain he did, and sure that I didn't. Not that I contributed a whole lot, but I think he was glad to have me there." He'd cracked a smile a few times and thanked her for her help when they'd packed up for the day. From what she knew of him so far, it was glowing praise.

Reeda peeked her head around the kitchen wall, then joined Kate at the table. She looked freshly showered, but there were dark smudges beneath her eyes that Kate didn't remember seeing before.

"Have you been sleeping okay?" asked Kate, straightening in her chair to study her sister more closely.

Reeda shrugged. "Not really. But what's new?"

"What do you mean?"

"Hey, what did you think of the contractors we interviewed?" asked Reeda. "We didn't really get a chance to talk about them because you had to scurry on back to work with the hot horse guy."

Kate's cheeks flushed with warmth. "He's not the hot horse guy, he's Alex, and he's one of our employees."

Reeda's eyes flashed. "Of course he is. So... what did you think?"

"Of Alex?"

Reeda sighed, irritation pursing her lips. "No, what did you think of the contractors. I'm fairly certain I know what you think of Alex." She waggled her eyebrows.

Kate knew Reeda, and her sister was never going to drop the subject of Alex's good looks once she got a hint of any attraction between he and Kate. Not that there was a hint, there was nothing between them. He worked for them, and he was good-looking. So what? Lots of people were good-looking, it didn't mean anything when she was already firmly ensconced in a loving, committed relationship.

Although, it was strange that she hadn't heard from Davis in days. Where was he? She'd tried his office and home numbers so many times she was beginning to wonder if something was wrong with his answering machine. Perhaps she should duck home to Brisbane for the weekend, before the renovation on the inn began in earnest.

"I liked Baron Moore..." replied Kate.

"Bruno, I think his name was Bruno," said Reeda.

Bindi slid into the seat across from Kate. "Who's Bruno?"

"Where have you been all day?" asked Reeda.

Bindi tipped her head to one side. "I went for a drive."

"Are you feeling okay?" asked Kate, resting a hand on Bindi's arm.

Bindi sighed. "I'm fine. I miss Nan."

"We all do," added Reeda. "It's so strange to be here without her."

"I keep thinking I hear her singing in the garden," added Kate. "It's so strange, I smile and start toward the back door, then realise it's all in my mind. She's not there, and it hits me all over again."

Bindi nodded. "I know what you mean. So, who is Bruno?"

"He's the contractor Kate liked. We interviewed four of them today, I thought you were going to join us."

Bindi shrugged. "You guys are capable, and I trust your instincts."

"You're the one who doesn't want to sell," replied Kate. "I thought you'd want to be part of it, the renovation, running the inn... isn't this what you wanted?" Sometimes Bindi could be so frustrating. Whenever she was feeling down about something, she withdrew from the world. Kate couldn't tell what her younger sister was thinking, or what she wanted.

"Yes, it is, I'm sorry. I still don't want to sell."

"Even though it makes the most sense," muttered Reeda, with a shake of her head that flung wet tendrils of hair that clung to her bare neck.

"She's right," interjected Kate. "I don't think we should sell either. The best thing would be to keep the inn closed for now until we can get it in top shape, then have a grand reopening or something. We can do this."

"And I believe the two of you would be better at managing the renovation than I would," added Bindi with a smile. "I'm happy to look after the books and all the administrative side of things. And when the inn is back up and running, I'll handle the day to day, take care of the guests, and all the things Nan used to do."

"Well, that's fine with me, I like the idea of managing the construction, if you'll help me," replied Kate, inclining her head in Reeda's direction.

Reeda nodded. "Okay, I can do that. But I can't stay in Cabarita forever, I do have a husband and a business back in Sydney. I don't want to be away for too long."

"I'm sure he misses you," replied Bindi with a sad smile.

Reeda dipped her head and mumbled something beneath her breath like, *He'd better*, but Kate couldn't be sure what she'd said. Kate shook her head. What was going on with her sisters? Not that she could say anything, her entire personal and professional lives were a hot mess.

She sighed. "I can help Mima in the kitchen."

Mima glanced over her shoulder with a chuckle. "And I would sure appreciate it. My legs get tired these days, and I'd love the company."

"That's perfect," said Bindi, with the most genuine smile Kate had seen her offer in weeks.

"And I can handle the interior design and pick out all the furnishings and decor for the place," said Reeda with a nod.

"I'd hoped you would say that," replied Bindi. "It's going to be perfect."

"I don't know about perfect," replied Reeda, "but we'll do our best and see how we go."

"I have a good feeling about it," replied Bindi.

"Me too," added Kate. "After all, when the money comes through from Nan's estate, we'll have plenty of funds to sink into the place. And who knows, with a bit of a facelift, maybe it'll turn into a hot destination for holiday makers."

"Well, between us, we can certainly get a few people from the major cities to come and visit, and then maybe word-of-mouth will help us," responded Reeda.

"Once Reeda and I head home, it'll be you, Mima and Jack taking care of everything," Kate prompted Bindi. "Are you sure you'll be able to handle it on your own?"

Bindi laughed. "You still see me as the baby of the family, don't you?"

Kate shrugged, her lips puckered. "I guess so, I can't help it. You're my little sister."

"I'll be fine. I'm more capable than you realise."

"I know you're capable, I worry about you, that's all." Kate didn't like the perpetual gloom that'd lingered on her sister's face over the weeks they'd all been living at the Waratah.

"Don't worry about me. I've got everything under control," replied Bindi.

✲ 15 ✲

CABARITA BEACH

Kate's stomach was so full she couldn't lay on it to read Nan's diary at bedtime. She groaned and rolled onto her back, patting her tummy gently with one hand. Perhaps she shouldn't have gone back for seconds, especially when Mima was serving pavlova with cream for dessert. She'd have to slow down on the delicious food if she was going to be able to fit into her clothes.

She reached for the wooden box on the bedside table where she'd left it earlier and pried open the lid. The letter from Nan rested on top of the journals as though taunting her to read it.

She still hadn't opened the letter. No doubt, Reeda and Bindi would've read theirs already. Reeda's curiosity would've driven her to it, and Bindi always did the right thing without having to think about it. Kate was the one who took her time, weighing her options, wondering, hoping, worrying.

She still wasn't ready to see what Nan had written. Guilt played through her gut, making it turn over. Would Nan remind her of how little time she'd spent with her in recent years? The pain of that reminder was too much to think about.

Besides, there were plenty of other things to do, busy things, urgent things, now they were keeping the inn. Although, Reeda was still determined to try and change Bindi's mind on the subject. Kate was certain she'd fail, and they might as well face the task ahead — perhaps the renovation would be more than all three of them could manage anyway, and the Waratah would be sold off whether they wanted it or not.

Kate pressed her lips together. She couldn't put it off forever. Something inside her wanted to postpone reading Nan's final words, since once she read them, she wouldn't ever hear from Nan again, even if the sound of her voice was only in Kate's mind.

With careful fingers she pried open the envelope, not wanting to destroy the seal placed so lovingly by Nan on the flap. Then she tugged two sheets of paper free.

The writing, more familiar than ever, since she'd begun reading Nan's journals, stood out in black ink on the white page.

Darling Kate,

If you're reading this, then I've gone on ahead of you to the next stage in the great journey of life.

I wish... so many things. I wish we could've had more time together, shared more laughter and tackled greater adventures.

I've left the Waratah to you girls, as I'm sure you knew I would. You're my family, the only family I have left, and I couldn't imagine anyone better to carry on taking care of the one last piece of earth that holds my heart.

The inn was my salvation at one time. It was a dream I had as a girl, that took me a long time to claim and changed a few times, but once I did, I never looked back.

I know you might be divided over what to do with the place, but can I ask this one thing of you? Please take care of it. Bring it back to its former glory. Don't leave it as it is. I couldn't bring myself to do anything to change the place once your Pop, Dad, and Mum were gone. There were too many memories haunting each room that I didn't want to let go of.

I long for your sisters and you to become the family you once were again. It breaks my heart to think of you facing life alone. You need each other, now more than ever; make sure you do your best to restore those connections.

If you decide you want to sell it, I trust your judgement. I'm so proud of you, my darling granddaughter. Prouder than you can imagine.

You have so much life in you. Don't settle for second best, always shoot for the stars, because that's where you belong. I wish I'd done more of that myself — wish I'd never let go of my dreams, never second-guessed what was in my heart. If only I'd believed in myself and the ones I loved. But none of us can go back in time, we can't rewrite the past. So, treasure each moment, my darling.

With love, Nan xo

TEARS DRIPPED FROM KATE'S NOSE AND CHIN, HITTING THE paper, and leaving wet marks where they landed. She folded it quickly away and pushed it into the envelope, then lay back on the bed, hands pressed to her face.

Oh Nan, I wish we had more time too. I should've visited, taken you on a trip to Europe, sat in the breakfast nook and had tea with you one last time.

With a sigh, she set her feet on the floor and straightened, then wiped the tears from her cheeks. The box was still on the bed beside her and she picked it up to push the envelope back inside, this time next to the journals, along one edge.

Her fingers pressed to something rough on the bottom of the box. She turned it over and saw something etched there. It wasn't in the neat style of the carvings that covered its surface, but as though it'd been whittled with a blunt knife.

She held it up to the dull glow that emitted from the bedside lamp and squinted.

Letters, there were four letters with the shape of a heart drawn around them.

CJ
  EW

Charlie Jackson and Edith Watson, it had to be them. Kate traced the outline of the initials with the tip of one finger, her heart pounding. Had Charlie made this box for her grandmother?

Kate shook her head and set the box on the bedside table, her stomach already churning with nausea at the thought of what was to come if she continued reading. Not tonight — not after reading Nan's letter. She wasn't sure how much more emotional turmoil she could take. And with everything that was going on in her own life, she had no more tears to cry that day.

Mum and Dad were gone, she barely knew Reeda or Bindi any longer. Something was going on with both of them but neither seemed to want to talk about it, and she had no right to pry. She'd lost that right when she let herself drift out of their lives, years earlier. And then there was Davis, the man she'd agreed to marry, but who wasn't returning her calls. Her heart felt heavy thinking about him — was it right to marry a man because he fit all the criteria on paper? Or, should she hope to find the kind of love Nan and Charlie had shared?

She stalked to the window and peered out into the darkness. The sound of the ocean calmed her spirit and she inhaled a long, slow breath, her pulse returning to a normal pace. The gum tree outside her window had grown over the years until one of the branches almost touched the wall by the window and another, higher up, brushed the third-floor roof.

Two bright eyes above the nearest branch reflected the light from her room back to her. She squinted and tried to focus her eyes in the gloom. A pink nose, a bushy tail and reddish fur — it was the possum. *Her* possum. The one that'd destroyed Nan's garden and scratched around in the inn's roof.

"Go find a tree to live in," she hissed, waving a hand at the creature.

It stared back at her, unmoving.

"Go on, get outta here!"

The possum looked away, as though it'd grown bored of her, then walked down the branch to the trunk and disappeared down beneath another branch. Kate frowned, there had to be something they could do about that possum, even if Mima didn't think there was. Maybe she could find out where it was getting into the roof and block up the hole. She'd have a word to Bruno when he began construction, likely he'd be able to find and plug the possum's entry into the Waratah Inn.

❧ 16 ❧

BATHURST

Waves of heat emanated from the farmhouse's tin roof. Sheep dotted the parched paddocks, and the leaves on some of the peach trees curled in on themselves. Inside the farmhouse, shouts bounced off the walls.

Edie covered her ears with her hands, her eyes squeezed shut. She couldn't take it anymore. Why didn't Father understand? He didn't know Charlie, not the way she did. Charlie wasn't the person he thought. Why couldn't he see that?

She straightened, and pressed her hands to her forehead, her father paced back and forth across the dark, cramped living room in front of her.

"But Daddy, we love each other," she cried, her voice wet with tears.

Her father stopped pacing and stood in front of her with his hands on his hips, his face thunderous. "You love each other? You're sixteen years old."

"Plenty of people get married at sixteen," she objected.

"I thought you wanted to finish school. That's all I've heard from you for years — you want to finish school and go to university, as if money grows on trees!" He spat the words like they were poison.

"I can get my certificate at the end of the year. We'll be married after that. And then we'll go to university in Sydney together."

"How are you going to pay for university?" shouted her father. He faced her mother with an upward wave of his hands. "This is the kind of daughter you've raised?"

Her mother stood in silence, both hands laced together in front of a white apron.

"I don't know how we'll pay for it," Edie continued, "but we'll find a way, I guess." He was being unreasonable. These weren't the things that mattered. Love was what mattered.

"Well, don't come asking me for money. I'm not throwing my hard-earned money down the drain by sending a girl to university to study science, of all things."

Edie spun about, tears streaming down her face. She saw Charlie then, through the gap in the curtains and her eyes widened. He gave her a nod.

The sight of him strengthened her resolve. It didn't matter what Father and Mother thought, or what they said. She and Charlie loved each other. They'd get married, go to University, and build a beautiful life together. They'd be successful and happy, and they'd do it far away from here.

When Father had finally finished yelling at her, he strode outside and slammed the door behind him. She peered through the curtains and saw him heading for the shed. He'd be there until teatime if history was any indication.

Mother disappeared into the kitchen soon after, without a word. She didn't like to get involved in conflict, but Edie knew what she thought. Mother supported whatever Father said, regardless of what Edie wanted. She wished Mother would support her, just this once.

As soon as Mother was out of sight, she hurried out the front door, being careful not to make a sound. She crept across the verandah and down the timber steps, then ran down the hill towards the creek.

Tall yellow grasses waved in the summer breeze. The sun beat on her head and sweat trickled down the sides of her face. Through the peach orchard, with trees whispering overhead and birds calling and swooping between their branches, she considered their future, and a smile crept across her tear-stained face.

When she reached the creek's bank, she saw him. He'd pulled off his suit jacket, undone his tie and shoved it into his pants pocket, opened the first few buttons of his shirt, and rolled up his sleeves. Then, he'd flung himself in the grass, plucked a long piece of it from the ground, and chewed on the juicy end while he waited.

She threw herself at him, kissing his face, his neck, his lips, all at once, while tears slipped from her face. She tasted their salt. Her hands cupped his cheeks, and she straddled him, her skirts splayed out around them, her knees pressed into the dirt on either side of his body.

He laughed and kissed her hard. "Whoa, slow down." He pressed his forehead to hers, their eyes connecting.

"Did you hear him? He says we can't get married, he's never gonna let us be together," she cried, pain ripping at her heart.

"I heard him, but he won't always have a say in how we live our lives."

She shook her head. "I don't know what to do. I love my parents, and I don't want to hurt them."

"Why does he hate me so much?" questioned Charlie.

"He says you're a bad influence. I don't know why. He's

wrong, I know he is. I don't know why he can't see you the way I do." She kissed him again, all at once feeling frantic and bold.

He sighed against her mouth. "He'll come around, they both will. Soon as you're old enough, we'll marry and then they won't be able to say a thing about it."

She blinked, and her eyelashes shone with tear drops. "We should get married now. I don't care what they say."

His jaw clenched and he sat up, spilling her onto the ground beside him. Then he set his elbows on his knees, as he stared out across the fields beyond the creek. What was he doing? Something was wrong. There was a pain in his eyes she hadn't seen before.

"We can't."

She smoothed her skirts over bent knees. "Why not? Why can't we?"

"I enlisted," he said, simply. "I joined the airforce."

She cried and she begged. But it was too late, he told her. He'd done it, and he'd be leaving the next day. They should treasure the moment, their last evening together. He didn't know how long he'd be gone, but it shouldn't be later than Christmas. He'd be back in time to go to university, then they'd go to Sydney together and build the life they'd talked and dreamed about.

Charlie pulled her to her feet and tugged a wooden box from the satchel slung over his shoulder. He held it out to her. Its carved surface looked warm. She studied it, her tears slowing. He'd whittled some of her favourite birds on the sides and Eliza's long, slender face on the lid. She took it in her hands, her eyes still half-blinded with tears, and smiled.

"What is it?" she asked.

"Open it," he said.

She lifted the lid free and a small, tin ring shone in the harsh light of the sun.

He knelt before her, smiled as he took her hand in his.

"Edie Watson, will you marry me?"

She cried out, her heart filled with joy, and reached down to kiss him. They stood, both pairs of lips still joined, and he wrapped his arms around her.

"Did you say yes?" he laughed.

She nodded. How could she say anything else but yes? Her heart belonged to him. Always to him. "Yes, I'll marry you."

Then he slid the ring onto her small, pale finger. "I'll come back for you, I promise. We'll get married, and we'll be together forever, and no one will be able to stop us."

She sobbed against his chest and issued a muffled wail into his shirt. Then, when she calmed and the empty hollow feeling of resignation stole away her tears, he stroked the hair from her face and they talked about all the things they'd do, where they'd get married, what they'd name each of their four children and how their life together would look.

Then, as the sun set beyond the sweeping fields of dry, brown grasses and the cicadas set up a chorus of humming, they kissed and held and loved each other for the first time beneath a line of blooming waratah trees with the sound of the creek bubbling and chattering over rocks at their feet and with tears wetting both their cheeks.

❧ 17 ❧

CABARITA BEACH

Two weeks were spent in negotiations with their new contractor, following up on financing with the solicitor, and endless discussions about paint chips, crown moulding, flooring, and curtains.

When Kate wasn't arguing with Reeda over armchairs or trying to understand Bindi's explanation of various accounting terms, she was holed up at the stables every afternoon with Alex.

By the end of the fortnight, the new stables were complete and every muscle, ligament, and tendon in her body ached, or screamed, depending on whether she was laying down or walking.

Kate had a clear idea of how she wanted the inn updated, but so did Reeda, and often their ideas clashed. On one thing they agreed, the bedrooms in the inn needed private bathrooms or modern-day holiday makers wouldn't be interested in spending their hard-earned money to stay there.

There were eleven bedrooms on three levels in the

Waratah, and they had decided to reduce that number to seven, three on each level with the master suite on the ground floor. The extra rooms would be converted into walk-in closets and spacious en-suites for the remaining bedrooms.

Reeda had suggested they opt for a lighter colour palette, with subtle variations for each of the rooms, rather than the eclectic, garage sale vibe Nan had created throughout the inn. She'd used whatever colour paint she'd felt inspired to use for each wall, with no apparent theme. Kate liked the idea and added that they should remove any unnecessary walls and change out the old, square windows for more modern, rectangular ones to let in more natural light.

Even though they couldn't agree on carpet or hardwood, fabric couches or leather, they both loved the idea of modernising the inn without sacrificing too much of its historical feel.

When Bruno came back to do the walk through with them, pen poised above his clipboard, he jotted quick notes as they spoke. He'd suggested they refinish the timber floors, since with a lighter stain, they'd be both modern and fresh, while keeping the inn's heritage intact. That had ended the question of flooring, since both Kate and Reeda loved the suggestion.

The contractor offered several more pieces of advice in his gentle voice as they paced through the inn. Each time, he encouraged the sisters to retain as much of the inn's character as they could, since that was what guests would be looking for when they booked the Waratah over the more lavish resorts farther north on the Gold Coast.

Bruno was right. Kate could tell he loved the idea of working on the Waratah by the way he ran his hand up the balustrade, or gazed down the length of the hallway, stepping out a measurement here, or cocking his head to one side to calculate options there. He was the right man for the job, and she felt a weight lift from her shoulders when he stepped into his truck and waved goodbye as the sun dipped below the horizon. She and Reeda exchanged a relieved smile and walked arm-in-arm back into the inn.

Kate made dinner that night, since Mima had gone to bed early with a headache. She'd carried a bowl of pumpkin soup into Mima's room, with a plate of fresh baked bread, and set it on the bedside table to check on her. She was sleeping peacefully, and Kate hated to wake her. She studied her a moment, then pulled the door shut. How long would Mima be able to keep up the pace of work required of a cook at what they hoped would be a busy boutique bed and breakfast?

After they'd cleaned up the kitchen, Reeda and Bindi disappeared to their rooms, and Kate tugged the office phone out of the wall and carried it up to hers. She'd noticed a phone jack in the wall when she was last up there and wondered what had happened to the telephone that was likely plugged in for guests to use at one time or another.

That was another thing they'd have to rectify as part of the update.

She plugged the phone into the wall, lay on her bed and dialled Davis's home number. The phone rang out. She slid the earpiece back into place and squeezed her eyes shut, her heart falling. Where was he?

Just then, the phone rang in her hands. She jolted in place, then juggled the earpiece back and forth between both hands like it was a hot potato before answering.

"Hello? I mean, good evening this is the Waratah Inn, how can I help you?"

"Katie?"

She breathed out a rush of air. "Davis, there you are."

He chuckled. "Sorry, I know I've been difficult to catch lately. It's been busy around here."

"I really needed to talk to you."

"I know, honey. I'm sorry. I'm here now. What's going on?"

"We picked a contractor, and he's going to start renovations on Monday."

"So, you're keeping it?" asked Davis, surprise lifting his voice to a higher pitch.

"Nan wrote us all letters about how she hoped we would renovate it. We don't have to keep it after we're done if we don't want to... but the three of us talked about it and agreed to honour Nan's wishes to make it look the best it can before we decide."

"Okay, well that's good news I suppose," encouraged Davis, stifling a yawn.

"Am I keeping you up?" asked Kate.

"No, no, it's fine. I'm tired, that's all. I've been working long hours. We've got this project that won't seem to end. But you don't want to hear about that... tell me about your contractor."

She sighed. "He's great, but the problem is, I think I need to be here to supervise. Reeda's capable, I know that, but I don't want to leave everything to her and Bindi. Besides, at some point she's going to have to head back to Sydney, and Bindi can't do this on her own."

The silence extended between them. Davis cleared his throat. "So, how long do you think you'll be there?"

"I don't know... but it'll probably be a while yet."

"What about your job?" he asked.

She shook her head, burying her face in her hands. She hadn't told Davis yet. She hadn't wanted to hear the words from his mouth — she should've fought for her position. Shouldn't have let it go so easily. He wouldn't have. She knew that. "Marco already replaced me."

He sucked in a breath and she waited for his response, her heart in her throat.

"I shouldn't be surprised. He's a selfish jerk, and always will be."

She exhaled. "He is. But I'm looking at it as my chance to change direction, do something different. I think renovating the inn is something I have to do. Nan left me a letter, and she asked me to restore the inn, to make it my priority. I don't think I can ignore that."

He sighed. "I get it. Look, I've got to go, honey. I've still got a ton of work to do, and I'm exhausted. So, maybe we can talk tomorrow, eh?"

They said their goodbyes and she hung up the phone, her heart heavy. Telephone conversations weren't the same as seeing each other face-to-face. She'd have to take some time to visit Davis soon, she only wondered why he hadn't made the trip yet himself. Cabarita was beautiful, and they could take long walks on the beach together, go horse riding, have a small holiday at the inn. She'd suggested it to him more than once, but he'd always found an excuse not to come.

As she pulled the curtains shut, she noticed a light on in the newly constructed stables. An electrician had come by that afternoon to set everything up, and she'd been delighted to see the glow from the overhead bulbs switch on and off again. She felt a pride she'd never experienced before in the strength and beauty of the structure she'd helped Alex construct. But one of them must've left a light on after the electrician packed up.

She skipped down the staircase and padded outside. The chill of the night air bit through her thin pyjamas, and she wished she'd thought to grab a coat. Her feet flopped about inside the enormous gumboots she'd found by the back door. Perhaps they were Jack's, she wasn't sure, but her small feet swam in them.

It was the storeroom light. She marched into the stables, reached around the storeroom wall, her fingers feeling their way, then flicked off the light switch, throwing the building into darkness.

The horses hadn't moved back into their stalls yet. She and Alex planned on filling the stalls with hay and setting up water troughs the next day. After that, the animals could take up residence. She hoped they'd enjoy their new, spacious stalls.

"Hey!" called a masculine voice from within the storeroom.

She startled, clutching at her heart. "What on earth?" She flicked the switch, flooding the room with light.

Alex stepped forward, his eyes wide. "What are you trying to do, kill me?" He held a saw in one hand.

She blinked. "What are you doing here? It's late."

He turned back to the piece of timber he'd been sawing and set the saw back in place. "I thought I'd hang around, get a bit more work done. There's nothing worth watching on the telly."

She shook her head and sat down on a bale of hay to watch him. "You just about gave me a heart attack."

"Ditto." He grinned up at her.

She sucked in a slow breath. "So, what are you working on?"

"Putting some shelving in here."

"Don't you have to teach tomorrow?" she asked, squirming in place to find a more comfortable position on the hay bale.

He shrugged, setting the newly cut shelving on the ground. "Yep. But I love being here with the horses, working with my hands. It's one of the few things in life I really enjoy, that and my garden."

She chuckled. "You don't look like the kind of man who has a garden, or a greenhouse."

He snorted. "What kind of man do I look like?"

Kate's cheeks flushed with heat. "I don't know... definitely not a maths teacher either."

"Well, I guess you've got me all wrong then," he replied, with a wink.

Her heart skipped a beat.

He reached for another piece of timber and began sawing it in two.

"So, you're engaged?" he asked, his eyes still fixed firmly on the timber and saw.

She stared down at her ring finger. The diamond sparkled, reflecting prisms of light against the storeroom's walls.

"Ah... yes. I'm engaged."

"Who's the lucky guy?"

Her stomach tightened. "His name is Davis, and he's an Operations Manager with a big firm in Brisbane."

"Sounds fancy," replied Alex with the flash of a dimpled smile her way.

"Yes, he is, I guess."

"And where is this Davis?"

"Huh?" she asked, not sure where he was going with this.

"I mean, your Nan died, and you're here trying to figure out what to do with this inn you've inherited — where's Davis?"

She couldn't be sure, but it sounded like a criticism. Only he'd said it with a warm smile painted on his lips, and dimples flexing in his cheeks.

"He's busy with work. He wanted to be here, but he couldn't make it."

"Shame," replied Alex.

As she walked into the inn and shucked off the gumboots by the back door, she couldn't shake the feeling that something had changed. Something inside her felt empty, weak, rattled. Where was Davis? She'd thought herself unfair for her disappointment in him not being there, but perhaps she wasn't. If Alex thought the same, maybe it wasn't her own insecurity talking. Maybe it was normal to expect your fiancé to be there when you needed him, like she needed Davis now. She padded back up the stairs to her warm bedroom, an ache in her chest. And as she fell to sleep, she dreamed of possums climbing through bedroom windows and horses running free on the beach as she chased them with a bridle yelling after them to stop.

❦ 18 ❧

MAY 1942

BATHURST

Eddie climbed onto her bicycle and fixed her skirt so she could peddle, by shimmying it up her legs as far as she dared. If only Father would let her wear pants like many of the other women working in the small arms factory alongside her.

She tugged the hairnet from her head with a sigh, and shoved it into her pocket, replaced it with her tattered straw hat, then pushed down on the pedals.

As she rode past the row of new cottages, built for the women working in the factory, she waved at some of the familiar faces who offered her tired smiles in reply.

She'd never seen so many women gathered in one place before, let alone working together, side-by-side, in a factory. Almost two thousand workers gathered in this factory every day, most of them had come from outside of Bathurst — surrounding towns and far off cities. She was one of the few who returned home each day, something she was grateful for and dreaded all at the same time. There were hours of chores awaiting her when she reached the farm, now that Bobby had joined the Royal Australian Navy.

Bobby had shipped out not long after she received the first letter from Charlie. He'd written home before he left, assuring them all that he'd take care. Her mother had gone to bed for the entire day and her father hadn't said a word about it. They'd tried to talk Bobby out of going.

"Leave it to the men who don't have a property to run. You have responsibilities here, it's up to us to feed and clothe the soldiers, son," her father had said.

He was right. Bobby had an exemption, if he wanted it. They ran a herd of sheep and the wool was already being sold to the army to make uniforms for the boys over on the front line. And they grew peaches in the orchard too, food for people in the cities, and for the cans and jars of fruit and preserves that'd make their way to feed the men on the front line.

Father had used every argument he could think of, then he'd spoken about the men he'd known, his father included, lost, or forever changed by the Great War. But it hadn't mattered. So many of Bobby's friends were gone, either in Sydney training for battle, or already stationed in North Africa, Papua New Guinea, or Malaysia. *Stone the crows*, he'd shouted, he wouldn't stay behind, like a wowser, and let them do all the fighting. So, he'd left. The house was quiet now. And the quiet bit at her sanity like drips from a leaking tap.

She'd heard from Charlie as well. He'd sent the letter before his ship pulled out of port, but for some reason it'd taken a roundabout passage to reach her, and she'd worried she wouldn't hear from him, wouldn't know where he was headed.

He was in good spirits, it seemed. Soon to leave Sydney, bound on a ship to join the North African campaign. He'd let her know when he arrived. They'd made him a pilot in the

Royal Australian Air Force, and he'd trained in Bankstown for several months before departing for Egypt. He said they'd be joining the Pommies there to send Hitler's goons home for good, and she could expect him back in a few months. His letter had been full of promises, declarations of love, and apologies for leaving her.

She pressed a hand to her chest, where she'd stored the letter inside her brassiere. It crackled against her skin, one corner of the folded page digging into her flesh. Since Bobby left for war, her parents didn't want to hear Charlie's name on her lips. They blamed him for Bobby enlisting, as though Charlie had somehow been the cause. She knew it wasn't true, they had to know it as well, but they wanted someone to blame and he supplied a ready target for relieving their pain.

Edie only wished she'd been able to speak to him before he left. How could she tell him that a baby grew inside her? When would she get the chance to let him know she and the baby were waiting for him to return home, to join them, to become a family together?

She'd suspected she was pregnant when she threw up her morning porridge in the yard by the stables a few weeks after Charlie left for Sydney. It wasn't long before her fears were confirmed, and the nausea remained as a constant reminder that everything in her life was about to change.

What would she do when her stomach grew too large to hide beneath skirts, dresses, and aprons? Her parents would find out then, and they'd be furious. Maybe they'd throw her out. She didn't want to go to the nuns. She'd heard stories about what happened to the girls who were sent to those cold, hard convents. Her heart hammered at the thought of it. No, if it came to that, she'd run away first. She and the baby might starve to death, but at least they'd do it on her terms.

Finally, Edie huffed up the long driveway to the house. It

perched high on the sloping hill, peeling white paint, rust-covered tin roof, looking older and more worn every day, as though the pain of losing Bobby was more than the house itself could bear. She felt the same way, she missed him already. The house echoed as though hollow without him, her life was dull without both of them — Bobby and Charlie. Not to mention the fact that Mima had moved to Sydney.

Mima was training to be a nurse, she'd stated, right before she climbed onto the bus that was headed for the big city. They'd need all the nurses they could get, so she wasn't going to miss out on the fun. Besides, she'd said, all the good-looking boys had left Bathurst, why would she stick around to be bored, doing needlepoint and such, when she could entertain the troops. She'd already packed her piano accordion under the bus with the rest of her luggage.

Edie had waved goodbye, a sad lump in her throat. Everyone was leaving, and she couldn't do a thing but stay behind. The quiver of butterfly wings fluttering in her stomach reminded her that a life was forming there, and she'd need her parents' help in the coming months whether she wanted it or not. She hated that she'd have to rely on them, unsure of how they'd react to the news once she broke it to them. But what else could she do? With Charlie gone, and Mima in Sydney, she had nowhere else to turn. She'd have to count on them.

She stowed her bicycle in the rickety old shed beside a few bales of hay and her riding tack, hung on nails against the wall. Her saddle sat astride a timber stand her father had crafted for her years ago when she'd first begun to ride. It was worn, weathered, and faded now, but she loved it just the same. She ran a hand over the saddle's smooth leather, kept supple by the regular oiling she gave it. It was a bit small for her now, but she could hardly ask for a new one given the way things were. She'd have to make do and hope that the war would be over soon.

Inside the house, she hung her straw hat by the front door, then sucked the ends of her fingers, worn almost raw by sorting bullets for hours on end, while she scanned the room.

"Mother?" she called.

Pots banged together in the kitchen and she followed the sound. Her mother was looking for something, her brow furrowed and nostrils flared in the way that Edie knew meant trouble.

"What's wrong, Mother?"

Her mother straightened, pressed her hands together and exhaled a short, sharp breath.

"Your father has enlisted in the Militia."

Edie's eyes widened. "What?"

"Yes, he will be leaving us as well, it seems." Her mother's eyes flashed, but otherwise she retained her cool, calm demeanour. She was a lady, and a lady kept her temper, something she'd tried hard to impress on Edie, without as much success as she would've liked. She'd never said as much, but Edie knew it was true.

Her father strode into the kitchen, dressed in a brand-new militia uniform. He brushed his shoulder with one hand, as though dust might have settled there on his walk down the stairs.

"What do you think?" he asked her mother, with a head dip in Edie's direction.

"It's very handsome," Mother replied, with a tight-lipped smile.

Father nodded. "Good afternoon, Edie."

"Father — are you really joining the Militia and leaving us alone?" she asked before she could think of something more fitting to say.

"You'll have each other, and I can't think of anyone more

capable of running this farm than the two of you. Besides, I'll be back whenever I can. I don't believe I'll be stationed too far away, so I'll try to see you every now and then."

"You don't know where they'll send you," snapped Mother.

Edie's mouth gaped. She'd never heard Mother say anything other than a gentle or kind word to Father before in her life. It wasn't like Mother to behave that way, and her breath caught in her throat as she waited on Father for a reaction.

He surprised her by cupping Mother's cheek with one hand, more affection than he'd shown in as long as Edie could remember. "Oh Diana, don't worry so."

❧

THE BASKET SWUNG ON HER ARM AS SHE WALKED THROUGH the orchard. The year's harvest was over, but Father had asked her to walk between the trees to make sure there were no peaches left in the branches or laying on the ground. They'd mummify or rot and cause trouble for the next year's crop.

Father had already set the ladder out for her against one of the trees. She climbed it and studied each branch, plucking any old or half-grown fruit that remained behind, and setting it in her basket.

How would they manage this place without Father or Bobby? She'd always worked hard and done chores, it was one of the things her parents had stressed for both their children over the years, but her chores had been more to do with managing the house and feeding the family. She'd learned to darn, knit, crochet and mend. But not to crop sheep tails. She knew how to polish the timber floor so it shone, and the best way to remove a stain from a shirt. But had never called out the dogs to round up their herd for shearing or dipping. Never pruned the peach trees or fertilised them with the right mixture of... she wasn't sure what Father used.

She'd seen it done of course, many times over the years, but was watching the same as doing? She pushed her fingers to her lips and made a breathy sound — she didn't know how to whistle the way Father and Bobby did when they were sending out the sheep dogs around the back of the flock. Would the dogs listen to her?

And what would she do when the baby came?

She inhaled a sharp breath as she climbed down the ladder. Then she set the basket on the ground to move the ladder to another tree, resting it up against the tree trunk with a shake to make sure it held fast.

She'd only recently turned seventeen and the idea of having a baby, of raising it, sent a shiver up her spine. She didn't have nieces or nephews, no younger brothers, or sisters, no one to show her how to do it. No one other than Mother, and she knew Mother wouldn't be happy about the baby coming.

Despite all that, it sent her pulse racing to think about the little bundle growing inside her. Edie was happy. Fear pulsed through her veins alongside anticipation — she and Charlie were having a baby. They'd love it and raise it together and be a family. If only he were here now, everything would be all right. He'd hold her, stroke her hair away from her face and tell her so.

She climbed the ladder as high as she could manage and picked the shrivelled and stunted peaches, stacking them in her rapidly filling basket.

One brown looking peach hung out of reach. She'd have to move the ladder again, or perhaps she could stretch a little farther. It tickled the end of her fingertips and she grabbed for it, lurching farther to one side. Beneath her, the ladder swayed, and Edie clutched at it with both hands to steady it. But the bottom of the ladder slid out from under her and she came crashing to the ground with a loud squeal, as her basket flew from her arm.

Peaches scattered in every direction as Edie landed with a thud in the dirt, her stomach impacting hard on the ground, her hands splayed out on either side.

"Edie?" her mother's voice floated from the direction of the house. "Edie? Where are you?"

She couldn't respond. The wind had been knocked from her lungs by the impact and she winced as she rolled onto her side and gathered her knees to her chest.

The baby.

Pain shot through her side like a knife slicing at her gut. She clutched at the pain, rolling back and forth as groans erupted from her mouth. Was that noise coming from her? Darkness flooded her vision making it seem as though she was at the end of a long tunnel with only a pin prick of light at the other end. Then she caught sight of her mother's feet running in her direction, and it brought a sob to her lips.

"Edie!" called Mother again, as she dropped to her knees by Edie's side. "Did you fall? Are you hurt?"

Edie couldn't answer, only rolled from side to side, clutching at her stomach and groaning. The pain was too much. She felt a wetness soak against her back where her skirts were clumped beneath her.

The thudding of footsteps as Father joined them.

"What happened, Diana?"

"She fell, Frank. Let's get her to the house."

Then darkness closed in and the light faded as Edie's conscious mind flitted away from the pain.

❦ 19 ❦

CABARITA BEACH

It took two tries to get Kate's Honda to start. The key turned and the engine made a whirring noise but didn't ignite until the second try. It'd been sitting out in the cold for too long without being used. She hardly had need for a car at the inn. Nan's truck was best suited to most things that needed doing around the place, and Reeda had her hire car. Bindi had returned her car to the carhire office at the airport, since she planned on staying at the inn permanently. She'd asked Reeda to drive her to a car dealership to pick out something suitable, which meant that Kate and Mima were home alone at the inn on a Saturday morning.

With the renovation project well underway, Kate and Mima had plenty of mouths to feed, and since it was the weekend, Kate had decided to drive to Tweed City to stock up on supplies for the week ahead. She'd tried to tell Mima they didn't need to feed the workers a hot lunch every day of the week, but Mima wouldn't hear of it. She said they'd do a much better job if they were warm and satisfied rather than cold and hungry, and Kate couldn't argue once she caught a glimpse of the determination in the older woman's eyes. She knew better than to pick a fight with Mima — the woman's gentle, good-humoured stubbornness was a force to reckon with.

Kate had promised to show Mima how to make Thai Beef Massaman on a bed of coconut rice from scratch, using the inn's slow cooker and a handful of fresh herbs and spices. Mima was intrigued, but not entirely convinced they should introduce some of the Asian influenced food that was Kate's specialty into the Waratah's kitchen. Kate wasn't sure it was the right fit either, but she'd been working on putting together a menu that fit the historical atmosphere of the elegant, old property, along with some Asian fusion influences to give it a more modern, typically Australian, edge.

The car crawled along the gravel driveway and out through the gates. The sign that hung by the gate was held in place only by one rusting chain from a timber post, the other chain had broken and hung limp from the top of the sign that now swung, lop-sided, with the wind.

Jack stood on a step ladder next to the sign, hammering a second post into place beside the old, weathered one. This one was fresh, new and had that raw timber look that the stables had since she and Alex rebuilt them. She slowed to a halt and wound down her window to offer him a wave.

"Everything okay?" she asked.

He tipped his hat in her direction. "She'll be right, love. Just getting the 'closed' sign fixed up."

The inn had been officially closed for weeks now, but every now and then they still had the occasional foot traffic coming in from the main road, looking for a place to stay. They hoped this sign would turn people away before they tromped through a construction zone, seemingly oblivious to what was going on around them.

She gave Jack the thumbs up, and stepped on the accelerator, heading north along the narrow highway as she wound the window back up.

Winter was over and spring was definitely making itself known. The cold weather had been replaced by a steady, stifling heat.

Nan used to say, there's no spring up here, only a few weeks of winter, a week of perfection, then a long nine-months of summer. She was right, as always. Summer was the default setting for northern New South Wales, and it was worse in Brisbane. Hot, dry, and humid all at the same time.

She slipped out of her cardigan and threw it on the passenger seat as she drove. Then she fidgeted with the air conditioner settings to see if she could get the car to cool down. It'd been colder inside the inn, all those dark rooms and cracks between the wide, timber floorboards. The contractor assured them he'd be working on better insulating the building as part of the renovation, and she was looking forward to lower heating and cooling bills. From what Bindi told her, the electricity used at the inn was a major financial drain on the Waratah's profitability. They intended to install solar hot water and gas to run the brand-new stove they were having shipped from Melbourne.

Just as she got the air conditioner set to the right temperature, a car whizzed by her in the other direction, buffeting her own vehicle and sending her onto the verge. Gravel shot up behind her car, ricocheting out from under the wheels and into the brush that lined the road.

She swore beneath her breath, then steadied the wheel, steering the compact SUV back onto the road, as her mind raced to identify a nagging thought. She recognised the car, and the driver behind the wheel.

Her eyes widened — Davis!

By the time she'd slowed the car to a halt and turned

around, there was no sign of his car. He must have been headed to the inn, but why hadn't he told her he was coming? She set off after him, even as she glanced in the rearview mirror and ran fingers through her lank hair; she could've done with some warning.

Up ahead, she found the car pulled onto the verge. He must've recognised her as well. She aimed the Honda to park behind his Lexus, gave her hair one last fluff, and climbed out.

His door opened and a blue-jean clad leg emerged, followed by the rest of Davis, with his perfectly groomed brown hair, wide brown eyes, and pale, smooth skin. There was a crease between his brows below a pair of reflective Ray-Bans, pushed up onto his forehead.

She waved, as nerves wrestled in her gut. What was he doing here? And without saying a word to her about coming?

She kissed his lips, a soft peck, and he patted her back. The exchange felt a little awkward. She pulled away and offered him a warm smile. "Davis, I wasn't expecting you. Why didn't you tell me you were coming? I could've... well, brushed my hair for one thing." She laughed, a little titter that warmed her cheeks with embarrassment. He was her fiancé for heaven's sakes, she was acting like a schoolgirl who'd never seen a boy up close before.

Granted, it'd almost been two months since she'd last seen him. She'd been planning on visiting him in Brisbane tomorrow. He knew that, they'd talked about going out to eat at their favourite restaurant, taking a walk at Southbank, rock-climbing at Kangaroo Point in the evening. So, why was he here?

"I wanted to surprise you."

She laughed again. "Well, you did. I was coming to see you tomorrow..."

"It was time I drove down. I should've come sooner. I know I said I would..."

"Multiple times," reminded Kate, her throat tightening. Almost every weekend he'd promised to travel south, but always gave an excuse at the last minute. She didn't want to hold it against him, but something inside her said there was a reason for it. He loved her, at least he said he did. He'd asked her to marry him, and yet he hadn't been able to find the time to drive two hours south to see her in two months.

It had to mean something.

"Where does this path lead?" he asked, pointing to a sandy trail beside them. It meandered through patches of spiky grass and disappeared between two large sand dunes.

"It goes to the beach, I expect," replied Kate with a shrug.

"Let's take a walk," said Davis.

She frowned. "Here? Now?"

He nodded, then locked his car and pushed the keys into his jeans pocket. He reached out a hand in her direction and she took it, then followed him down the path.

"What's going on, Davis? Why don't you come back to the inn with me? I'll brew a pot of tea and pull out some of Mima's scones, we can sit outside under the gum tree in some uncomfortable and very rickety garden chairs and talk there."

He laughed. "This is fine. Actually, there's something I want to talk to you about, so I'd rather not go to the inn and face everyone yet."

"No one's there but Mima," she continued.

He shrugged, but didn't say anything else, just continued trudging forward through the sand.

When they reached the beach, he released her hand and pushed his fingers through his hair, staring at the curling waves, the spray of water and the swooping gulls. His gaze travelled up and down the length of the beach before he sighed, his shoulders drooping. He slid the sunglasses back into place over his eyes.

"It's so beautiful here."

She inhaled a sharp breath. "That's what I've been trying to tell you. You need a holiday. We could fish, eat, talk, swim... whatever you like. It's what we both need. Since I lost my job, my stress levels have dropped... some time out is what I've been wanting."

He faced her, pressing his hands to his narrow hips. "No, it's not what I need. Look, Kate, I don't know how to say this, so I'm going to come out with it." He sucked in a deep breath, running his fingers through his hair until it stood wildly on end, completely unlike its usual, smooth, brown styling.

Her breath stuck in her throat. She fixed her gaze on his face. "What is it?"

"I've met someone else."

She blinked. "What?"

He shook his head. "I'm sorry, Kate. It hasn't worked between us for a long time. You've been gone for two whole months, what did you think was going to happen?"

She frowned, then swallowed. "I thought my fiancé would be supportive of the fact that I have a lot going on here. Things I have to take care of. I can't run away back to Brisbane and forget about my responsibility to my family."

He snorted. "Family? Kate, I've barely heard you mention any of these people before now. You're hardly a close-knit family, are you? And I'm assuming you've decided to let your career go entirely?"

Her eyes widened. "What does it matter to you?"

"I proposed to a beautiful, smart, connected up-and-coming chef, Kate. Now look at you? You've lost your job and from what I can tell, you're not looking for another one. What are you doing with your life? Are you going to stay down here and run a bed and breakfast? Is that who you are now? You haven't brushed your hair..." He threw both hands in the air.

She glanced down at the shorts and T-shirt she was wearing. There was a smudge of yellow paint on one knee. Her hair fell loose around her cheeks, and she knew there wasn't a stitch of makeup on her face, since she hadn't worn more than lip gloss in weeks.

"I thought you loved me," she whispered.

He sighed. "I did love you, Kate, but it was a different you. And you haven't been around. I've met someone else, moved on. You should too."

As tears pooled in the corners of her eyes, she tugged the diamond ring from her finger and handed it to him. "Here, you'll need this for your new girlfriend."

His lips tightened. "Don't be like that..."

She crossed her arms over her chest, as the stone in her gut grew. "Go home, Davis. You don't belong here."

He took another look around, then cocked his head to one side. "It *is* really beautiful."

She huffed. "Goodbye, Davis."

He walked away as the tears slid down her cheeks. She didn't want him to see her cry, so she brushed them away with the back of her hand and pushed out her chin. He turned back to wave, then disappeared around the bend of the trail. Then, she let the tears fall.

How could she have loved a man like that? He wasn't the person she'd thought he was.

She spun about to face the water, inhaled a long breath, slowing her heart rate back to a normal pace. She was better off without him if that was how he felt about her. Like she was some kind of trophy for him to parade around to his corporate friends. No wonder he'd been so frustrated with her in recent months when she'd chosen to spend her evenings relaxing at home in front of the television rather than attending his many, upscale soirées. She'd hated those parties. Always the same people, the same conversations, and the latest fashions. She couldn't keep up with it all and had no desire to.

She stepped forward, strode along the beach, her head down and hands pushed deep into her shorts' pockets.

Anger burned in her gut, and tears continued to wet her cheeks. Nan was wrong about love, all wrong. Love only hurt. It meant letting someone get so close to you, they could tear your heart out and stomp on it.

Although, if she were being entirely honest with herself, she wasn't as hurt by the breakup as she was by the way he'd done it. He'd met someone else, no doubt someone thinner, more fashionable, younger. She was twenty-eight years old, probably over the hill as far as he was concerned. He'd proposed when she was still in her mid-twenties, maybe he wanted a younger model.

She laughed through the tears. Good riddance. She didn't need that kind of pressure. What she wanted was someone like the boy Nan had loved all those years ago, someone who could accept her the way she was, love her for all her quirks, without makeup caking her face or an expensive dress that showed off her curves just so. Even when she hadn't thought to run a brush through her hair or had streaks of paint on her knees.

In fact, she didn't need a man at all. Perhaps her career was in the toilet, and her relationship was over, but she still had her sisters, Mima, Jack, and a broken-down bed and breakfast. Another laugh turned into a wail, and she buried her face in her hands. What was she doing with her life?

"Kate? Are you okay?"

She raised her head to find herself face to face with a half-naked, dripping wet Alex. He had a surfboard tucked under one arm, his tanned torso flexed as he shifted the weight of it, and concerned hazel eyes fixed on hers through several wet strands of hair that dripped saltwater down his nose and cheeks as she watched.

Her heart skidded to a stop.

"Ah... yep. I'm..." Who was she kidding? There wasn't a person on earth she could fool into thinking she was fine in the state she was in. Her usual bluffs wouldn't work this time.

"I thought you didn't surf anymore?"

"It was time I got back into it... time for a few changes, I think. Are you sure you're...?"

She stared at him, her eyes still filling with tears at the thought of what Davis had said. Was she so replaceable? So undesirable?

She walked up to Alex, curled a hand around behind his neck, pulled his head down toward her and pressed her lips to his. He tasted like salt and smelled like the ocean.

His eyes widened in surprise, then hers drifted shut as he dropped his surfboard in the sand and wrapped his arms around her waist.

Her lips parted as he explored her mouth. The wetness from his bare chest leached through her shirt, making her shiver. She pushed up onto her tiptoes to deepen the kiss, and moaned against him, making him grip her harder still.

Then, she pulled back, ran a finger over her lips and smiled.

"Kate... what happened?"

She turned on her heel and marched back up the beach.

"Kate? Kate!"

She spun about, walking backwards, to grin at him. "I'll see you back at the Waratah later."

He shook his head as he watched her go, his hands hanging loose at his side, above an abandoned surfboard. Then, she turned and ran to her car.

❧ 20 ❧

BATHURST

When Edie came to, she was encased by two strong arms, and carried through the yard. Her face was pressed to her father's chest. It smelled of tobacco and sweat, a familiar scent that brought tears to her eyes.

"Daddy?" she whispered.

She never called him that, not anymore. Not since she was a young girl.

He glanced down at her, his eyes wide. "Edie love, what happened? What hurts?"

She shook her head, squeezing her eyes tight. "I fell from the ladder."

"It's going to be all right." A muscle clenched in his jaw as he pushed backwards through the front door of the house and carried her over the threshold.

She clutched a handful of his shirt and held on tight. Gently he lay her down on the sofa in the living room. Her mother hovered close by, until he stepped out of the way, then reached for her hand.

"You're bleeding," she said.

Edie squeezed her eyes shut for a moment.

Mother glanced over her shoulder to where Father paced back and forth, his boots dropping clods of dirt on the living room rug.

"Frank, your boots," admonished Mother.

He stared at them like he'd never seen muddy boots before, then startled and hurried outside.

"Are you pregnant?" Mother asked in a whisper, the moment he was out of sight. Her lips pulled taut.

Edie sobbed. "Yes, Mother."

Mother's face fell, but only for a moment. She pulled herself together and tugged a lap rug up over Edie's dress, tucking it around Edie like she was an infant again, and Mother was putting her to bed.

"Well, you may have lost the baby today," said Mother, not meeting Edie's eyes. "We'll know more in time. I'll send Father to get May Hobbes from next door, she's been a midwife enough times."

Edie sobbed into her hands, the pain in her abdomen intensifying with each moment. She doubled over, groaning with the cramp that tightened in her gut.

Mother took Edie's hand in hers again, holding tight while the cramp subsided.

"There's nothing more we can do now, but rest and wait. You'll get through this, my dear," she said.

Edie couldn't speak, couldn't think, there was only pain and the need to breathe, great big gulps of air.

When the cramp passed, she fell back on the sofa, sweat trickling down her brow.

"I don't want to lose the baby, Mother," she said, meeting her mother's gaze with a steady look. "I want it to live."

Mother's eyes softened. "Of course you do. And now is not the time for reprimands. But you should know, if you keep the baby, the father isn't here. He won't be marrying you anytime soon and won't be around to care for either of you. So, you'll have to do things my way."

Edie swallowed and tried to sit up, but the pain was too great. She grunted and squeezed her eyes shut tight.

"Your way?" she asked.

"If this baby lives, I'll raise it as my own. That way, you can live without the shame you'd otherwise face, and do all the things you've hoped to do with your life."

"But Mother..."

Mother squeezed her hand and leaned over to kiss Edie's forehead. "Shhhh... I never had the chance to do things my way, to live the life I wanted. I had dreams too, you know. Dreams that never could come to anything, because I got married and had Bobby and you." Mother offered her a warm smile, as she brushed Edie's hair out of her face. "And I don't regret that, I love you both, but I don't want you to have to give up everything you've wanted for a baby, especially not your reputation. I don't want that for you." Mother's eyes took on a hard look and she stared beyond Edie, into some distant memory Edie couldn't see.

"It's for the best," she said. "Don't you see? It will be for the best, for you and the baby."

Something inside of Edie wanted to scream, to cry, to wail that the baby was hers, that she would raise it herself and didn't care sixpence what anyone in town thought of her or Charlie. They didn't need anyone else, they only needed each other.

Except Charlie wasn't there, she was all alone. And she couldn't raise a baby by herself. She had a job now but would lose it the moment her supervisor saw the bulge beneath her dress.

She needed her parents. And if Mother said it was for the best, she couldn't see how Mother could be wrong.

"Yes, Mother," she said.

"And you'll leave that job at the small arms factory and stay here at the farm until the baby comes. We can't have people talking about you." Mother pushed out her chin. "You're a Watson, after all."

May Hobbes visited and confirmed there was nothing they could do but wait while Edie rested. Soon after May left, the bleeding stopped, and the pain subsided enough for Father to help Edie upstairs to her own bedroom. She changed slowly, with Mother's help. Mother bathed her with a gentle, warm cloth, and helped her beneath the covers then kissed Edie on the forehead and left the room, pulling the door shut behind her.

Edie reached beneath her mattress to find the box Charlie had whittled for her. She fingered the carvings on the lid and sides, marvelling at the intricacy of his design and the hours he must have spent carving it with her in mind. She slipped the silver ring onto her finger, then back off again, setting it in the bottom of the box.

Downstairs, the sound of her parents arguing filtered beneath her bedroom door. Father yelled something she couldn't understand and was answered by Mother's steely, calm voice. They were talking about her.

She knew, with a calm certainty, that nothing between them would ever be the same again. Father wouldn't see her the same way, and from that moment on, her life would be contained within the walls of the small, white farmhouse. For months, or maybe longer, if Charlie didn't hurry back soon to rescue them. She clutched the box to her chest and fell asleep with tears leaving streaks in the dust on her cheeks.

🦋 21 🦋

OCTOBER 1995

CABARITA BEACH

The sitting room was a disaster. Already the walls between it and the living room, dining room and breakfast nook had been torn down. Plaster lay scattered across the drop sheets that covered the hardwood floors. Only a few support beams remained in place. Sunlight filtered through the gaps in the window coverings, giving the entire area a light, spacious feel.

Kate stood with her hands on her hips, surveying the damage. It was hard to imagine how anything beautiful could come from all this mess and destruction, but Bruno had assured her it would.

She couldn't seem to focus on the task at hand. When she went to bed the previous night, running over and over her conversation with Davis and the kiss she'd shared with Alex, her stomach twisted in knots and adrenaline continued to pump through her veins, regardless of the fact that she was lying on her side, in bed, with her eyes pressed shut. In the end, she'd groaned, rolled onto her back, and stared at the

197

ceiling, the faint scratching of the possum in the roof cavity her only companion. Then, she remembered Nan's journals, and she'd sat up, cross-legged in bed, reading until her eyelids finally drooped and she was ready to sleep.

One thought kept nipping at the edge of her mind — Pop wasn't Dad's father. Not his biological father anyway, if she was reading Nan's journal right. The timing fit. She'd done the calculations using a precise finger counting method. If Nan lost the baby, perhaps Dad came soon after. But how could that happen? Especially now that Charlie had left for the war? She shook her head and pushed thoughts of Nan, Charlie, and Dad out of her mind. She wouldn't find the answers in the demolished sitting room and wasn't ready to talk to her sisters about what she'd discovered yet. Not until she knew the truth.

Reeda stood in one corner, a measuring tape in both hands. She pulled one end of the tape out, pressed it to the wall, then stretched the tape as far as she could reach in the other direction. She muttered something beneath her breath and made a note in the notepad she carried everywhere she went now that the renovation was well underway. Her hair was caught up in a messy ponytail, paint smudged one cheek and her eyes sparkled. She was in her element.

"I'm going shopping for furniture. I have to put in orders now so that they'll be ready in time for the opening," said Reeda, tucking the tape measure into the tool belt that hung from her hips.

Kate nodded. "Do you think you could pick up some lunch while you're out?"

Reeda shrugged. "Okay, that's fine. Sandwiches?"

"Sounds good to me."

When Reeda left, Kate looked for Bindi. She found her in the office, going over the accounts. There was a crease between her eyes and her chin rested on one hand, almost as though in defeat.

"Hey, sis. What's going on?" asked Kate, sitting on the edge of the desk.

Bindi shook her head. "I'm trying to understand Nan's accounts. I don't get it. What is this account? Personal. That's all it says, 'personal'. And there are tens of thousands of dollars listed under the account. Meanwhile, the accounts for electricity bills, food purchases, furnishings... are almost entirely empty." She groaned and sat back in the chair, her eyes shut.

"Sounds like Nan was skipping corners when it came to reporting what her expenses were for."

"But personal? She's probably been missing out on tax deductions for years, by the look of this."

Kate sighed. "That's Nan for you."

"I'm not sure where to start," began Bindi, leaning forward again and squinting at the screen.

"Maybe start from now. We can't go back and change the past, but we can do our best for the future."

Bindi grinned. "Wow, that sounds like a Chinese fortune cookie quote."

Kate laughed. "Well, I'm all about gleaning wisdom from food."

A knock on the inn's front door startled them both. Kate brushed her hair back from her face and hurried to meet whoever had made it past the closed sign and through the stacks of tiles, timber, and men in hard hats.

"Hello?" she called, sensing Bindi right behind her.

A man stood in the open doorway. He wore a navy business suit, white shirt, and multi-coloured tie. He scraped the soles of his black, patent leather shoes on the dusty welcome mat, and glanced up at Kate with a ready smile.

"Hello there, I'm Howard Keneally," he said, extending his right hand toward her.

She took it and shook. "I'm Kate Summer. Is there something I can help you with? As you can see, we're closed at the moment…"

He scanned the bedlam with a chuckle. "Yes, I know. Actually, I'm here to help you."

Great, just what they needed, someone wanting to sell them the latest two-thousand-dollar vacuum cleaner or a stake in a religious cult she had no interest in joining.

"I'm a developer, and I'm planning a resort down the road from this property. I spoke with the former owner here…" He glanced down at a folder in his arms. "An Edith Summer… about buying the place. I want to include this property in my development proposal. It'd give me the opportunity to really make my vision a reality. And I'd pay you well for it."

Kate exchanged a look with Bindi. "Oh? You're building a resort nearby?"

"I'm planning on it," he replied with a smug grin.

"I don't think we're looking to sell…" began Bindi.

He interrupted her, lifting a hand to quiet her. Bindi's cheeks reddened. "I promise, you won't get a better offer than the one I'm willing to make. This place is falling apart, and before you sink another cent into something that, let's face it, can't bring in the kind of serious cash I'm talking about, let's make a deal that could change your life forever." His white teeth gleamed.

Kate wondered whether his blond tips were an homage to a boy band or if he liked to look as though he'd stepped off the beach, with his fake tan and glaringly bright teeth.

"Would you tear it down?" she asked.

"What? This building?"

She nodded. "Yes, the inn. Would you have to tear it down to make way for your resort?"

He laughed. "Of course, we couldn't keep it. It wouldn't... fit with the look we're going for. All modern, all white, suave and sophisticated."

Bindi's face was red, and her nostrils flared. She pushed out her chin and opened her mouth, but Kate stepped in front of her and stuck out a hand toward Howard.

"Thanks Howard."

He shook her offered hand.

She patted his shoulder and ushered him away from Bindi, down the stairs and through the cluttered yard. "Thank you for coming over. We're not looking to sell, but we appreciate your offer."

"I'll fax over the details," he continued. "I promise, you won't be able to say no, once you've seen it."

She smiled. "Well, we're in the middle of refurbishing what is, for us, a very beloved and sentimental building. But if we change our mind, I'll be sure to let you know."

He climbed into his BMW and drove away, one arm waving out the open window as he passed through the inn's gates.

Bindi came up behind her. "I don't like him," she said.

Kate chuckled. "I can see that."

"He wants to destroy the place."

"Don't hold that against him, I've wanted to do the same more than once since Bruno and his men arrived," muttered Kate.

Bindi huffed. "Be serious."

Kate faced her, resting her hands on Bindi's shoulders. "Okay, okay. I seriously didn't like him either. There, does that make you feel any better?"

Bindi nodded. "Yes, thank you. You're not going to change your mind and try to sell the Waratah again, are you?"

"Not this week."

"And I don't think we should tell Reeda about slimy

Howard. She'd see it as the perfect opportunity to get rid of the inn."

"Well..." It was the kind of chance that didn't come along often. They could sell the place, take their share of the proceeds and each return to their old lives. But what kind of life would she go back to? Brisbane wasn't home any longer. She had no job, no fiancé, and her friends had given up on calling to see how she was going. She'd had enough of that life.

"Please. Let's keep it to ourselves, for now, at least. We can tell Reeda, just not yet. I want to give us a chance to see what we can do with the Waratah, and if it doesn't work out, then we'll call Mr. Sleazey."

Kate laughed. "Tell us what you really think, Bindi."

"Please?"

"Okay. Fine, we won't tell Reeda. But so you know, I'm not comfortable keeping things from her."

Bindi grinned and embraced Kate. Kate groaned. "You're squeezing the life out of me."

Bindi laughed. "You're such a drama queen."

As Bindi walked away, Kate's heart lifted at the sight of her sister's happy, swinging gait. Lately, Bindi had seemed low, so out of sorts, it was good to see something lift her spirits.

"I'm going to Brisbane in a few minutes to pack up my unit," she called after her sister.

Bindi waved a hand above her head and kept walking. She'd already offered to help, but Kate had turned her down. They needed Bindi to stay here, keep things going while Kate was gone. It'd probably take her a few days to get everything packed up and put away. She'd move most of it to a storage unit she'd rented in Tweed Heads, and the few things she needed she'd move into the inn. They weren't renovating upstairs yet, so the bedrooms were still liveable.

With a sigh, she took in the construction crew, busily

hammering, sawing and lugging equipment across the dust-covered grass. She hoped Nan would be happy about what they were doing, though she'd likely have been horrified by the amount of demolition involved. Still, if they wanted to build a modern structure enticing enough to attract tourist dollars, sacrifice was necessary, as Reeda had explained to Bindi when she'd cried over the removal of the internal walls.

So much about her life had changed over the past few weeks. And yesterday she'd lost Davis and kissed Alex. Her face burned as the memory of the startled look on his face leapt into her mind. She shouldn't have done it. But he'd looked so appealing, standing in front of her dripping wet, eyes dark with compassion. And she'd been rejected, only moments earlier, by the man who said he'd love her forever. It'd been an impulse, nothing more. She'd apologise — but maybe not yet. Not until enough time had passed for the shock to wear off. Or perhaps he'd forget the whole thing and she could pretend it'd never happened.

Thankfully, Alex wasn't at the inn today. He was no doubt teaching impressionable teenagers about things like polynomials and equations. She wondered what kind of teacher he was. She was certain that she and her high school girlfriends back in Sydney would've had an enormous crush on him. By the time she'd moved to Kingscliff High, she'd been too swamped in grief to think about romance or cute teachers.

Kate headed for the house to find her purse. It'd be strange to go home and not see Davis. She'd lined up coffee dates with a few of her closest friends over the next two days, but otherwise needed to focus her time and energy on getting everything packed up. The movers and cleaners were coming in two days' time and she had a lot of work to do before then.

As she glanced around the bedroom, mentally checking off the list of things she'd need for the trip north, she spotted Nan's wooden box on the bedside table. She pulled out the journal she'd been reading and slid it carefully into her purse. She'd need something to do this evening when she was exhausted with packing and was dying to find answers to some of the questions she couldn't shake. Like what'd happened to Nan's baby? Did it survive the fall? Was the baby Dad, like she'd thought, or was he Pop's child after all? Did Charlie have anything to do with their family or was he simply Nan's one-time, and long forgotten, lover?

OCTOBER 1995

CABARITA BEACH

Ginger's hooves pounded along the hard, wet sand and Kate held on tight with her legs, her hands clutching a bunch of Ginger's mane along with the reins.

It'd been a long time since she'd ridden anywhere bareback, but she'd decided to take a ride along the beach with the sun setting behind her. It was a delicious evening. She hadn't gone riding nearly often enough since she moved back to Cabarita and didn't want to bother with the saddle. After all the work she'd done around the inn that week, gap-filling, painting, and sanding the upstairs hallway, she could barely move her arms, let alone lift a saddle onto a seventeen-hand-high horse's broad back.

Above her, the sky had turned a dark blue with patches of cloud, but behind her it was all pinks, yellows, and streaks of white. She glanced over her shoulder, her hair swishing in her face with each stride the horse took beneath her. It was beautiful. If only she could hold on long enough to get back to the inn without tumbling off and breaking something. That was all she could hope for now, since she'd lost all control over Ginger.

She'd tried pulling the horse to a stop, but apparently the animal had dreams of hay, oats and maybe a good tail rub on the fence post by the paddock gate driving her on. Ginger had scratched against that post so often it leaned at an odd angle, as though it might tip over at any moment. And the fence wires woven around its girth held strands of chestnut hair sticking out in every direction.

Kate could try again, or she could hold on and enjoy the ride. The wind whipped at her face, cold and with a hint of sea spray. She saw the path that led back to the inn in the distance, they'd be there before long. She shivered as the sun continued its descent. She really should've worn something other than a summer dress. Although, it'd been so hot when she finished work that she hadn't considered it.

The visit from the developer had played on her mind over and over. Bindi was adamant they say nothing to Reeda, but she didn't want to keep anything from her older sister. She knew how much that kind of thing upset Reeda. Her sister valued honesty more than she did just about anything else. What would happen when she discovered they'd kept it from her? It was likely she'd push them to take the deal, which was what Bindi was afraid of, but it didn't mean they had to do it. As Nan requested, they'd all have to agree before they'd change course, and Kate couldn't imagine Bindi would budge when it came to the Waratah's fate. She seemed to have made her decision and from what Kate could tell, she was sticking to it.

At least the three sisters were genuinely beginning to get along. Better than they had in years. Perhaps it was why she didn't want anything, like hiding the developer's offer from Reeda, to get in the way of that. Nan was right, she needed her sisters now more than ever. Everything else in her life had dissolved in the blink of any eye. The career she'd spent years building, the relationship she'd invested her time, heart, and soul into, all of it was gone and now she only had her family and the inn.

She could go back to Brisbane tomorrow and start again, but she didn't want to. Losing Nan, inheriting the inn, finding the journals, and reading Nan's letter — it'd changed everything for her. Her perspective had shifted in a different direction. She couldn't, or wouldn't, see things the way she used to — success, prestige, money — none of it meant what it had. And it could be whisked away again in a flash, as it already had.

Suddenly, Ginger slowed, then stopped. She turned to the water, dropped her nose to the remnants of a wave that lapped at her hooves and sniffed. She jerked her head in an upward arc, pushing her jaw forward and loosening Kate's grip on the reins, then lowered her head and took a step.

The ocean lay still. The wind had died down and the water rose and fell like a woman sighing. Kate remembered taking Janet into the ocean on days like this when she was young. They'd swim together, Janet's legs propelling them forward and Kate holding on by a handful of mane, her body floating above the horse's submerged back.

If Ginger wanted to swim, she wouldn't stop her. She leaned forward and stroked the animal's neck.

"You want to go swimming?"

Ginger continued forward. A small wave splashed her whiskered nose and she shook her head with a snort. Then, stepped over it and kept going. Before long, the water had reached Kate's thighs. She gasped as the cold seeped into her dress and up to her waist. Then, she pushed her legs out behind her and floated, while Ginger pressed forward and launched into a swim, with steady, rhythmic beats. The horse's head hovered over the water and her nostrils flared, she panted hard and paddled in a circular direction back to the beach, heaving free of the water. When she reached the dry sand, Ginger stopped still, dripping.

Kate smiled, her heart soaring as she shivered. The freedom she'd felt brought a bubble of laughter to her lips. Her entire body was covered with goosebumps and her teeth chattered. The water had been frigid, and now the sky was filling with angry-looking clouds that churned and hustled overhead, jostling each other for space. The wind picked up and Kate smelled rain in its gusts.

"I think we should head back to the inn," whispered Kate, sliding her hand across Ginger's dripping coat.

She pressed her heels to the horse's sides and Ginger broke into a trot. Before long, they reached the stables. Just as Kate slid from Ginger's back, there was a crack of lightning. Her heart stood still, the sound of the thunder that came on its heels making Ginger dance in place. Then, the rain poured from the heavens like water tipped from a bucket. Giant, fat raindrops landed on her face, shoulders, chest, immediately plastering her hair to her head.

She undid the bridle and set Ginger free to run with the other horses in the paddock. Ginger galloped to meet the group, her tail swishing. Kate stood in the rain watching her go, then peered up at the sky. The clouds had a faint greenish hue to them, it could mean hail. She should bring the horses into the new stable and rub them down.

Kate jogged into the stables, then through to the storeroom. She found a bucket, threw some corn and oats into it, then hurried to stand on the bottom rail of the fence. She shook the bucket and called to the horses. They didn't hear her at first. The rain pummelled the stable's tin roof, drowning out the sound of her voice to her own ears. The horses milled about at the far end of the enclosure, then Ginger saw her and pricked her ears forward. Kate raised the bucket higher still and shook it again, shouting to Ginger as loud as she could.

Ginger plodded toward Kate, then broke into a trot, her ears flicking back toward the group then forward to Kate. The other three horses watched with interest, then followed. And soon Kate had all four of the animals secured in stalls, munching happily on their own buckets of corn and oats.

She stepped into Ginger's stall with a towel and rubbed the animal down. When she was done, she headed for the next stall, but stopped when she heard the roar of an engine above the thunder of rain. There was a carport beside the stables. They'd built it for Nan's truck, but it had room for two vehicles in case they ever had need to buy a tractor or four-wheeler. The last had been Kate's suggestion, but Reeda and Bindi hadn't gone for it. There were so many other things they needed first, they'd said. Kate had grumbled over it but agreed. She'd thought it would be fun to ride on the beach but could admit it wasn't strictly a necessity.

Alex's truck pulled into the space beside Nan's, its red paint gleaming with rain. He switched off the headlights and the gloom of a rainy twilight settled back into place. Kate's pulse accelerated. What was Alex doing here? She'd planned on avoiding him, but she could hardly make a run for it now. He'd already seen her, besides which it was bucketing down.

Instead of hiding, she waved. He climbed out of the truck, a crease between his brows.

"Kate? I wasn't expecting to see you out here."

She hugged herself, suddenly aware that she was in only a summer dress and that the dress clung to every part of her body. She was soaked, her hair painted against her head and drops of water dribbling down the sides of her face.

"I went for a ride and got caught in the rain," she explained, her teeth still knocking together.

"You're freezing," he said.

He opened the back door of the truck and pulled out a blanket, then wrapped it around her shoulders.

She held onto it and offered him a grateful smile, tugging it tighter around her numb body. "Thanks."

"I'd offer you an umbrella, but I don't have one," he said with a shrug. "But I could drive you back to the inn — door to door service."

She nodded. "Thanks, but I think I'll be fine. I can't get any more wet than I am."

He chuckled. "That's true."

"I didn't know you were working this evening..." Her teeth had stopped chattering, but she still shivered, and it made her voice sound thin.

"Ah... I'm not. Actually, I saw the storm rolling in and was worried about the horses."

Just then, there was a loud bang on the roof overhead, followed by another. Soon, the clatter of hail on the roof filled the air. Rough edged balls of it bounced against the ground around the stables. Another crack of thunder made her jump.

"Wow, that was close," she said.

"I can't see the horses, so I guess you brought them in already?" he asked, his gaze making a quick sweep of the sodden paddock.

She nodded. "They're in the stalls."

"Good." He strode around the stables, checking on each of the animals, stroking a neck here, fixing a bucket there and speaking gently to them in a low voice.

Kate watched the hail slow, then it was replaced once

again by rain with only the occasional hailstone.

She pressed her back to the stable wall and slid down until her rear rested on the ground. She'd wait it out. While there were still hailstones falling from the sky, she wouldn't risk the hundred metre dash to the inn.

Soon, Alex joined her. He lowered himself onto the hay-strewn ground beside her and rested his elbows on bent knees, hands linked together between them.

"So, thanks for taking care of the horses," he said.

She shrugged. "I was here..."

"Still..."

She smiled. "You're welcome. And thank you for always taking care of them. It helps take a load off my mind to know you've got it under control."

"You have a lot going on," he replied.

"I wanted to apologise," she said, suddenly.

He turned to her. "Oh?"

"For kissing you the other day on the beach... I shouldn't have done that. I'm sorry. I don't know if you're single, and it was inappropriate..."

"Forget it," he responded. "And I am."

Her brow furrowed. "You are what?"

"Single," he replied with a laugh.

"Oh, good to know. Me too... newly single."

He quirked an eyebrow, and she waggled her newly nude finger at him.

His lips pursed. "Ah... I'm sorry to hear that."

Her cheeks burned. "No, I'm sorry. For the kiss, I mean."

"If it makes you feel any better, it was a really good kiss," he replied.

She turned to him, her face still flushed, and met his gaze. "Yeah?"

"Yeah."

She grinned. "It was... really great."

They stared at each other, both smiling, gazes entwined. Electricity crept up into her gut and then her chest, her breaths deepening. "So, why are you single? A guy like you, a hot high school teacher, you should have your pick of the single women in Kingscliff." It was the nearest town. Cabarita itself wasn't more than a hamlet or village, but Kingscliff had shops, restaurants, the high school where Alex taught. Compared with Cabarita it was a virtual metropolis. There was bound to be plenty of single women vying for his attention.

He sighed and leaned his head back against the wall, staring vacantly into the falling rain. "I've been married. I guess I haven't wanted to jump back into anything. Not yet anyway."

That surprised her. She hadn't considered that he might be divorced, although it made sense. Now that she was in her late twenties, whenever she met a single man, she had to assume he had a past. Some kind of serious relationship that hadn't worked out for whatever reason.

"Ah, you're divorced?" she asked.

He shook his head. "My wife died of cancer about three years ago. We were living down south, in Coffs Harbour, both teachers at the same high school. I'd lived there my whole life, apart from the years I spent at uni in Newcastle. But after she died, I couldn't stay any longer. Too many memories, too much sadness. That's when I moved up here."

Kate's throat tightened. "I'm so sorry. I didn't realise."

"It's fine. It was a long time ago."

She bit her lower lip. Why had she blurted out that question about divorce?

He met her gaze. "She'd want me to be happy, I know that, but I can't seem to get there. It's better now than it was. Time heals, they say. And I guess it does, but only because the memories fade. At first, every time I laughed or smiled, I'd feel bad, like I was betraying her somehow. Now, I can do those things without guilt, but I think I've forgotten how."

Kate set her hand on his arm. "You'll figure it out."

"You reckon?" he offered her a wan smile.

"Yeah, I do. You're strong, I can tell that already. You'll find your way back."

He looked down at her hand, then lifted it with his own pressed his lips to the back of it. Goosebumps travelled up her arm and her heart skipped a beat.

When he met her gaze, her entire body quivered with anticipation. He wanted to kiss her; she could see it in his eyes. But it might be a mistake, would be a mistake. He was grieving, she was newly single — and she was his boss. She'd already apologised for one inappropriate kiss; she shouldn't let it happen again. Only, she couldn't seem to move. Her body was frozen to the spot. He inched closer, his stare drifting to her lips.

When he kissed her, sparks bounced from her lips through her body, all the way to her toes. She'd never been kissed like it before — soft, gentle, yet firm and demanding all at the same time. Her eyes drifted shut and her hands curled around behind his neck as he shifted toward her, his own hands cupping her cheeks. Their first kiss on the beach had left an impression, but this kiss took her breath away.

She understood in that moment what Nan had described in her journal. The chemistry between them shook her and left her feeling depleted, yet exhilarated. He was like a mystery and yet something so familiar. Like coming home and embarking on an adventure all at once.

When he pulled back, she missed his lips on hers. Her eyes blinked open and she found him watching, the corners of his mouth crinkled in a half-smile.

"Are you going to apologise again?" he asked.

She spluttered. "But you kissed me."

He laughed. "Well, I'm not sorry."

He looped his arm around her shoulders and pulled her to him. She nestled into his side, resting her head on his chest. And while the rain fell, they talked about the past, the future, their hopes and dreams, and soon it felt like she'd known him all her life.

❧ 23 ❧

SEPTEMBER 1943

BATHURST

Edie strode toward the lambing pen, a bucket of water sloshing against her leg and dripping into the top of her gumboot where she'd tucked her pants leg, wetting her stockings.

She set down the bucket and studied the lambing ewes. The sun was rising, throwing orange and yellow light over everything, and making the ewes look like a cluster of golden cotton balls, their thick winter coats overgrown and framing long, white faces with puffs of wool.

Pink snouts sniffed the air, no doubt hoping she had something for them to eat. Two pink ears stood out on either side of the ewes' heads, flicking away flies and listening to hear what it was she had to say. Then, when she didn't speak or give them food, they lost interest and focused instead on lipping at the scraps of hay scattered over the hard ground.

"I think we're going to see at least three lambs tonight," said Mother, coming up behind her with a shepherd's crook in one hand and a coil of rope in the other.

Edie nodded.

"We can watch them in shifts," continued Mother.

"I've got nothing else to do," replied Edie.

"Mumma, mumma," Keith's sweet voice brought smiles to both their faces.

Edie found him seated on a picnic blanket beside the garden that wrapped around the front of the house. He waved chubby arms in their direction, a smile between his rosy cheeks.

"Hello, little one," replied Mother, waving a hand in his direction. "We'll be having brekky soon, my darling. What a good little boy you are."

Edie swallowed back a retort. Mother had never spoken to her that way. But what good would it do for her to say anything? Mother made daily sacrifices to raise Keith as her child. She'd told everyone in the neighbourhood, all their family and friends, that Keith was the son of a dear friend who'd died during childbirth and whose family all lived far away. Most believed her because Diana Watson was a woman of her word. Though some suspected the truth. A secret like that was hard to hide in a small town like Bathurst. Still, so far, they'd gone along with the ruse, at least to Mother's face. Edie had heard the whispers behind her back whenever she went to town alone and knew the cause of the gossip. Still, what did she care? He was theirs — hers and Charlie's — and he was healthy. That was what mattered.

Edie was grateful, had to be grateful. She had no other option than to swallow her own desires, dreams and wants, because Keith was all that mattered now. And this was what was best for him. He wouldn't be accepted if people knew, rather than suspected, the truth. She couldn't do that to him.

To those around them, Keith had appeared, it seemed, out of nowhere. Everyone in Bathurst was well aware of Frank Watson's strict rules when it came to his daughter, and most thought little of the fact that he'd kept her at home for seven full months, hardly seeing another soul. If they'd found it strange, they kept the thought to themselves.

Everyone had their own fair share of troubles in these uncertain times and didn't feel the need to go borrowing it elsewhere. Those who'd visited the farm during her pregnancy, or had heard the gossip, had plenty of their own concerns to deal with. The war had caused the small town's occupants to pull together, putting any grievances or judgements aside, united in their fear of losing loved ones abroad, or of being unable to feed those who'd remained behind.

"I'll make breakfast, if you'll take the first shift," said Mother.

While Mother took Keith inside, Edie set to work, checking each of the ewes to see if any looked ready to birth. By the time she was done, she'd found three in the early stages of delivery, but nowhere near ready to push. She had time before she'd be needed and there was something else on her mind.

She hadn't heard from Charlie in four months. The letter she'd received then had been dated two months earlier. Which meant that she didn't know anything about where he was, or what he was doing, if he was still alive, from the past six months of war.

The last thing she heard was that Charlie was flying with the Royal Australian Air Force in the Mediterranean Theatre as part of the Desert Air Force offensive. She didn't know for sure what any of that meant, but Father said he was likely flying over Italy, but he didn't expect they'd be posted there much longer. Father had furlough two weeks earlier and he'd said they were bringing many of the boys home, in preparation for the Japanese attack that could come any day.

Darwin had already come under attack, he told them. He'd read it in an old issue of *The Sydney Morning Herald* he'd borrowed from another militia man. Even Sydney was shelled, he'd told them. The militia had been hustled out of bed to respond but found that none of the shells fired from the Japanese submarine had exploded.

"They got as close as the Macquarie Lighthouse," he said. And Mother had pressed her hands to her forehead as if in prayer.

Edie was glad no one was hurt. Still, it didn't make her feel any better knowing the Japanese fleet had made their way so far south. The last they'd heard from Bobby, he was stationed in Guadalcanal fighting back the Japanese assault there. She saw the look in her parents' eyes when they spoke of it and knew how much they fretted over what might come should the Japanese invade Australia.

Since then, Father told them he'd taken to watching Movietone newsreels whenever he could buy a ticket to a local cinema. Edie hadn't been to town in so long she hadn't had the chance to see the newsreels herself, and Mother said she had no desire to fill her head with such nonsense. So, the two of them remained on the farm, relatively oblivious to what was going on in the rest of the world, but Edie was anxious all the same since Charlie, Bobby, and Father were out there, in the midst of it all.

She stuck her head inside the front door of the house, not wanting to remove her boots.

"Mother?"

Mother replied from upstairs. "I'm changing Keith's nappy."

"I thought I might ride into town and visit the Jacksons. Perhaps they've had a letter from Charlie," she shouted.

There was no response. She could picture her mother's stoic expression, disapproving of the idea but unwilling to cause conflict. She didn't care, she was going now whether Mother wished it or not. Since Keith's birth, helped along by the capable Mrs. May Hobbes from the next farm over, slowly but surely Edie had begun doing whatever she wanted, throwing off the desire to please as the war worked to strip her, and everyone she knew, of hope.

Now, she shouted if the situation called for it. She sat with her knees apart while eating her midday sandwich. She sang at the top of her lungs in her bedroom, at least when Keith wasn't sleeping. And she'd secretly begun teaching herself how to drive the truck, when Mother wasn't paying attention.

She'd found the keys on the kitchen table one day. After eyeing them for a full minute, she'd shoved them into her pants pocket and hurried to the shed. When she climbed in and figured out how to get it running, she'd almost squealed in delight before remembering to keep it down. She didn't want Mother to know what she was up to, at least not until she'd managed to navigate the long driveway on her own.

Her tongue stuck out the side of her mouth, she ground the stick until she found the right gear, let out the clutch, and pressed down hard on the accelerator. The first time she did it she'd bumped and shuddered halfway down the drive before the truck sighed and gave up completely. It'd taken every last ounce of patience to figure her way back up the hill so she could park the vehicle behind the shed where it stayed. Mother had been visiting a neighbour on foot, and hadn't missed the keys, since Edie put them back right where she'd found them.

Edie wiped her palms down the front of her trousers and smiled. No more working the farm in skirts and Mary Janes. No more tiptoeing around. She'd saddle Eliza and ride to town in pants to see the Jacksons and watch a newsreel if she wanted, and no one would stop her.

MONIQUE JACKSON WAS SMALLER THAN EDIE REMEMBERED. Her shoulders were more rounded, her arms thinner, and there were streaks of grey in her thick, black hair that hadn't been there two years earlier.

"Would you like a biscuit with your tea?" she asked, poking her head around the kitchen wall to smile at Edie. Tension seemed to pull her shoulders high.

Edie nodded. "Yes please, that sounds perfect."

"I see you rode your horse," continued Mrs. Jackson, carrying a tray with a teapot and plate of biscuits to where Edie was seated at the small, dark timber dining table. "Will she be okay, do you think? Or can I get her something?"

"She's fine. It's not far. And I'll be heading right back home again as soon as I leave here." The Jacksons didn't own horses and had turned their stables into a carport. They'd embraced the modern age and were one of the few families in town who owned a sleek, black car.

Mrs. Jackson tugged off her apron and hung it over the back of her chair before sitting across from Edie. "It's so lovely to see you, Edie. I was beginning to wonder what'd happened to you. How are you?" She furrowed her brow as though she wanted to say more but the words had gotten stuck in her throat.

Edie coughed. What could she say without being dishonest?

"I'm well."

"And your... little brother?"

Edie's cheeks flamed. "Keith is growing quickly, thank you. He's a cheeky little monkey."

Mrs. Jackson smiled quickly. "That is good to hear. I'd love to see him sometime."

Edie nodded. "I'm sure Mother would love to catch up with you."

"You must all be missing Bobby, and your father, of course."

Edie took a sip of the hot tea, then set the white china cup with a pink rose pattern back in the saucer before answering. "Yes, we miss them a lot. Especially now it's lambing season."

Mrs. Jackson's eyes widened. "Indeed. Will you and your mother manage that alone?"

"We don't have much of a choice."

"And how is your mother?"

Edie was dying to ask the one question she'd ridden into town for. Where was Charlie? Had they heard from him? But she knew her best chance at getting an answer was to push through the small talk that made her skin itch.

"She's very well, thank you. And Mr. Jackson?"

"Business is slower than usual, but that's to be expected of course." Mrs. Jackson held the teacup to her lips and drank, her eyes fixed on Edie's face.

Edie sucked in a slow breath. "Actually, the reason I came was to see if you'd heard from Charlie."

"Oh?"

"Yes, he wrote to me some months ago, but I haven't heard anything lately..."

"He wrote to you?" Mrs. Jackson's lower lip quivered.

Edie had always wondered how much Charlie's parents knew about their relationship. Her questions about Keith suggested she knew more than she was willing to admit.

"Have you heard anything? Anything at all?" asked Edie, leaning forward in her chair.

She squeezed the table edge between her fingers, her knuckles whitening.

Mrs. Jackson's face fell, and Edie wondered why she hadn't noticed the dark circles beneath the older woman's eyes before that moment. Mrs. Jackson stood stiffly and walked to the kitchen hutch on the other side of the small, dark room. She opened a drawer and pulled out an envelope, then held it to her chest.

"We received this telegram only a few days ago."

Edie leapt to her feet, her heart beating like thunder in her ears. "What? What is it? What's happened." She rushed to Mrs. Jackson and reached for her hands. "Tell me."

Tears pooled in the corners of Mrs. Jackson's eyes. "They say he's been shot down over Crete or The Gulf of Tunis. Missing in action — that's what it says. He's missing. They don't know where he is, he's been missing since July."

Missing.

The word rang in Edie's ears, over and over. Missing. Charlie was lost. Somewhere in North Africa, thousands of miles away from her and Keith, he was dead, injured, alone. And there was no way for her to know which, or when or how it'd happened. If only she'd been able to see him one last time, for him to meet Keith and them to hold each other.

"Is that all it says?" she asked.

Mrs. Jackson nodded. "I'm sorry, my dear. I know the two of you were friendly..."

"We were engaged," murmured Edie, her eyes glazed. "We'd be married now if he hadn't left."

Mrs. Jackson's hand pressed to her mouth.

Edie stumbled back to the table and slumped into her chair. "Thank you for telling me."

Mrs. Jackson nodded.

"Please let me know if you hear anything else."

Mrs. Jackson crossed the room and rested a hand on Edie's shoulder. "Of course, my dear. Of course I will."

As she rode Eliza home, she thought about everything Mrs. Jackson had said. About Keith, the lambs, and the farm. It was all too much, she couldn't deal with it, nor could Mother really, not with Keith to care for. It wasn't fair.

Charlie could be lying dead somewhere, might have been dead for months, and she hadn't known about it.

Back at the farm, there was a truck parked in front of the house. Mr. Ken Hobbes stood on the front steps speaking with Mother, while she held Keith in her arms, a white cloth slung over her shoulder.

"Edie, darling, Mr. Hobbes has come to help us with the lambing. Isn't that kind of him?"

Edie smiled as Eliza clip-clopped by. "That is very kind, thank you Mr. Hobbes."

It was then the idea formed in her mind. She mulled it over while she fed the ewes and checked on their progress. Then again as she inspected the peaches to see how they were progressing and watered the trees. All day long she laboured, and all day long she thought and planned.

Over tea that night, she spoke up. "Mother, I think we should ask Mr. Hobbes to come and help on a more permanent basis. He could run the farm and take a portion of the proceeds. We can't do it alone and besides I think I'm going to stay with Mima in Sydney for a while."

Mother's brow furrowed. "Sydney?"

"Yes, she wrote in her last letter that they're desperate for more nurses, and I think I could do well there."

Mother nodded. "I suppose that's true. Although, Keith and I would miss you."

"Maybe you should move into town to stay with Aunty Estelle and Uncle Don for a while. Mr. Hobbes could take over the farm while Father is away."

Mother's lips pursed. "That is a thought. It would be good to see more of Estelle, and if you leave there isn't much reason for Keith and me to stay out here all alone."

"So, it's settled then." Edie's mind was made up, she was going to Sydney. There was nothing to keep her in Bathurst any longer. Keith didn't need her, he had Mother. Charlie was missing, perhaps dead. The thought settled a stone in her gut and pricked at her throat, catching her voice. If his parents heard anything different, they'd promised to pass on the message — something they could still do no matter where she lived. And if he was wounded and returned to Australia, maybe she'd find him if she was nursing at the Army hospital.

"I'll have to speak with Estelle, but I'm sure she won't mind. She's mentioned the idea herself a time or two since your Father left, but I didn't want to unsettle you," said Mother in a clear voice.

She could see her mother warming to the idea with each moment that passed. She'd go to Sydney and see Mima. After that, she had no idea how she'd deal with everything, but it was movement, a way to keep going forward, it gave her something else to focus on and that was what she needed right now; a distraction from the pain of not knowing.

❧ 24 ❧

CABARITA BEACH

"**B**runo wants us out of the inn today," said Reeda, "so I've booked a flight to Sydney. I'll be back in two days. Do you think you can handle things while I'm gone?" Reeda sat at the dining table, elbows resting on the white, embroidered tablecloth.

Kate flipped the slices of bacon in the pan beside the eggs, sunny side up. "Piece of cake," she said with a grin.

"Don't forget, if they deliver the floor rugs, leave them rolled up against the wall. We've got to get the floors sanded and stained before we can put down rugs."

"I know, don't worry, I've got it all under control," replied Kate with a wink.

"Why doesn't that make me feel any better?" asked Reeda, her brow furrowed.

Kate shrugged. "I don't know... maybe because you have control issues."

Reeda cocked her head to one side. "Very funny. But seriously, call me if you need anything. I'll be home most of the day today, so you should be able to reach me. I have to pop into the office and get a few things done tomorrow, but today I'll be home with Duncan. He's got an entire day with no surgeries scheduled since he was supposed to be attending a conference in Singapore, but I convinced him to stay home to spend time with me instead."

"He's such a romantic."

Reeda smiled, but Kate couldn't help noticing the way her sister fingered the edge of the tablecloth, as her foot tapped a fast-paced rhythm on the floor.

"I'll be here to help, so whatever happens, we'll handle it," said Bindi, pulling her nose out of the newspaper spread wide between her hands for a moment.

"Okay, good." Reeda's foot kept tapping. "Bindi, don't forget to pay the painters."

"I won't," replied Bindi, her voice a monotone.

"And the plumber."

"On it." Bindi gave Reeda the thumbs up without looking at her.

"We're all over it like a sand rash on a half-naked surfer," said Kate.

Reeda shook her head. "Jeez."

Bindi laughed, then took a bite of cereal. "Have a good time, sis."

Reeda stood and smoothed her skirt against her toned legs. "I've got to get moving, I'll see you when I get back. Call me, okay?"

Kate embraced her sister and kissed her cheek. "Relax, enjoy some time with your husband. Everything will still be here when you get back."

Kate watched her leave then scooped the eggs onto pieces of toast, setting the bacon beside them on four plates.

"Mima, Jack, breakfast!" she called.

While they ate, Kate stared out through the kitchen

window. White lace curtains framed the window and through the brand-new, sparklingly clean windowpanes she could clearly see the garden shed and Nan's kitchen-garden.

"Nan's garden's looking a bit sad these days," she said.

Mima nodded, then swallowed a piece of toast. "She worked in that garden almost every day. It takes a lot to keep something like that going. It's too big now, with no gardeners living at the inn."

"I can downsize it for you, if you like. Or we could replace the whole thing with sod." Jack spoke around a mouthful of bacon.

"No, definitely not. I don't want to get rid of Nan's garden. I was thinking I might take a look at it today, since Bruno wants us all to make ourselves scarce while they work on the downstairs walls and upstairs bathrooms. Besides, I've been wanting to see what I can do to stop that possum from getting in through the fence and eating everything down to the ground. It's spring, so I thought I should plant some vegetables to get ready for the summer season, but there's no point with the possum around."

Jack nodded. "Edie used wire netting, but I think it's all fallen or been blown out of place."

"I'm going to take a look, see what I can do." Now that she'd said the words, Kate was resolved. She'd pull Nan's garden back into shape. She'd always wanted to grow a kitchen garden so she could use the fresh ingredients in her cooking but living in a unit in the city hadn't given her the opportunity. Now she had the chance to build as large a garden as she wanted.

The first thing she did was pull on overalls, gumboots, and an old straw hat she'd found hanging on a peg by the back door. She remembered Nan wearing the hat when she worked in the garden, and it felt right to set it on her head, like she was taking on the gardening mantle.

Then, she stepped through the gate and paced up and down the narrow pathways Nan had built into the rectangular space. Most of the produce had died away to only wisps of brown stems, or shrivelled leaves. Some parts of the garden had been cleared, tilled, and prepared for the winter months before Nan died. And a few of the evergreen flowers and bushes along the back rows of the garden were sagging, the soil around them hard and washed away in places.

She spotted Nan's waratah trees almost immediately. The brilliant red flowers were partially hidden beneath a mesh netting that'd fallen over them. She remembered Nan hanging it above the bushes to keep them sheltered from the harsh, summer sun, but it'd fallen and now smothered the plants.

Kate tugged on a pair of gloves and set to work freeing the bushes. Soon, the striking flowers were exposed and reaching skyward. Kate smiled, setting her hands on her hips to admire them. Nan loved those plants. She'd named the inn after them since she'd brought the plants with her and Pop when they moved from Bathurst. They were the first thing she'd planted when they moved in, and she cared for them like they were her children.

Kate wondered if Nan thought of Charlie Jackson when she looked at those flowers or walked through the doors of the inn. Waratahs were special to her, that much was clear enough. But were they special because of Charlie? How could she spend all those years of her life with Pop, when her heart belonged to Charlie?

Kate still hadn't finished reading the journal entries. She told herself it was because she'd been busy with the renovations, or spending time with Alex in the afternoons and on weekends. But the truth was, she was reluctant to keep reading.

It hurt to think of the pain Nan went through, knowing

her baby's father had been shot down, most likely killed in action. Believing she'd never be able to raise the child as her own. Nan had called her son Keith; Kate's father's name. Kate knew now that Charlie was her biological grandfather. She wondered if Dad had known — she didn't think so. She couldn't remember him saying anything about it and was sure he would've if he'd known. Or maybe he wanted to keep it from them. It wasn't likely she'd ever discover the truth now.

Besides that, sometimes it felt as though she were peering through the curtains into Nan's life. She shouldn't do it, shouldn't keep prying that way. Nan kept a lot of secrets from them, from all of them. It didn't seem right, since some of those secrets had a lot to do with the family, but for some reason Nan had chosen to do it. And she should respect Nan's wishes.

Once the waratah trees were free, she got to work tearing down all the netting that'd either disintegrated from the weather or had been blown free of the garden beds. Then, she pulled weeds. After three hours of back breaking work, she sat on her rear end in the dust to guzzle water from a drink bottle she'd brought outside with her. She knew she should really go in search of some food, but that would mean standing up and walking and she didn't have the energy for either.

As if reading her mind, Bindi emerged from the back door and headed in Kate's direction, a white plate in her hands.

"I hope that's food, or I might eat you," called Kate as Bindi pushed through the gate.

Bindi laughed. "I brought you a sandwich. I'm afraid it's not gourmet, the way you'd make it, but it's the best I could do."

"Thank you." Kate took the plate, set it on her lap and began eating. The tuna and salad sandwich was what she needed, and when she was done Bindi pulled two plums out of her jeans pockets and handed one to Kate. The other she bit into, letting the juice drip down her chin.

"How's it going out here?" asked Bindi.

Kate shrugged. "It's taking a lot longer than I thought. But look, Nan's waratahs are flowering."

Bindi grinned. "Wow, those things bring back memories."

"I know. For some reason it makes me feel good to see something of Nan's like that, and they're still going strong."

"How long do you think Reeda's going to stick around for?" asked Bindi suddenly.

"I'm not sure. Why?"

"Don't you think it's strange that she's staying? I mean, she's planning on coming back north in two days and her husband lives in Sydney. She's been here for months and barely talks about him, or about going home."

She had a point.

"It's a bit odd, that's true. Do you think something's wrong?"

Bindi sighed. "I don't know. I've never been married, but from what I understand, married couples usually try to live in the same state."

"I know Duncan works a lot."

"Yeah, maybe you're right. Still..."

"What about you?" asked Kate.

Bindi's cheeks flushed pink. "What about me?"

"Is everything okay with you?"

Bindi's green eyes met Kate's then she stared at the ground in front of her. "I lost my job."

"What?"

"That's why I wanted to stay here," continued Bindi. "Why I didn't want us to sell the inn."

"Why didn't you say anything?"

Bindi shrugged. "I was embarrassed. You guys always talk

about how proud of me you are with my big career in television journalism, and now it's over."

"It's not over. You'll get another job... if you want to. I mean, you can stay here and run the inn, if that's your dream, but don't give up on your dream for this."

Bindi's eyes filled with tears and she shook her head. "No, I won't get another job. There aren't any jobs going at the moment, and I've interviewed dozens of times. There are rumours that the industry is changing, they won't need as many journalists, and maybe they're downsizing because of it. But I was out of work for six months before Nan died."

Kate reached out and held Bindi's hand. She squeezed it. "I'm so sorry, Bindi. I didn't know."

Bindi wiped the tears from her eyes. "It's not your fault. I should've said something. I'm kicking myself that I didn't pack up and come home to the inn sooner. I could've spent that time with Nan instead of trekking up and down the streets of Melbourne looking for work."

"And what about Brendan? I've been wanting to ask you about him, but you didn't seem like you wanted to talk about it."

Bindi sighed. "We're taking a break."

"What does that mean?" asked Kate.

"He wants some space to think about his life, about us," replied Bindi with a smirk. "That was about a month before Nan passed. So, when I moved to Cabarita, it was as though it was meant to be."

"Do you think you two will patch things up? You've been together a long time."

"Too long," replied Bindi.

"Sorry?"

"He didn't want to marry me. We talked about it and he always diverted the conversation to another topic. We've been dating for six years and he doesn't want to get married. I should've known something was wrong years ago. I just thought he was taking his time."

"So, it's over?"

"I don't know. I guess we'll see. But for now, yes, it's over."

Kate stood with a grunt, then wrapped her arms around Bindi and pulled her close, kissing the top of her head the way she had when they were kids. "It's all going to be okay," she said.

Bindi sobbed against her overalls as she wrapped her arms around Kate's shoulders.

⁂

WHEN KATE FOUND ALEX IN THE STOREROOM BEHIND THE stables that afternoon, she crept up behind him and surprised him by sliding her arms around his waist without speaking. When he spun to face her, she pressed her lips to his, as his eyes flew wide.

"Good to see you," she whispered.

He laughed. "You too. You can surprise me like that any time you want."

She let him go and wandered over to Ginger who stood in her stall munching hay. Kate ran her hand down the length of the horse's face. "So, I guess we should get to know each other better," she began.

He grunted. "I guess so. What did you have in mind?"

"Music. What kind do you like?"

He chuckled, leaned back against the stable wall, and crossed his arms over his chest. "Nirvana, Pearl Jam... the usual suspects. How about you?"

"The Cranberries, of course, and Tracey Chapman. But I don't mind a bit of Lenny Kravitz either."

"Huh, different," he said.

She nodded. "I'm a different kind of girl."

"What was your first tape?" he asked.

She frowned, thinking back. "I think it was Johnny Farnham, but Mum and Dad bought it for me for my birthday, so not really my taste."

"He does have a good voice," replied Alex with quirked eyebrows.

"Very true. What about your first tape?"

He shrugged. "Pink Floyd."

"Wow. Good taste." She smiled, head nodding. "I'm glad, otherwise I don't think it would've worked out between us."

He laughed. "Oh really? My taste in music is that important to you?"

She took a step toward him, reached for his shirt, and tugged him close. "Very important. I have to know what kind of man you are, and nothing says that more than the music you listen to."

"What about the car I drive?" he asked.

She shrugged. "I don't care about your car."

"Good. Because it's old and ready to break down at any moment."

Kate laughed, pushed up on her toes to kiss him. Her heart thudded against her rib cage and tingles ran up and down her body. As he wrapped his arms around her, she melted against him.

🏵 25 🏵

DECEMBER 1981

PENNANT HILLS

Kate stood on tiptoe, trying to reach the angel that perched on the tip of their perfectly green, perfectly fake Christmas tree. They'd tried using a live fir tree the Christmas she was five years old, but it'd been such a dry summer that the tree was a crackling brown by the time Christmas Day rolled around and Mum had deemed it too much of a fire hazard to keep in the house. So, it'd sat outside in the yard gathering dust, dew, and the occasional bird poop.

This fake tree was pushed into the corner of the rumpus room in front of the psychedelic, swirling brown and green wallpaper, beside the record player with all its records stashed upright, the black vinyl peeking through the slits, and wedged beside the bookcase holding their entire set of Encyclopaedia Britannica, a collection Dad was so proud of. Kate loved to sit by his side on their emerald green, woollen couch, and flick through the pages of one of the volumes. Perhaps they'd start with the letter P and read all about penguins, or the letter L and travel to Lithuania for half an hour.

She huffed and hoisted herself a little higher in her Converse shoes, reached the angel and tugged it down with a victory shout.

The angel's dress was falling off and she'd seen it every time she walked by the tree. It'd been bugging her for days. She straightened the dress, then poked her tongue out the corner of her mouth as she worked to set it back in place.

"You fixed her dress?" asked Mum, coming in behind her.

Kate nodded.

"Thank heavens. It was driving me nuts." Mum laughed and looped her arms around Kate from behind, hugging her tight.

"So, what'd you get me?" asked Kate, studying the brightly wrapped gifts beneath the tree.

"I finally got that Barbie Dream House you asked for when you were six."

Kate rolled her eyes and spun to face Mum. "Thanks, exactly what every fourteen-year-old girl wants."

Mum grinned. "Come on, you can admit it to me — you'd love a Dream House. Wouldn't you?"

Kate couldn't deny it. She'd always wanted one, and though she knew most girls her age were over the Barbie craze, she still played with her dolls when no one else was around.

"Fine, just don't tell anyone," she said.

Mum laughed and drew a cross over her heart with a fingertip. "Your secret is safe."

"Where's Dad?" asked Kate.

"He's sleeping off the turkey he ate at lunch. Of course, he'll never admit he wants to take a nap so he's sitting upright in the lounge room..."

Kate loved Christmas Day, especially when Nan and Pop

came all the way from Cabarita Beach to visit. They brought the kookiest gifts with them and were so much fun. Mum and Dad had to cook, clean, and do so many things around the house all the time, but Nan and Pop gave the three girls their undivided attention.

Nan buzzed into the rumpus room with Pop, Reeda, and Bindi in her wake. "Who wants to play Scrabble?" she cried.

Kate smiled. "I do."

Mum nodded. "Sure, I'll join you as soon as I finish cleaning up in the kitchen. Then I have to get the potato casserole in the oven..."

Kate huffed. "Come on Mum, can't all that wait? You never play..."

Mum seemed to grapple with the pull of the dirty dishes for a moment, then smiled. "Okay, sure I'll play a game. But then..."

"Then you have to wash the dishes." Kate rolled her eyes.

"And for that, Missy, you can dry..."

"Fine," Kate grumbled.

"Come on, grab a seat," said Pop. He patted the chair next to him and Kate slumped into it.

He offered her a sideways hug. "Come on Pumpkin, you can be on my team. Let's slaughter these suckers."

She grinned, her spirits rising. "They haven't got a chance."

He laughed, his green eyes twinkling.

In the lounge room, Dad coughed. He poked his head into the rumpus room. "Scrabble?"

"Yes! You wanna play?" asked Bindi, jumping up and down in place.

She was such a child. Kate rolled her eyes again.

"I'd love to. I'm going to grab a drink first. Who wants eggnog?"

※

DECEMBER 1995

CABARITA BEACH

Kate tapped a red and gold ornament with her fingernail. It hung from one branch of the Christmas tree that decorated the newly refurbished sitting room at the Waratah Inn. She studied it, then took a step back to look at the entire tree. It was decorated with a subtle mixing of reds, golds and white. It had Reeda's handiwork written all over it.

Kate would've chosen an eclectic mix of classic, modern, pretty, and humorous ornaments, then covered the whole thing in colourful, twinkle lights. But Reeda's decorating was stylish, tasteful, and understated. Just like Reeda herself.

A large bag hung from Kate's arm, piled high with gifts. She pulled one out, wrapped in blue and red with small, red Santas all over it, and pushed it gently beneath the tree, beside the stack of gifts already waiting there. One by one, she placed her gifts beneath the tree, then folded the bag and set it on a side table.

"*When my heart finds Christmas*" played softly in the background. Bindi had hooked the CD player in the office up to the new sound system, with speakers in the various downstairs rooms, including the dining room, sitting room, and breakfast nook. Harry Connick Junior's sultry tones soothed her spirits. It was their first Christmas without Nan. She kissed her fingertips and pressed them to a framed photograph of Nan that stood on the side table.

"Merry Christmas, Nan."

"Eggnog?" asked Reeda, coming up behind her.

Kate laughed. "It's a bit early for me, but thanks anyway."

"Are you joining us in the kitchen?"

"Yep. On my way."

Mima, Jack, and Bindi were waiting for them in the kitchen. Bindi sat on the bench, a cup of coffee held tight between her hands and close to her lips. Her sandy blonde hair was pulled into a ponytail. She wore shorts and a T-shirt, and had her legs crossed at the ankles.

"Merry Christmas, Katie," she said with a smile.

Kate nodded. "Merry Christmas everyone." She kissed cheeks all around, then poured herself a cup of coffee.

Mima stirred a batch of pancake batter and hummed along to Harry Connick, Jr. Jack took a seat at the table, spread open a newspaper and buried his nose in it, one leg crossed over the other. His grey hair was mussed on top so it looked as though he'd just crawled out of bed.

There was a tap on the back door. Kate opened it, her heart thudding. Every time she saw Alex the same thing happened. Her heart raced, her stomach tightened, and excitement pumped through her veins. Was this how it was supposed to be?

She threw her arms around his neck and kissed him hard on the lips. His still-damp hair smelled like coconut.

"Merry Christmas," he whispered against her ear.

"Merry Christmas yourself. I hope you're hungry, Mima thinks she's feeding breakfast to a small army."

He laughed. "I'm starved."

They ate pancakes, bacon, eggs, and toast while they sat around the brand-new, hewn timber dining table Reeda had picked up from a local craftsman somewhere in Pottsville.

The air smelled of coffee, syrup, and fried bacon, and they shared good conversation and plenty of laughter. When they were done, they all helped clean up and made their way into the sitting room to open gifts.

Kate carried the coffee pot into the room to refill everyone's cups, then settled herself in front of Alex's armchair, his feet resting on either side of her. She tilted her head back and he kissed her lips in an upside-down smooch that had her skin tingling.

Alex gave her a new watch, which she badly needed. She hadn't worn a watch in a month since her last one died, and she felt lost without it. She gave him a new wetsuit. She'd found him trying to sew his old one up where a seam had split along one leg weeks earlier.

He kissed her again. "I love it, thank you."

She grinned and spun her watch around in place on her wrist. "Me too, thanks."

She'd been dreading what Christmas might look like with no Nan or Pop, no parents, and no fiancé, but the day was relaxed and filled with warmth, and she found herself happy.

After breakfast, they all sat in the breakfast nook. Reeda and Bindi played chequers with Mima, a pedestal fan buzzing back and forth, lifting Reeda's hair as it went. Jack snoozed in an armchair, his Akubra hat tilted forward over his face, his soft snoring a soothing backdrop to the women's laughter. Alex sat on a long, wicker sofa, a book in his hands, legs draped along the sofa's length.

Kate perched with her feet looped over his legs, reading a book as well. She fanned her face every now and then with the open book. Alex rested one palm gently on her bare feet. And she felt as much peace as she imagined was humanly possible. Every now and then she stopped reading to take it all in with a smile.

Jack sat in an armchair in the sitting room, in view of the kitchen. He held a magazine between his hands, his chin rested on his chest and a light snore emitted from his gently gaping mouth.

Kate chuckled as she finished scraping the scales from a fish Alex had caught an hour earlier and brought up from the beach for her to include in their Christmas seafood lunch banquet.

"So, how are we going to cook this snapper?" asked Bindi, eying it with a curious and somewhat worried expression.

"We'll fillet it, then we'll stuff it with garlic cloves, slices of onion and lemon, and marinate it for a few minutes in lemon juice, butter, salt and pepper. It'll be great on the BBQ. I've got a smoker box in there, and I'll set it to a low heat, it'll come out fresh, tender, and moist." Kate's stomach growled at the thought, though she'd barely had a chance to digest breakfast.

"Mmmm... sounds delicious. I have this prawn salad ready... anything else I should do with it?"

Kate shook her head. "It goes in the fridge. Then, you can help me fillet this fish. Ever done it before?"

"Nope. But I've already learned how to take the heads off prawns, and pull the meat out of a crab's claw, so I guess filleting a fish is the next lesson."

Kate winked. "You'll be a chef in no time."

"And what's for dessert?" asked Jack from his perch in the sitting room. He smacked his lips together and wiped the corner of his mouth with one finger.

Kate laughed. "Well, look who's awake. We're having lemon meringue pie with fresh lemons from Nan's garden, and pavlova with whipped cream and fresh slices of peach, nectarine, kiwi, and figs."

Jack hobbled over and rubbed his hands together. "Ah... dessert's my favourite part. Although of course I don't usually get a feast like this. Half of the time I spend Christmas on my own and find a pie shop or something to eat at."

Kate sliced the fish, taking a thick fillet off one side. "A pie shop? Why is that?"

"Well, I liked to let Edie and Paul have Christmas with all of you... you didn't need me hanging around during family time. And then, once Paul died, it was you girls and Edie."

"You don't have family nearby?" asked Bindi.

He shook his head. "I do, but they're not always around at Christmas."

He didn't offer more, and Kate didn't want to pry. She'd never thought much about Jack's family, although she'd assumed he had some, somewhere. It was sad to think that during all those joyous Christmas celebrations they'd had at the inn, he was at a lonely pie shop somewhere, biting into over-cooked pastry.

"Well, not anymore. You're always welcome at the Waratah Inn for Christmas from now on, Jack. This is your home and we're your family."

His eyes gleamed. "Thanks, Katie."

"Of course you are," added Bindi. "I hate to think of you all alone, I didn't realise..." Her voice faded away. Kate knew how she felt.

Mima was seated at the dining table. She'd complained of knee pain earlier, and Kate had sent her to sit down. She had one foot propped up on another of the chairs and a cross-word puzzle book open in front of her, pen poised above the page. She smiled without raising her eyes from her crossword puzzle, and Kate bit back tears. Mima and Jack were the only family the three of them had left, besides each other. And they'd make sure to include them both in every family activity from now on.

"You too, Mima," she stated.

Mima met her gaze. "You're my family too, sweetheart. And I wouldn't have it any other way."

. . .

AFTER A LIGHT LUNCH, SEAFOOD AND SALAD, THEY ALL decided to take their party down to the beach. The heat of the day had set in, and they were all bathed in sweat. The new air-conditioning unit for the inn wouldn't arrive for weeks yet, so they'd made do by opening all the windows and setting pedestal fans in strategic locations to blow the humid air around the space. But finally, it'd become more than they could bear.

Kate and Alex set up two umbrellas and some short beach chairs for Mima and Jack, who took their places immediately. Bindi carried down a picnic rug, and Reeda brought a jug full of freshly made lemonade and a handful of plastic cups.

Kate stripped down to her bikini and strode to the water. Alex followed, and when they reached the waves, he sprayed her with a handful of the salty water.

She laughed and splashed him, then he dove for her, pushing her beneath an oncoming wave. When she breached the surface, she was laughing and coughing all at the same time. His arms wrapped around her and pulled her close, then his lips found hers and she revelled in the salty taste of his mouth, and the strength of his arms around her waist.

After their swim, they took turns showering in the only bathroom that hadn't been completely pulled apart by the construction crew. The one in Nan's room was still entirely as it had been. It wouldn't be long before it was redone, but they'd needed it to remain functional while the upstairs bathrooms were being worked on.

While Alex was taking his shower, Kate retrieved the journal she'd been reading from the wooden box in her room and carried it down to where Reeda and Bindi were sitting. They were reminiscing about past Christmases when she took a seat on the long sofa. Mima was taking a nap and Jack had gone back to his cottage.

She set the journal on her lap. Her heart raced and her

palms were bathed in sweat. How would they react when they found out she'd been keeping this from them all this time? Worse still, that she'd read Nan's personal diaries?

After she'd sat in silence for several long minutes, Reeda finally glanced her way. "You're very quiet."

Kate pursed her lips. "I want to show you both something before Alex joins us again."

Reeda shifted in her seat toward Kate. Bindi's brow furrowed.

"You're worrying me," said Bindi.

"It's nothing to worry about, but it is something... it's a big deal and I'm not really sure how to tell you."

Bindi bit down on her lower lip.

"Okay," replied Reeda.

"When we were looking for photos for Nan's funeral, I found this." She held up the journal, then returned it to her lap.

"That looks old, what is it?" asked Reeda.

"It's a journal, Nan's diary actually. And, there are more of them."

"Wow," said Bindi.

"Have you read it?" asked Reeda, gesturing toward the journal she held.

Kate nodded. "Most of it."

"What does it say?" asked Bindi, leaning forward.

Kate swallowed. "I'm sure you'll want to read it your-selves, but there is something in this one we should discuss."

"Go ahead," encouraged Reeda.

"It says that Pop wasn't our real grandfather."

"What?" asked Bindi, hurrying to sit by Kate. "It says that? Where?"

Kate shrugged. "It's all through the diary. This one is from when Nan was a teenager. She was in love with a boy called Charlie Jackson, and she got pregnant right before he went off to fight in the war. He was a pilot with the RAAF. It says he was shot down in 1943."

Reeda's mouth gaped. "But that doesn't mean he was our grandfather..."

Kate inhaled a slow breath. "Nan wrote that he was Keith's father. And when Dad was born, Pop wasn't in the picture from what I can tell. Nan was still living at home with her parents on the farm outside Bathurst."

"Are you sure Nan wrote that?"

"Who else could it've been?" asked Kate. "It talks all about her life in Bathurst, her parents, her horse Eliza... Mima is in there too."

"Mima?"

"Wow," repeated Bindi.

"I wonder if Dad knew," mused Reeda, staring at her hands.

"I don't know, but I don't think so. Surely, we would've heard about it if he and Mum knew," Kate said.

Bindi shook her head. "This is crazy. I can't understand why Nan wouldn't have told us. It doesn't make any sense."

"So, all this time, Pop knew he wasn't Dad's father, or our grandfather, and yet he didn't ever let on. I'd never have guessed. He loved us so much, he was always happy, full of life... and he and Nan were so much in love," said Reeda, a wobble in her voice.

"I know," replied Kate. "He was our grandfather, but not our biological one."

"So, did you find out anything about this Charlie fellow?" asked Bindi. "Did you look him up or anything?"

Kate shook her head. "I haven't been game to. It says in the diary he was shot down over The Bay of Tunis, but I don't know anything else. Well, other than the fact that he grew up in Bathurst, his mother was apparently really pretty, and his father was a solicitor. Also, he wanted to be an engineer and asked Nan to marry him. But he left for the war before they could get married."

"Sounds like an amazing guy," said Reeda.

"Oh, and Nan's parents didn't like him for some reason. They wouldn't agree to her marrying him. So, when Dad was born, Nan's mother told everyone they'd adopted him when a friend of hers died during childbirth."

Bindi gasped and Reeda covered her mouth with one hand. "Really? Poor Dad."

"Poor Nan," added Bindi.

"I can't believe you found all of that in an old diary." Reeda hugged herself, her eyes wide. "I wonder what we'll find in the others."

"I don't know. I didn't want to keep reading after I found out what happened to Charlie." Kate's throat tightened. Even now, she hated thinking about what Nan must've been through, the grief and pain she must've suffered. And the fact that Kate would never get to meet him. "So, you guys aren't mad that I read it? I was worried you'd think I was invading Nan's privacy or something," Kate blinked back tears that threatened to spill onto her cheeks.

"Well, of course you're invading her privacy," began Reeda, rubbing a comforting circle on Kate's back, "but I would've done the exact same thing. I wish Nan was here to tell us about it herself, then we could ask *her* our questions."

"So, he was killed in the war?" asked Bindi. "You're sure?"

Kate shrugged. "I'm not sure... but Nan's diary says he was missing, shot down over the ocean. And he never came home, as far as I know, so I guess he must've been killed."

Reeda slumped to sit on the desk by Kate's hand. Bindi leaned against the wall behind them with a sigh. Kate's throat closed over. They sat that way, silent, processing, for several long minutes.

"Well, I guess that's that." Reeda broke the silence, then stood to her feet, brushing her palms together.

"I guess so," replied Bindi.

"It's sad," said Kate, her voice breaking.

"What're you all talking about?" asked Alex, poking his head through the sitting room doorway.

Kate shook off the sadness and stood to her feet with a smile. "Nothing, we were talking about the past."

He laughed. "Ah, I see." Alex lay his arm on her shoulders and kissed the side of her head.

Kate shot a sympathetic backwards glance at her sisters.

Reeda nodded and Bindi blew her a kiss. She swallowed the lump in her throat and forced cheer into her voice. "So, who wants eggnog?"

✢ 26 ✢

CABARITA BEACH

The Waratah Inn stood tall and proud, gleaming like new beneath the blazing summer sun with its pale-yellow paint, white trim, and shiny new windows with matching white shutters.

The wide verandahs were also painted white with a natural timber stain on the floorboards and brand-new wicker furniture scattered about with the kind of decorative flair Kate imagined *Better Homes and Gardens* would envy.

She stood at the bottom of the steps, hands pressed to her hips, and surveyed the structure from top to bottom. It'd turned out better than she'd hoped it would. It'd been difficult for her to picture in her head when they'd been arguing over whether it should be pale blue, sea-glass green, or yellow, but in the end Reeda had been right. Yellow perfectly suited the eucalyptus grove where the inn sat between reaching branches and beneath scattered leafy shadows that cast dancing patterns across its surface as the sun drifted slowly down the pale blue sky toward the horizon.

"It's perfect," she breathed.

Reeda grinned. "Do you think so?"

Kate faced her, a lump in her throat making it difficult to speak. "I really think so." She threw her arms around Reeda and hugged her tight. "You did a great job."

"You did too." Reeda's voice was muffled by Kate's shirt.

"We make quite the team," added Kate, pulling back to study her sister's face.

"Who would've thought?" quipped Reeda, wiping a stray tear from her eye with one finger.

"And it's done... finally," declared Kate with a sharp exhale.

"Yes, it's done. And I can go home... to my husband and my life." Reeda didn't sound nearly as excited as Kate thought she should.

Her sister hadn't said much after her last visit to Sydney, though when she got back from the airport, she looked a little like a balloon that had lost some of its air.

Bindi skipped down the stairs and turned to peer up at the inn as well. "Wow."

"Do you like it?" asked Reeda.

Kate looped an arm around Bindi's shoulder and leaned her head toward her sister's. Bindi smelled of lavender and fresh baked bread. Mima was inside baking up a storm in her new oven. When Kate had left her, she'd been exclaiming over the buttons and dials, declaring she'd never seen anything so lovely nor confounding.

Bindi shook her head slowly. "I love it. It looks how I remember it... you know, from when we were kids. Different colour of course, but full of life again."

Kate nodded. It did, although better than before, since Nan had never decorated in anything other than an eclectic, beach style mixed with garage sale chic.

She smiled at the memory of Nan bringing home a secondhand sofa in the back of the truck from one of the many garage sales she'd attended on a Sunday. Pop had slipped his hat from his head and scratched his balding pate as he watched her back up to the inn's side door.

"Now, who in tarnation does she think is gonna carry that thing inside?" he'd asked, his white moustache twitching.

Kate had smiled, all blind faith and love for the man standing beside her, who in that moment seemed like the strongest man in the world in her eyes, second only to Dad. She'd slipped her hand into his giant paw. "You are, Pop. But don't worry, I'll help you."

He'd laughed at that and kissed the top of her head. "Of course you will, Pumpkin. You're all the help I need."

Her heart had swelled with pride at his words and they'd managed it, with the help of a furniture dolly and some bungee cords. Nan had re-covered the old sofa with some leftover upholstery fabric she had in the attic, and until a few months ago, that sofa had rested in the sitting room, a reminder of Nan's quirky shopping habits and Pop's faithful love for her. Although by then the fabric was old and faded and had several small holes where hundreds of rear ends had worn through to the cushions encased within. She'd wanted to keep it, but Reeda had said they couldn't keep everything. So, each of them had selected one or two small things that reminded them of Nan, and of happier times, and stored them in the attic, everything else was gone.

Kate's eyes smarted at the memory of that sofa, and the way Pop had sighed, then kissed Nan's weathered cheek when she climbed from the truck with a shout of victory. Paul Summer hadn't been who she thought he was, but he was the only grandfather she'd known. He'd adored Nan, and he'd loved her. That much she was sure of. And it was all she needed.

KATE WIPED THE STOVE WITH A CLOTH, THEN SMILED AT the gleaming surface. There wasn't anything more satisfying than a brand-new kitchen wiped clean until its surfaces shone. Well, not much anyway. She'd never had children, she imagined that would probably bring with it a sense of satisfaction she had yet to experience, but surely a clean kitchen came close.

She tossed the cloth into the sink, crossed her arms over her chest, and leaned against the counter.

Would she ever have a family of her own? She'd never been like other girls, dreaming and longing for marriage and family. She'd always assumed it would happen but hadn't given it much thought. Still, now that she was twenty-eight and single, the idea that maybe she'd never have children loomed on the edge of her mind.

Of course, there was Alex, but at this early stage in their relationship it was so difficult to tell where it might go. They had amazing chemistry, but was he looking for a serious commitment, a family? They'd hadn't yet spoken about it.

A shout came from the office, startling Kate from her reverie.

She straightened, her brow creased, waiting to see what the fuss was about.

Soon, Reeda marched into the kitchen with Bindi trailing in her wake.

"What's this?" she demanded, tossing several pieces of fax paper in Kate's direction.

Kate jerked, caught the paper before it drifted to the floor and held it up to read.

From the office of Howard Keneally

Kate inhaled a sharp breath. The developer hadn't been in touch with them again since his visit to the inn all those weeks ago, and she'd almost forgotten about him. She'd hoped that would be the end of it, that he'd listened when she told him they weren't interested and had decided to leave them be.

Apparently, he hadn't.

Reeda crossed her arms over her chest, her face red. She tapped a foot, waiting for Kate to speak. Bindi stood beside Reeda, her lips pinched together.

"It's from a developer," replied Kate, in a calm voice. "It's nothing. Don't worry about it."

"A developer who wants to buy the inn," replied Reeda, waving one arm. "He says here, that he visited back in October and made you an offer that he's now following up on. Is that true?"

Bindi's eyebrows knit together, and she shook her head in a quick, abrupt motion. Kate ignored her.

"Yes, it's true. He came here and said he wanted to buy the place. We told him we weren't interested."

"We?" Reeda's voice rose to a new pitch.

"Bindi and I." Kate wasn't about to get sucked into Reeda's flair for the dramatic. She'd spent a lifetime in her sister's tornado of emotions, she knew how to manage a blow up — stay calm and on point.

"So, you're both in on this?"

"We didn't mean to upset you," began Bindi. "But we thought we'd wait... you know, to see how things went."

"Wait? We could've skipped the entire renovation and sold the inn. I could be back in Sydney right now with my husband, keeping my business afloat instead of here in the middle of nowhere picking out wallpaper patterns."

Kate rolled her eyes. "You don't seem to be in a very big hurry to get back there."

Reeda crossed her arms over her chest. "What did you say?"

"Nothing. Forget it. Just don't turn this into something it's not, Reeda."

Reeda's head shook from side to side and she blinked. "I can't believe you didn't tell me."

"I can't believe you still would've sold it — look at this place. It's magical, you should be proud of what we've done. We all should," replied Bindi, her eyes glimmering.

"You didn't give me the chance to decide," snapped Reeda.

"Do you want to sell?" asked Kate.

Reeda's nostrils flared. "I don't know. It'd be easier..."

"No, we're not selling," cried Bindi. "We already decided."

"It's not right that you get to decide for all of us," replied Reeda, her eyes flashing. "What about what I want?"

"You don't care what I want. Why should I care what you want?"

Kate's mouth gaped. She'd never seen Bindi so angry before, or so ready to give Reeda a piece of her mind.

Reeda's eyes filled with tears, she exhaled a quick breath, then turned on her heel and stormed inside, letting the screen door thud shut behind her. Kate hugged herself, then offered Bindi a wry smile.

"Don't worry about it. She'll calm down, and everything will be fine."

"Stop trying to protect me," blurted Bindi. "I'm not a child anymore."

Bindi's feet slapped up the timber stairs and across the verandah. Again, the door banged shut.

Kate found herself alone. Kookaburras laughed in the distance and a lone curlew called a mournful tune as the sun blinked behind the branches of a tall gum tree, casting her and the inn into shadow.

She scrubbed her face with both hands and sighed. Then, climbed the stairs with reluctance. This was the family dynamic she remembered. It was familiar and jarring all at the same time and made her wish for a hideaway. Somewhere she could run to, a place to calm her thoughts and fears.

Upstairs she changed into her bikini, thinking for a moment that it was high time she went shopping for a new swimsuit. This one was beginning to lose its shape and had faded from bright yellow to a pale, lemon colour under the harsh summer sun.

As she slipped on her wetsuit, she considered what Nan would say. Would she tell her to make amends? Or perhaps she'd say they should part ways and forget the whole thing. No, she could almost hear Nan's voice in her head: "Give Reeda some space. She's a passionate one, your sister, like your old Nan. She'll come around. She needs to know you're on her side."

Kate bit down on her lip as she tugged the zipper on her wetsuit. She missed Nan's wisdom, missed hearing her voice and having her there to make the peace. Still, she knew what she had to do.

"Family's hard," Nan often said. "But everything in life that's worth something is difficult. It's the things we have to work hardest for that bring the most reward."

Kate hurried down the wide, smooth staircase, appreciating the newly polished floors and spacious open living areas of the downstairs. She could see it all from the second level. She glanced up to take in the large, crystal chandelier she'd fallen in love with and had to talk Reeda into buying. Now Reeda loved it as much as she did.

If Reeda really wanted to sell the place, perhaps they should go along with her. She didn't want to be in business with someone against their will. Then again, it'd break Bindi's heart, and she wasn't sure she was ready to part with Nan's dream yet. The inn was beautiful, she was certain it'd attract plenty of guests now that they'd remodelled it. What was going on with Reeda that she couldn't see that? Or didn't want to?

She jogged across the yard to the garden shed and retrieved her surfboard from the corner. Then, she set it on two sawhorses Jack had left out and rubbed wax over the surface for a few minutes, before tucking it beneath her arm and heading for the beach.

The inn had become her home again all these years later. Was she ready to move on? To go back to her old life? Something within her rebelled against the idea. She'd tried living in the city and going after her dream to be a renowned chef, engaged to one of the city's up and coming young businessmen. And now that it was in her past, she felt a sense of relief that it hadn't worked out. It was everything she thought she wanted, but she couldn't remember why.

Now she had the inn and she and Alex were seeing more of each other. She was happy, or at the very least, content. But the thought of what Reeda might want stirred the nerves in her gut. She stood on the shore, watching as the waves rolled in. They beckoned, as though whispering a welcome, and she ran into them.

❧ 27 ❧

SYDNEY

When Edie arrived in Sydney, Mima had squeezed the breath out of her then promptly taken her out dancing. For the first time in her life she was free to do as she pleased, and she revelled in that freedom.

She'd been issued a bed in the same dormitory as Mima, and a job as a Nursing Orderly Grade Three at the Yaralla Military Hospital, or 113 Australian General Hospital, a brand-new facility built on the old Yaralla estate. Everything was new and clean, and the two-thousand bed hospital was one of the tallest buildings in Sydney and the largest of its kind in the Southern Hemisphere. Edie was proud to work there, although she quickly found she'd had no idea what she was getting herself into.

She was immediately put to work washing walls, lights and floors with Lysol, scrubbing enamelware with monkey soap or sandsoap, cleaning copper sterilisers with oxalic acid and shining them with monkey soap and Brasso, filling autoclaves, sterilising gloves, cleaning bedpans, and sorting linen.

The ward Sister inspected everything she did, and if she wasn't happy with how something had been completed, she'd make Edie do it all over again, regardless of how many hours Edie had spent at the task or how long it'd been since her last meal.

She'd found herself exhausted and sore at first, then over time her strength and stamina improved. She was fortunate. Some of the women she worked alongside had fallen ill with tuberculosis or other ailments and had to leave the hospital in those first months, but she'd managed to keep going.

The entire nursing staff worked long hours, doing back-breaking tasks, and as an orderly she had much less to do with the patients than she'd wished — other than to give them sponge baths and help move them when needed — and more to do with scrubbing, shining, and washing things.

Still, she kept her chin up. Mima had been at it longer than her, and always sported a smile on her round face. When she first saw her at the train station, Edie had been flabbergasted at how slim and muscular Mima had become in the short time since she'd left Bathurst. But within a few months on the job, one glance in a mirror revealed to Edie that she looked much the same.

However, it wasn't until the two of them were sent to rookie training that they really understood the meaning of pain. Somehow Mima had managed to avoid it until then, but neither of them were able to get out of it once the Sister had it in her mind to send them. The amount of route marching they did gave both girls blisters on their heels and they fell into bed, overcome with fatigue, at the end of each day until Mima devised the ingenious plan of bagging a bath right when it was time to do the route march each day. Still, Edie wondered if they wouldn't shrink, taking so many baths day after day.

After rookie camp, Edie and Mima returned to the hospital and resumed work. Edie was glad to be back and took to the work with gusto. Major Swanson seemed pleased with how she was doing and offered her a place in the training programme to become a full-fledged nurse, though she'd have to attend the lectures during her own time outside of her work hours. She agreed and found that she enjoyed learning about anatomy, physiology, dressing wounds and the dangers of infection.

She still hadn't received word about Charlie. She'd written a letter to Mother to ask for news, and Mother had told her that no one had heard anything more. She did her best to push down the thoughts that threatened to overwhelm her. She could only keep working, keep moving, if she believed he was still out there, alive somewhere, doing his best to get back to her. And as soon as the war was over, he'd be home and they could start their lives together.

Although, whenever she pictured them together, a stone of regret would form like a lump in place of her heart, since Keith wasn't with them. In her imagination he was still on the farm near Bathurst with Mother and Father.

She couldn't think about that either. So, she went to work, studied, read everything she could get her hands on, and spent any spare time she had going to the newsreels or out with Mima.

Mima had talked her into singing and dancing for the troops on furlough or recovering from injury, and so the two of them often went out, around Sydney, performing for the men. Mima played her piano accordion and Edie sang. She learned to ham it up for the crowd, especially when she drew wolf whistles and shouts from the men watching, pulling a performer from within she hadn't realised was there.

Over the sadness and the stone in her chest, she tugged a blanket of liveliness, warm smiles, and laughter that didn't reach beneath the surface, but was enough to fool most.

Only Mima didn't buy it, though she knew what it was that ate at Edie, so didn't say much about it. Only every now and then she'd wrap her arms around Edie's thin body, squeeze her and plop a wet kiss on her forehead.

"We'll get through this, you and I. One day this bloody war will be over, and life will go on. You'll see."

Edie couldn't speak when she did that, but she'd give Mima a peck on the cheek in return. She knew that Mima understood her in a way that no one else in her life ever had. They bickered like sisters, then made up with hugs and smiles until Mima would braid her hair and Edie would thread her fingers through Mima's and tell her stories of how it would be when the war was over and all the young men came back for good.

Edie ran a hand over her hair, poking stray pieces beneath her white hat. A film of sweat coated her palms and she rubbed them down the front of her apron. Her shift was almost over for the day and she'd promised Mima they'd entertain the recovering troops outside on the green. Some of the men without serious injury gathered outside in the afternoons to play cards, exchange small talk, or listen to the radio when the weather was fine.

She hurried down the long hallway and into the emergency ward. The Sister had called for her. They'd had an influx of local and American casualties at around the same time, since the US Army Hospital had been overwhelmed with patients, and now they were shorthanded as well.

Since she was training to be a nurse, and Sister Durham was the one who'd recommended her for it, she liked to give Edie what she called *opportunities to grow*. In other words, she gave Edie more than she knew what to do with, and then hurried off to attend to her own tasks.

Edie scanned the room and drew in a sudden breath. The place was abuzz with activity. Bloody bodies lay prone on every surface, men groaned and cried out for help. Her stomach tightened into a knot and the air caught in her lungs.

"Nurse, here, help me with this," said Sister Durham.

The Sister's hands moved swiftly to examine a young man, who to Edie's eyes looked more like a boy. The uniform he wore had gaping holes in it and blood seeped out of each wound, but his head had fared the worst. He rocked it from side to side, moaning out his agony.

"Can you hear me?" the Sister asked, close to his ear. "I'm Sister Durham, and you're in a hospital. We're going to take care of you. Can you tell me your name?"

Edie hurried to the other side of the bed and began cutting the soldier's clothes away.

"I'm Sam Spencer," he said, between moans. "What's wrong with me? Why can't I see anything? Is it dark?"

Edie's throat tightened and she tugged the remnants of clothing free, leaving him stripped on the bed in only his undergarments. She was relieved to see the wounds to his body looked to be superficial and given a few stitches would heal. She bathed him quickly while Sister Durham continued asking him questions.

He was from Wagga Wagga, he said. Eighteen years of age, he'd been a truck driver before he enlisted. He'd barely begun to sprout a beard and his body, now wiped clean, was thin, hairless, and pale. He hadn't received more than the most basic rookie training when the Army sent him to Borneo to beat back the advancing Japanese forces. He'd stepped off a landing barge at Balikpapan and had a hand grenade thrown in his face. Pieces of shrapnel stuck out from all over his face like echidna spines.

Sister Durham told him to lay flat and still on the bed. Then she asked Edie to run and find two sandbags. Edie brought them, one at a time, balanced over her shoulder. Huffing under the weight of each bag on the wide staircases, she set them on the bed, against either side of his head.

"You shouldn't move," the Sister explained to him with a gentle voice. "We'll take out as much of the shrapnel as we can, then we'll have to wait for the rest of it to work its way free. In the meantime, these sandbags will keep your head steady. Do you understand?"

He said that he did. Sister Durham turned to Edie. "Nurse Watson, please remove the pieces of shrapnel you can see — but leave his eyes. Then bathe him. Be gentle, there are pieces lodged deeper than we dare attempt to remove."

"Yes, Sister."

"Please, can I have a drink of water?" asked the boy.

Edie poured him a cup and held a straw to his lips for him to sip from.

He smiled at her. "Thanks."

"You're welcome," she replied. "I'm sorry if this hurts."

His lips pursed. "Never mind."

She did her best to extract the pieces of shrapnel she could see. And Sam winced and bit down on his lip but didn't say much of anything. He moaned once or twice, but it was a marvel to Edie how well he held back from complaining or crying out.

"We're almost to the end of it," she said, tugging softly at the last piece.

"Thank you. You've been very kind."

Her throat ached at his words. How could he be polite? Why didn't he cry out and rail against the injustice of it all? He'd likely never see again. Tears threatened and she swallowed them down.

"Do you think I'll see anything soon? I'd like to know

where I am, look around, and see if any of my mates are here with me."

She swallowed. "I don't know. I'm sorry. I wish I could tell you."

"No worries."

"The eye specialist will be here to see you as soon as he can. There're a lot of people needing his attention right now, so I'm not sure how long he will be."

"I can wait," he replied. He linked his hands together over his chest.

"I'll finish your bath and get you something to cover up with," said Edie. "Then, we'll see about finding you a ward so you can have a bit of peace and quiet. It's like a zoo in here."

By the time her shift was over, Edie felt as though she needed a cup of tea, a Bex, and a lie down. Perhaps she'd cancel on Mima. Besides, all the blood and gore she'd encountered in the emergency room, not to mention Sam's swollen but earnest face, had made her think about Charlie and she couldn't shake the lump from her throat. The image in her mind that Charlie was lying injured some-where, with no one to help him, no one to bathe his wounds or tell him everything would work itself out, made it hard to breathe.

She found a chair in the hallway and sank into it, pressing her hands to her head.

Deep breaths.

He'd been shot down. The horror of that gave her night-mares, still, during the day she tried to think of things other than the picture of his face in her mind's eye as his plane fell from the sky; anything other than that.

Oh Lord in Heaven; what if he'd crashed into the deep, dark ocean?

Was there anything worse than the image of him gasping for breath as the waters swallowed him whole?

She couldn't catch her breath. No matter how hard she tried, the air wouldn't fill her lungs.

Mima bustled past her, stopped, skipped back, and grabbed her up. She linked her arm through Edie's with a laugh. "Come on, let's go and entertain some troops."

"I don't want to," replied Edie with a sigh, as she stumbled along beside Mima.

"You always say that and then you feel better after we do it. It'll be fun. I promise, we can go back to the dorm and you can curl up in bed and turn the lights out when we're finished."

Sometimes Edie really hated the way Mima pushed her around. Still, perhaps Mima had a point — all Edie really wanted to do was curl up in bed and get lost in the memories swirling through her head. Something inside her knew that wasn't any way to live. So, she followed Mima to their room to shower and change.

She'd go with Mima, she'd sing, she'd dance, and she'd pretend to the world that everything was grand. But she didn't want to do it. Not when Charlie was out there alone somewhere, maybe dead, and Keith was living in Bathurst with Mother and her aunt. Mother had written he'd taken his first steps right after she left for Sydney. She'd spent the rest of that morning in bed, until Mima dragged her out to go to the beach with a group of friends from the hospital.

She'd become good at pretending. And perhaps that was all there'd ever be. A smile plastered to her face; her eyes dull behind the cheap sunglasses she'd bought from a stand at the newsagents.

When they reached the green, recovering soldiers were already scattered about the lawn in chairs and on picnic rugs. If they didn't have either, they sat on the grass and risked the wet seeping through the seats of their pants. Sunshine warmed their faces as they played cards, chatted, smoked, and laughed together. Some stared into the distance, blankets pulled over motionless legs, others wrote letters, faces pinched and pale, or read books or letters, forgetting all they'd seen and done for a short time as they travelled in their minds to distant lands or small hometowns.

They were convalescing, the men who were almost well, or had lesser injuries. Many would be returning to the fight before much longer, their time at the hospital a respite from the storm. And while Edie and Mima sang, danced, and played for them, their faces brightened, even if only for a little while. Seeing them light up that way was the reason Edie was there instead of curled up in her bed, the curtains pulled to cover the light shining in through the dormitory window.

They walked amongst the group, several of the men calling out greetings as they went. Edie smiled, patted shoulders, asked questions about how certain patients were progressing and then joined Mima on the edge of the lawn. Mima had taken her piano accordion out of its case and was warming up her fingers by playing a few notes, humming softly as she did it.

She winked at Edie, then broke into a lively rendition of *The Boogie Woogie Bugle Boy*. The men who could stand, jumped to their feet and smiles swept across faces. The song was always a crowd pleaser. Edie joined in, singing the melody and dancing along to the song, flipping the skirt of her red and black polka dot cotton dress around her nylon-clad legs as she moved in time to the beat. Her strong voice built until it soared and echoed over the lawn. Men cheered and hooted, and those who could clapped along.

Edie's heart warmed and the smile she'd faked slowly turned real. There was some truth to Mima's words — she always ended up enjoying it. No one could bring joy to another without feeling some measure of it herself. She knew it was true, and yet when dark thoughts swamped her at the end of a long day, she couldn't seem to fight the desire to run, to hide, and to give in. Singing, dancing, and watching the faces of the men as they forgot their troubles for a precious few minutes was the salve she needed to bring comfort to her soul.

The next song Mima played was a slower one and Edie took the opportunity to grab a cup of water from a tray brought around by one of the orderlies. She seldom drank enough water during her shift and was often desperately thirsty afterward. As she gulped down the last mouthful of water, she felt a gentle tap on her shoulder.

She spun about to face a man, at least a head taller than her, with dark brown hair, wide green eyes, and thin cheeks.

He blinked. "Excuse me, ma'am, I was wonderin' if perhaps there'd be any dancin' today?"

His thick American accent wrapped around her like a wool blanket.

"Dancing?"

"Yes, dancin'."

She nodded. "If you like."

"Would you dance with me?"

It was the last thing she felt like doing, but his eyes were so eager, his grin so shy, and as he crushed a white naval hat between his hands, she smiled and reached for his hand.

"Of course, why not?"

His eyes brightened. "Thank you kindly, ma'am, it's been so long since I danced with a girl... a woman... I'm afraid I won't be much good."

He tapped the cast that wrapped his leg from his toes to his hip in white plaster. He wore a pair of blue hospital issue pyjamas and one leg of the pants had been shorn off, leaving the plaster exposed.

"Then, you'll match me just fine," she replied with a chuckle. "Because I've never been much good at it."

He laughed, took her outstretched hand, and pulled her toward the middle of the lawn. A few of the men wolf-whistled, others called out that it would be their turn next. Her cheeks flamed as he spun her around and she landed with a gasp against his strong chest.

One hand pressed to the small of her back, the other grasped hers and he moved, or more like bobbed, along to the music, his eyes fixed on hers.

"I'm Paul Summer," he said.

"Edie Watson, Edith really, but nobody calls me that except my parents when I'm in trouble." Her cheeks warmed further still.

"Is that so? I'll remember to call you Edie, then," he replied.

"You're American?" she asked.

He laughed. "I guess there's no hiding it. Yep, I'm from North Carolina. I was on the USS Brooks when we got the stuffing... excuse me, ma'am, we were shelled by the Japs. The leg will recover, I'm told, so I guess I got off light. And likely they'll have the Admiralty Islands all taken care of by the time I get outta here." His face clouded over for a moment.

"I'm happy you'll be all right," she said.

His eyes sparkled. "I'm glad I got to be here, else I'd never have met you."

"Have we met before now?" she asked. She didn't always remember the faces that she passed in the wards.

He laughed. "I saw you earlier when I came in. You were busy fussin' over someone, but I couldn't help notice those pretty eyes and that sweet smile."

Her heart pitter-pattered at his words, but she wondered if he said the same thing to every girl he met. Sydney women were falling in love right and left with every Yankee serviceman who came to shore, but he couldn't know her heart was already taken.

Still, it felt good to be held, to dance, however awkward it might be, and to hear pretty words fall from such a handsome mouth.

"Thank you," she said. "But I think I should get back to Mima. I've left her all alone, and she'll be needing my help on the next song."

She stepped out of his embrace. He dipped his head, his eyes never leaving hers. She smiled. "It was nice to meet you, Paul Summer."

"The pleasure was all mine, Edie Watson," he said.

By the time Edie made it back to Mima, the piano accordion had fallen silent and been abandoned in the grass. Mima sat on a brick retaining wall, one leg crossed over the other, a cigarette hanging from one hand as she guffawed over something one of the men whispered into her ear.

"Are you ready...?" asked Edie.

Mima shook her curls, her red lips pouting. "I need a break, take a seat, there's someone I want you to meet."

Edie folded her skirts over her legs as she sat on the cold, hard bricks beside Mima.

"Edie, this is Oliver. He's from America," said Mima, her eyes wide.

"Pleased to meet you, Oliver." Edie shook his hand. He was handsome with sandy blond hair, brown eyes, and dimples. His muscular arms bulged beneath the sleeves of a plain white T-shirt.

"Pleasure, Edie. Your friend here has already told me so much about you."

Edie's mouth puckered. Mima never could hold her tongue. She'd blurt out every little thing to anyone who came along. It was what made people love her, but sometimes it was too much. Especially when Edie was holding tight to her feelings, clutching her own story to her chest, not wanting anyone else to see how vulnerable she really was.

"Oh? Mima, shouldn't we keep playing...?"

Mima shrugged. "I think they can do without music for a little longer. Oliver here was telling me all about California. Can you believe it? He's from California! He's been to Hollywood."

"That's astounding," replied Edie in a monotone.

Mima had always wanted to go to Hollywood and found anything and everything about the place enthralling in a way Edie didn't understand. In fact, the way she was feeling, she couldn't understand anyone or anything. How could they sit around, eating, singing, dancing, and acting like nothing was wrong when her heart and the whole world was a pit of horror and despair?

"I'm going back to the dorm, then," said Edie.

Mima nodded. "Righty-oh, I'll see you back there later."

Edie's heart hurt, her head pounded, and her throat ached. She stood and staggered across the lawn toward the dormitories. When she glanced back over her shoulder, she saw Mima leaning in close to the American. He whispered something and she threw back her head to laugh, like a kook-aburra on a branch. She pressed her hand to his arm, her eyes focused on his, her cheeks flushed.

Edie sighed, spun on her heel, and marched up the wide, concrete staircase. She'd never felt so alone.

❦ 28 ❧

CABARITA BEACH

Kate brushed the tears from her cheeks and set Nan's journal on the bedside table. She could feel Nan's pain, the depth of her grandmother's mourning sprang from the page and twisted Kate's heart into a knot.

So, it was true. Mima knew all about Charlie and Dad. She was there when Nan and Pop met. And yet when Kate had asked her about it, she'd hemmed and hawed like she could barely remember that period of her life.

But she'd been there. Right beside Nan when she danced with Pop on the green.

Kate had heard the story before, of how Nan and Pop had met at a hospital when Pop was injured in the war. Still, reading about it brought it to life in a new way. Hearing her grandparents tell their stories when she was a girl, was like listening to something that'd happened to strangers in another time and place she couldn't relate to in any way. But reading it in Nan's journal, she was given a glimpse into their lives as though she was watching it play out on the big screen.

Tears continued to streak down her cheeks and wet the pillow beneath her head. She rubbed her eyes.

Poor Nan.

She'd been mourning Charlie when she met Pop for the first time. That was certainly something she'd never related as part of the endearing meet-cute anecdote before.

Charlie was gone and she had no place in her heart for another. And yet somehow Pop had won her over.

She wasn't sure she could keep reading. Everything she'd thought she knew about Nan, Pop, and their family was a lie. Each journal entry she read shook her world in a new way. She couldn't take it anymore.

It wasn't fair for Nan to lose Charlie that way. She'd loved him, better than Kate had ever loved anyone until she met Alex. Her eyes widened. Did she love Alex? Sweat broke out immediately all over her body. She loved him. It'd come on so suddenly she hadn't been aware of it. Her breath caught in her throat. The impression swept over her, stronger than any feelings she'd felt for Davis, or anyone before him for that matter. She exhaled; a sharp release of the air held tight in her lungs.

The first time she kissed Alex was the beginning of understanding. It had given her a taste of how Nan must've felt about her childhood sweetheart. Still, she hadn't known Alex as long as Nan had known and loved Charlie, nor did she have a baby, or the rushing hormones of teenaged angst driving her.

And what was she doing with Alex, giving her heart to a man who was obviously mourning a loss of love the way Nan had mourned Charlie? Nan's words opened her eyes to the way Alex must feel — he'd lost the love of his life. Now Kate had come along, kissed him, essentially pushed him into a relationship. Maybe he didn't want it or want her. But she was there, and his wife wasn't.

Could that be enough for Kate? It wasn't. She wanted to be someone's first choice, not like Pop, twirling Nan on the green, falling in love while Nan's heart broke over her lost fiancé.

❦

THE GLOOM OF DUSK SETTLED OVER THE INN. WHEN KATE stepped outside, cicadas sang a loud chorus that overwhelmed almost everything else.

She stuffed her hands into her pockets and hunched her back to walk to the garden. She'd forgotten to water everything earlier, though in the heat of summer she preferred to leave the watering until almost dark, so the wet leaves didn't burn beneath the scorching sun.

She unwound the hose from around the tap and turned the handle until water dammed up behind the nozzle. Then she faced the garden and spun the nozzle until water spurted out in a long arc, wetting the dry plants. The dusty soil darkened beneath the spray, and Kate drew in a long breath, letting the sadness leech out of her.

She'd pushed Nan's journal back into the box and shoved it beneath her bed. It was too hard to keep reading, too emotional. She needed a break.

Was that how it was between her and Alex? She was Pop in their relationship. The one Alex would settle for since he'd lost the true love of his life. Poor Pop, how had he lived with that? Had he even realised?

Kate stretched her neck, leaning her head to one side, then the other, until her tired muscles released the tension that'd built there with everything that was going on. Between the argument with Reeda and Bindi, reading Nan's diary, and questioning her relationship with Alex, her shoulders had drawn higher with the stress of it all, until they seemed almost even with her ears.

She dropped her shoulders, squared them, and inhaled another slow breath.

She'd been to a counselling session once, at a particularly anxious period in her career. The counsellor suggested a technique for reducing her stress levels — she should look around and name the things she saw.

Kate glanced to one side.

Beans, peas, strawberries, carrots.

Then to the other.

Cucumbers, tomatoes...

Her brow furrowed. Bloody possum!

Half the plants had been eaten level with the earth. Bare stalks jutted up through the ground, cut jagged and leafless.

Her nostrils flared and she marched back to the tap to turn it off. With angry jerks she looped the hose around the post, then stalked in the direction of the stables.

She still had to check on the horses, make sure Alex had fed and watered them, before she returned to the inn. Then, she'd figure out what she was going to do about that nuisance of the possum. In the morning, she'd inspect the garden fence and netting to see how it'd wriggled through. It was too dark to see much of anything now. And knowing that the possum would likely return that night to finish what he'd started only stirred a burning anger in her chest.

All she'd wanted was to resurrect Nan's garden so that she could keep something of Nan for herself. Was it too much to ask that a possum didn't eat Nan's legacy? Maybe Reeda would want to sell the inn anyway, in which case there was no point trying.

So much for *that* relaxation technique.

Her neck seized with tension.

She hadn't seen Alex in days. He'd been busy with school

and the after-school soccer team he coached some afternoons. But he always made sure to visit the inn and get the horses settled for the night.

Before she reached the stables, she spotted his truck parked in the attached carport.

Why hadn't he come to the inn to see her? Perhaps she'd exaggerated his feelings for her in her own mind, simply because of the way she cared for him. Perhaps he didn't feel the same way. Something she'd only just begun to understand. It made sense. He wasn't the kind of guy who'd fall head over heels for someone like her.

She marched into the storeroom and found him putting lids on the feed barrels.

He glanced up, then smiled, his eyes lighting up. "Hey! How are you?"

He finished what he was doing then gave her a kiss. She pulled away.

"Is something wrong?" He frowned.

"Were you going to come and say hello? I haven't seen you in days."

His brow creased further still. "Yes, I was. But I haven't made it home yet today, soccer practice..."

"I get it, you're busy. Maybe you're too busy for me."

He studied her, his face unreadable. "Okay, Kate. What's up?"

She ran a hand through her hair. "Nothing. Something. Oh, I don't know. I don't think we're on the same page."

"And what page is that?" he asked, pressing his hands to his hips.

"I don't want anything serious and you do." That wasn't right. She hadn't meant to say it, but it slipped out. What she wanted to say was that she didn't want to be his second choice, that his heart would likely always belong to his deceased wife and that she wanted all of it, or none at all. She wouldn't spend her life like Pop, oblivious to the fact that her spouse was pining after a lost love.

"I see. If that's how you feel..."

"It is. I think we should end things now, before anyone gets hurt."

"I don't understand where this is coming from," he said, his cheeks flushing red.

"It's coming from me. Reeda wants to sell the inn, and I'll be moving back to Brisbane. My life is there, my career is there. I can't live here forever, I'm a chef, there's nowhere for me to go."

His shoulders drooped. "I can't believe you're doing this. I thought everything was going great between us. We're having fun, enjoying time together, getting to know each other. This isn't like you at all."

"Maybe you don't know me as well as you think you do."

"I guess not," he said, his eyes dark.

"I'm sorry."

"Nah, it's all good. I'll get out of your hair. I'm finished for the day anyway. I guess I'll see you later."

"Yeah, I'll see you."

He left then, the truck tires squealing as he pulled out of the driveway and onto the highway. Kate squeezed her eyes shut, a pain in her gut clenched her stomach muscles tight.

What had she done?

It was for the best. She couldn't be his second choice, the one he lived with but didn't love. She needed more than that, and she'd fallen too hard for him too fast to cope with discovering she didn't mean as much to him as he did to her when they were eighty years old. She couldn't waste her heart the way Pop had. He'd deserved more than Nan had been able to give him, and Kate deserved more than Alex could give her.

She wrapped her arms around herself and squeezed, then hunched her shoulders and wandered back to the inn.

❦ 29 ❦

CABARITA BEACH

Ginger snorted as Kate swung onto the horse's broad back. This time she'd added a saddle so they could gallop along the beach and Kate wouldn't feel as though she might be jolted off at any moment and trampled beneath the animal's hooves.

She was too old to be flung from a horse's back these days. When she was young, she remembered falling on a regular basis, onto the hard sand, into grassy hollows, into a patch of thistles on one particularly warm day, but she never had more than a few scratches or bruises to show for it. Now, at almost thirty, she knew she'd suffer far more if she fell so far.

They trotted down the path to the beach. The track branched off to one side to circumnavigate the timber stairs, and Ginger jostled slowly down the steep embankment, then took off at a trot again through the warm, soft sand.

Sweat trickled in a line down the centre of Kate's back. She wore a sleeveless white singlet over a pair of colourful board shorts, decorated with frangipanis and green leaves. A white helmet perched on her head like the end of a cue tip, and her straight brown hair was pulled into a low ponytail that slapped against her back with each bounce.

The inn was complete, they'd listed it with all the appropriate real estate agencies and travel agencies both locally and across the country. They were booked solid next week, their official grand re-opening week, and for a full three months after that. Kate had included a series of photographs with her listing when she sent it out, and she'd received a number of messages of congratulations from people Nan had worked with in the past, pleased with the inn's transformation.

Nerves buzzed in her gut. It was really happening. Finally, after all this time and work, it was coming together the way they'd planned. Reeda hadn't pushed the idea of selling the inn since their fight, and the inn's transformation was complete. She hoped Nan would've been pleased with what they'd achieved. She was certain Nan would've said something encouraging, then cracked a joke that they'd have laughed over. She didn't have Nan's easy wit, but Kate had done her best to tell Reeda and Bindi how much she appreciated their hard work over the past months.

She and her sisters had talked over the developer's offer and decided that, for now, they'd put it to one side. They were all curious to see how the inn fared once it was open for business, and if pre-bookings were any indication of success, it seemed they'd made the right choice. Reeda had apologised for her outburst and they'd made up over a pot of tea.

Ginger's hooves pounded along the water's edge, leaving half-circle impressions in the hard sand. Kate leaned forward, a smile on her face and the wind whipping strands of hair into her eyes.

Saltwater spray wet her cheeks as her legs held on tight to the saddle and the power of Ginger's movements radiated up through her body.

It'd been a month since she and Alex had split. She tried not to think about him, but it was difficult with him working at the inn. Bindi had offered to be the one to deal with him and Kate had taken her up on it, only visiting the stables when she knew he wouldn't be there.

She missed him, but she reckoned it was for the best. He'd be better off without her, especially if she didn't stay in Cabarita. And she didn't want to settle for a half-hearted attempt at love, the way Pop had done for all those years as Nan's second choice.

She'd kept busy with the re-opening of the inn, dealing with insurance, permits, licences and more. Thankfully, the money from Nan's account had come through in time to pay all the contractors, and everything had been taken care of. They'd used most of the funds to renovate, so they needed the inn to operate profitably within six months or they'd have to reconsider the developer's offer.

And maybe that would be for the best anyway. Then they could all return to their lives. Bindi would find another job. Reeda could go home to Sydney, and Kate could start all over again in Brisbane. Although the thought didn't sit well in her stomach. She grimaced. Starting a new life wasn't as appealing as it had been a decade earlier.

She'd worked so hard to build the life she thought she'd wanted, and now that it was gone, she felt more relief than anything. Relief that she didn't have to keep all those balls in the air any longer. That she could be herself, be real and take things as they came. With no one to impress, nothing to strive for, she could ride Ginger along the beach with the wind in her hair.

Still, she couldn't stay in Cabarita forever. Could she? There was nothing there but a general store, a fish and chip shop, a bait shop, and a Chinese takeaway restaurant. She needed more than that for a full life. She had dreams, goals, plans. All she was doing was taking a break, having a well-earned and much-needed rest. Then, she could go back to the city and tackle the mountain all over again.

She sighed and steered Ginger up through the soft sand to the top of the beach. They stopped, and Kate looked around, one hand shielding her eyes from the harsh sun. It was almost dusk, and the sunlight sparkled on the ocean's surface like jewels, ever moving, never settling anywhere for more than a moment.

Kate decided to ride back to the inn along the side of the road rather than the beach. She could stop at the General Store and buy a litre of milk to take with her. Otherwise they'd have nothing to put in their tea that evening.

She ended up buying an ice cream as well, a special treat she rarely indulged in now. She'd managed to fit back into her clothes more easily after a month of daily exercise and forgoing dessert. She tied the bag with the milk to her saddle, and licked the cone with slow deliberation as Ginger plodded along the narrow grass verge. The reins hung loose in one hand and Ginger's neck stretched out long and relaxed, her head bobbing with each step.

By the time she was in sight of the inn, the sun had settled beneath the horizon and shadows lengthened along the sides of the road where bushes and shrubbery clumped together in groups as though to comfort one another.

Something moved on the side of the road up ahead. Just where the Waratah's drive branched away from the main road. Dusk was too thick and the waning sunlight too dim to tell exactly what it was, but when it moved again, Kate squinted, then her eyes widened.

It was that possum. Her possum!

If she hurried, she could cut off its escape, shepherd it away from the inn and into the brush on the other side of the highway. Bruno's team had sealed up its entrance into the inn's roof and she'd thought they'd gotten rid of the creature until she discovered where it'd romped through her garden again. Surely the creature would be happier living on the other side of the road, in the freedom of the bush.

She kicked Ginger to a trot, leaning forward to urge her into a canter. A smile tickled the corners of her mouth. She would finally get the little so and so.

As she drew closer, the possum saw her and stopped still in the centre of the road.

Sure, it was cute. But it was also a menace. For months, maybe years, it'd scratched about in the roof cavity. She distinctively recalled hearing a chewing sound at various intervals, which made her skin crawl. Was it actually eating the building from the inside out? And it'd taken to destroying Nan's garden. That was something she couldn't allow.

Anger stirred in her gut. The creature watched her, seeming unable to move. She was close, if she could squeeze between the possum and the gates, she could scare it off — maybe for good.

The roar of an engine behind her came as a surprise. A white ute hurtled by, V8 growling as it scattered gravel from wide tires into her path. Several sharp rocks hit her leg and torso and she shouted in dismay as Ginger lay back on her haunches and reared onto her hind legs.

Kate held on tight, hunkering over Ginger's neck and threading her fingers through Ginger's mane. The ice cream had landed on the ground somewhere a few metres back, though she still tasted its sweetness on her tongue.

Ginger pranced in a circle as Kate fought to control her, the reins tight between her fingers. Finally, Ginger settled back into a walk.

Kate's heart jittered in her chest and her hands shook as she lowered them to rest on Ginger's withers.

She stroked Ginger's neck with one hand. "There, there, Ginger. Shhh. Good girl, everything's fine."

She squinted after the vehicle. In the distance its red brake lights blinked as it took the turn.

"Bogan!" she shouted after it.

Ginger trotted sideways.

"Sorry girl, it's just that I can't believe how inconsiderate..." she stopped there, staring at the road ahead.

Where was the possum?

She urged Ginger forward, and the horse trotted up to the inn's gates. A brand-new sign hung above the stone entryway, announcing *The Waratah Inn, Beachside Bed and Breakfast*, in soft, swirling white letters against a yellow background.

When she saw the possum, lying against the stone wall, she gasped. With one smooth movement she slid from Ginger's back and ran to it.

It lay on its side, eyes shut, blood splashed along its dark, smooth tail.

"Oh no," said Kate, dropping to her haunches to take a closer look.

Her throat tightened. The possum's sweet face was still, but its side heaved slightly with each shallow breath. It was still alive, but for how much longer?

She scooped it up gently and rested it in her arms. "Come on, possum, let's get you inside and take a look."

Its eyes flickered open and it struggled for a moment, its nails sharp against her skin, then gave in and watched her instead through one, dark eye, its mouth parted slightly as it panted.

She held the creature close to her body and led Ginger along with the reins looped around one hand. At the stables, she tugged off Ginger's bridle, but left the saddle on her back. She opened the gate and Ginger trotted eagerly into the paddock to greet the other horses. Kate only hoped Ginger wouldn't roll with the saddle on, but she couldn't manage to take it off with only one free hand and the possum was getting heavier by the second.

She carried it to the inn, through the back door and into the kitchen.

"What in Heaven's name?" Mima held a spoon over a saucepan on the stove, her eyes wide. "What do you have there?"

"A possum. Can you grab me a towel please, Mima?"

Mima hurried to comply and Kate lowered herself into a dining chair. Bindi was reading a book on the other side of the table and glanced up with a start.

"Bindi, can you please see if you can find a box? We must still have some empty ones lying around somewhere."

Bindi hustled from the room, her brow furrowed. "Don't you let that thing get away from you," she called over her shoulder.

By the time they had the box and the towel sorted, the possum had relaxed in Kate's arms. She lowered it into the box, and it lay there, unmoving but looking alert enough.

"Is it okay?" asked Bindi.

Kate shrugged. "I don't know. It got into a tangle with a ute, but I didn't see what happened exactly."

"Oh, poor thing," crooned Mima, bending to lean closer.

Kate squatted beside the box and ran a soft hand over the animal's sides, legs, and tail, hoping to find some sign of the creature's injuries. It reacted when she touched its tail, and that was where most of the blood was. And one of its hind legs seemed also to be hurt. An inspection of its chest and abdomen revealed a pouch, though it seemed to be empty.

"She's a girl," announced Kate.

"Oh, how sweet," said Bindi. "I can't believe she's letting you touch her like that."

"I think she's in shock," replied Kate with a frown. "The

only injuries I can find are this hind leg and her tail. She must've been almost clear before the vehicle went by."

Jack pushed through the back door with a grunt, tugged off his boots one by one with the toe of the other foot. He slumped into a chair, then spied the possum.

"Is that the same possum who lives in our roof?" he asked.

Kate nodded. "Lived. Past tense. She was almost run over, poor thing."

He reached out a hand to caress the animal's fur. "Hmm... heart rate's fast, but that's to be expected, I guess. Seems like she's in shock. Might be an idea to give her some water, help her calm down a little bit."

"Good idea," replied Kate. "How will I do that? A bowl or something?"

He chuckled, still stroking the possum's soft back. "I reckon an eye dropper would do the trick."

She found an eye dropper in one of Nan's medical supply boxes and filled a cup with water. Then she carried it all back to the box and lowered the eye dropper toward the possum's mouth. At first the animal paid no attention to the water dripping down her chin, then she began to lick.

"She's drinking." Kate smiled with triumph.

"Well, that's a good sign. Isn't it?" asked Bindi.

"I think so. If she's still unwell in the morning, I'll take her to see one of the vets in Kingscliff."

"I'll come with you," replied Bindi. "I need to get away from this place. Next week is coming far too soon and I know I won't get a chance to take a break for quite a while."

Kate continued giving the animal water, while Bindi helped Mima to cook tea. Jack disappeared into the media room, no doubt to watch the news. He had to get his fix of current affairs in the evenings.

Kate sat cross-legged beside the box, stroking the animal's soft fur every now and then. She couldn't believe she'd tried to chase her away; up close she was so pretty. Her brown, almost golden eyes remained fixed on Kate, and her dark brown and black coat faded to white around her soft belly.

"I think I'll call you Cocoa," she said. "Because of your cocoa coloured fur."

"Here you go," said Mima, offering Kate a slice of apple. "See if she'll eat that."

Kate set the apple in front of Cocoa's mouth, but the creature didn't move.

"Not quite ready to eat yet? That's okay. You'll feel better soon."

When Kate washed her hands for tea, she kept the possum in her box right by her feet. And when she went to bed, she carried the box to her room and set it against the wall. She wanted to be there in case Cocoa needed her. And besides, it was her fault Cocoa was injured. If she hadn't tried to chase her away, the possum wouldn't have frozen in the middle of the road like that. She lay on her side and stared at the box, her hands clasped together beneath her cheek.

❧ 30 ❧

SYDNEY

Edie's eyes blinked open to the sound of a door slamming. It jolted her out of a deep sleep. Every muscle in her body was tired and she ached from head to toe. Sister Durham had decided yesterday was the day to scrub the bedpans, surgical instruments, walls, floors, and furniture in every single one of the wards and operating theatres they covered, over again.

She groaned and tugged the pillow from beneath her head to wrap around her ears. The high-pitched chatter of feminine voices drifted in from the hallway, along with shrieks of laughter followed by noisy shushing sounds and cackling.

"Noise, too much noise," she croaked.

The springs in her bed squeaked as one side of the mattress dropped beneath someone's weight. She peeked out from beneath her pillow.

"Good morning," said Mima in a chipper voice.

Edie frowned. "It was until someone sat on me."

Mima chortled. "But I have something I want to tell you and it really can't wait."

Edie pushed the pillow hard against her face. "Yes, it can." Her voice was muffled by the goose down stuffing.

Mima pulled the pillow out of Edie's hands and away from her face. She set it on the end of the bed and faced Edie with a wide smile.

"Ollie asked me to marry him!" She squealed and clapped her hands together in delight.

Edie sat up, leaning her back against the wall behind her. "But you barely know him..."

Mima's smile faded. "We've been seeing each other for a whole month."

"A month is nothing..."

"Don't ruin this for me Edith Watson," pouted Mima.

Edie cocked her head to one side, then opened her arms. "Come here. I'm happy for you, Mima, really, I am. I'm sure the two of you will have a wonderful life together in Hollywood. I'll miss you..." Her voice broke and she couldn't finish.

Mima accepted her embrace. "In Hollywood? Do you really think I'll get to live in Hollywood?"

Edith pushed her friend back and held her by the shoulders. "You haven't talked about where you'll live?"

Mima shrugged. "Those things don't matter. We'll work it out after the war's over. For now, all that matters is that we love each other and we're going to be together forever, wherever that may be."

"I'm glad you're happy, I only hope your parents will be just as delighted." Edie knew Mima's family would be less than thrilled by the idea. They'd already expressed their horror at her travelling all the way from Bathurst to Sydney alone to live in a dormitory with what they called *a group of loose women with no moral compass to guide them*.

She also knew Mima didn't want to hear it. She loved her family but had taken to the single life, parties, concerts, theatre, dance halls, and independent living in Sydney with gusto. She had no desire to return to Bathurst and live under her mother's thumb again.

Mima grunted. "You're in a foul mood today, I'm going to tell the rest of the girls. They'll be happy for me." She trounced from the dormitory room, her curls bouncing against her back.

Edie called after her. "I'm grumpy because someone woke me from a deep sleep by sitting on me! And I *am* happy for you!"

She slumped down on the bed, her lips pinched together. Mima was engaged? It'd happened so fast her head was spinning. She wanted only the best for Mima, and Ollie seemed like a genuinely nice man, in fact Edie really liked him — he was handsome, funny, kind, and had so far shown Mima more respect than any of the other men she'd dated. She and Mima had spent a lot of time with him and his friend, Paul, over the past month, going to the movies, staying out late, dancing, or walking beside the glistening water, eating at the various restaurants that dotted the bustling harbour, and swimming at Bondi Beach.

It turned out that the man she'd danced with on the green was Ollie's best mate. They'd been stationed on the same ship together and were injured at the same time. And since neither of them had any serious ailments, they'd been allowed, or had taken, plenty of liberties during their rehabilitation in Sydney. Still, she knew nothing good lasted forever. Both men were scheduled to return to their ship the next day. No doubt that was the reason for Ollie's hurried proposal.

And when they were married, he'd take Mima with him to live on the other side of the world. With Charlie gone, that meant Edie would be left all alone. She might never see her friend again.

She lay on her side, reached for her pillow, and hugged it to her chest, her knees tucked up beneath her.

The sounds of girls showering, dressing, applying makeup and all the while talking in attempted hushed voices wafted down the hall and through the still-open doorway. Edie huffed and swung her feet to the cold floor. With her toes she searched out her slippers and slid her feet into them, then pulled on her dressing gown and cinched the belt around her waist.

She rubbed her eyes. There was a letter sitting on top of her bedside table. She had the bottom bunk, Mima took the top. They shared the table, and she'd set the letter there the day before, too tired to open it and read about all the things Mother had helped Keith do. All his first times were happening without her. It exhausted her to know what she was missing, so she often didn't read the letters until she'd steeled her nerves.

After Mima's news, she needed something to ground her. To help her feel as though she wasn't alone in the world. A letter from home might help.

She slid a finger beneath the flap of the envelope and tore it open. Then, tugged two loose pieces of paper free. They were covered in Mother's neat cursive. She never smudged the ink.

Her gaze flitted across the page, skimming over the words, looking for something, anything about her son. She could only think of him that way when she was alone. She'd never said the words out loud to anyone else. To the world out there he was her brother, in the private world of her mind he was her son.

Then something jumped off the page that stole the breath from her lungs.

Bobby was dead.

She gasped and clutched her throat with one hand. No, it couldn't be. She'd been so worried about Charlie, she hadn't thought anything could happen to her big brother. It couldn't, not when his best friend was already dead. It wasn't fair to take both of them. There must be some kind of mistake.

Her fingers frantic, she brushed them over the words as they sank into her mind. He'd been shot during the British takeover of Maungdaw, Burma when they pushed back the Japanese occupiers. He was gone.

Mother's words were stilted, as though she'd stopped and started writing more than once. There was an unlikely smudge on the edge of the page that might have been a tear. Mother stated that Father had received leave from the militia and would be coming back to Bathurst for a short time. She should ask leave to attend the funeral, it would be held in two weeks' time, as soon as they could arrange it.

She lay on her bed, pushed the letter beneath her pillow, and moaned into it, her mouth pressed to the pillowcase. As she rocked back and forth, tears cascaded down her cheeks, wetting the fabric, and tearing loose all the pain she'd been carrying around inside her heart for months.

Bobby was gone. She'd loved him, looked up to him, written him a letter every week of his service and received the occasional one from him in return, forwarded by Mother after her move to Sydney. But nothing had prepared her for this. To her he'd been invincible. Now the world seemed crueller than ever. She didn't know how she could continue to live in its crushing grasp.

EDIE COULDN'T GET OUT OF DOING ROUNDS. ESPECIALLY since she hadn't told anyone her news. How could she? She couldn't utter the words that Bobby was dead, that would make it real. She couldn't face it. It was her secret for now, hidden away in her heart, pushed out of her mind. Although it hovered in the shadows of her thoughts, causing an ache like there was a stone lodged in her throat.

"Are you okay?" whispered Mima, as she turned the top sheet around the bed corner, forming a crisp fold.

Edie nodded, her face numb.

"Because if you're worried about me, don't be. I'm going to be fine. Better than fine, actually. I'm deliriously happy — or I would be if my best friend in the whole world would get on board." Mima straightened, then smoothed her skirts with both hands.

"I'm on board," replied Edie, as she finished with her corner of the bed. "I'm completely on board."

"Good, because I want you to be my maid of honour and I can't have you sporting that miserable look on your face."

Edie squeezed her lips into a half-smile. "Don't worry. I'll do my part, I promise."

"Edie?" It was Paul. He'd come up behind her and stood with his hat in one hand, a bunch of wildflowers in the other. Some of the flowers arched toward the ceiling, others hung limp, and there were a few blades of wayward grass clutched between his fingers along with them.

She widened her smile, the physical pain of it almost too much to bear. "Hi Paul. Are these for me?"

He nodded, his eyes eager and bright. He handed her the flowers, then squeezed his white cap between both hands.

"Thank you, they're beautiful," she whispered, pushing them to her nose to smell their sweetness.

"I'll see you in a few minutes," said Mima with a knowing smile.

Edie nodded. "Okay."

When she focused her attention on Paul again, he'd fallen

to one knee. He reached for her hand and held it between his own, his gaze searching her face.

"I know we haven't spent enough time to truly get to know one another, Edie. But I've fallen for you — well and truly. You're the woman of my dreams, and I can't get you out of my mind. I'm going tomorrow, back to war, and I'd sure feel easier about it if I knew you'd marry me when it was all over."

Her mind was blank. Her mouth gaped, but no words came out.

"So, will ya? Will ya marry me? Make me the happiest man in the world?" asked Paul, his eyes burning with love.

She shook her head and pulled her hand free from his grasp.

"We haven't courted, Paul. I don't feel that way about you. I'm sorry."

He stood, his brow furrowed. "Oh. I understand. Sorry... I thought..."

"It's not your fault. That was a lovely proposal," she said. "But when I marry, it'll be because I can't live without the other person, and I don't feel that way about you. Maybe if things were different... another time, another life..."

He bit down on his lower lip.

"I'm sorry, I don't mean to hurt your feelings. It's just that, we're not right for each other. There's someone else — someone I'm waiting for."

He nodded. "Sure, I understand. I hope he comes back to you, because you deserve all the happiness in the world."

She offered him a genuine smile then. "Thank you, Paul. And I wish you all the best as well."

His lips pressed into a straight line as he turned on his heels and strode through the ward. His hands pushed deep into his pockets, his shoulders hunched, he stopped. With one last glance back at her, he inhaled a deep breath and stepped through the doorway.

She wouldn't see him again. He'd go back to the battlefield the next day, and if he survived, he'd return to America after the war was over. She felt nothing but emptiness in the space where her heart should've been.

❧ 31 ❧

CABARITA BEACH

Kate slapped the diary shut and stared at the ceiling. In her box, Cocoa rustled, then went quiet again. She'd taken her to the vet the day after the accident and the animal had a bright white bandage around her back leg and tail. Otherwise she was fine and eating them out of house and home. But Kate wasn't ready to release her back into the wild yet, not until she could remove the bandage and make sure the wounds wouldn't become infected. She'd had Bruno build a possum-sized enclosure on a long branch, near the place where Cocoa had previously pushed her way into the Waratah's roof cavity. Cocoa would have a home at the inn after all.

Kate pressed her hands to her face. Pop had proposed to Nan and Nan turned him down. She was still waiting for Charlie to return from the war, which he obviously never did.

Her heart ached and her throat tightened.

She flung her feet to the floor and stood, shook her head, and hurried down the stairs. She found Mima seated in an armchair in the breakfast nook. The black and white cat purred in her lap. It lay on one side, its eyes squeezed shut, a steady buzz emitting from its body. Mima's eyes were shut also, her head nodded forward, then jerked back up again.

"Mima?"

Mima's eyes blinked open. "Oh, hello love. What can I do for you?" Mima shooed the cat to the floor, and it scampered out of the room. "Don't mind Rooster, he's a mischief but he's got a good heart."

Kate frowned. "Rooster?"

"He's like an alarm clock. Tends to pounce on my feet while I'm sleeping, scares the living daylights out of me." Mima chuckled.

Kate sat on one arm of the chair next to Mima and leaned forward. "Can I ask you something?"

Mima cleared her throat. "You certainly can."

"I asked you once about Nan and Charlie..."

Mima's eyes widened and she wriggled in her seat. "Uh, well..."

"And you said you didn't remember much about it, or something like that."

"I don't recall exactly."

Kate quirked an eyebrow. "And now I have to tell you why I asked."

"Okay."

"I found Nan's journals, and I've been reading them."

Mima grunted. "You did?"

"Yes, I found them before the funeral actually. I've been reading them, bit by bit, this whole time. And I know all about her, about Charlie and how he was Dad's biological father."

Mima squirmed again, her cheeks turning pink. "Right, well you know..."

"I'm not here to rouse on you, Mima."

"Well, that's a relief." Mima chuckled, then offered her a wink. "So, what's up, buttercup?"

Kate sighed and rested a hand on Mima's arm. "The journals also talk about an Oliver... someone you once agreed to marry."

Mima's lower lip trembled and she pressed arthritic fingers to her mouth. "Oliver... yes, Ollie. He was a wonderful man." She swallowed.

"Whatever happened to him, Mima? You never married, so I'm assuming it didn't work out." Kate's voice was soft.

Mima stood slowly, working out the kinks in her back before straightening it. "He was the love of my life. I've never forgotten him, or gotten over him, as you young ones like to say." She paced to the open window and stared out into the darkness as the soft shushing of waves washed back to them through the stillness.

Kate's eyes smarted with tears at the pain in Mima's voice.

"He was killed in Papua New Guinea, I'm afraid. Right after he proposed, they set sail and he was killed within months. I didn't know what'd happened to him for the longest time, since I wasn't family. I had to write to his parents back in California, and finally they sent me a letter to tell me what'd happened. It broke my heart." Mima's voice wobbled.

Tears spilled from Kate's eyes and she wiped them away with the back of her hand. "I'm sorry, Mima."

Mima shrugged, then faced her with a wry smile. "Thanks, my love. I suppose it wasn't meant to be, although I often wonder how my life might've gone had he lived."

"I imagine it would've been very different."

Mima's eyes shone. "I could've lived in California," she said. Then laughed. "Of course, I've had a good life. And I wouldn't trade it for anything. Well, anything other than having my Ollie here with me, by my side."

"And what about Nan's Charlie? Did she feel the same way about him?"

Mima pushed up her glasses to dab a handkerchief at the corners of each eye. "She loved Charlie, that was for sure. Although I don't want you to think she didn't love your Pop. She did, and they had many good years together. They couldn't have children, you know, so they had to make a life for themselves with Keith. And they did that. There was a lot of joy in their little family. You should know that."

Kate's heart ached and she wiped away a few stray tears. "Thanks, Mima. I think I needed to hear that. It's been... unsettling to learn that Nan and Pop weren't the people I'd always thought they were."

Mima shuffled to Kate's side and raised a hand to brush against her cheek. "Your Nan and Pop were exactly the people you knew them to be, but with a bit more mystery and excitement in their lives than you were aware of. That's how it always is, my dear. The younger generation never considers that we oldies might've done a thing or two in our past." Mima chuckled, then continued past Kate and out the door.

"But Mima..."

Mima waved a hand without turning around. "I'm off to bed, sweetheart. We'll talk some more another time. All this talk about memories and the past has worn me out."

Kate called goodnight to Mima, then settled into one of the armchairs to think about what Mima had said. Perhaps Nan really had loved Pop the way she'd always thought, or maybe it was all a lie. She was confused and she wasn't sure Nan's diary would bring her the closure she needed. Reading Nan's words hurt too much. Hearing her heartache reverberate from each page was drawing Kate into a darkness that weighed her down with a heavy melancholy.

She should take a break from the journals.

She hurried up to her room, taking the stairs two at a

time. The diary sat on the doona where she'd left it. She slipped it into the box Charlie had made for Nan, pushed the box back beneath the bed and vowed not to open it again until she'd found her own path, recovered a sense of joy she'd lost when her parents' car slid from the road all those years ago. And that could take a very long time.

FEBRUARY 1996

CABARITA BEACH

Kate raised her aching feet with a groan and set them on the ottoman. She leaned her head against the fabric headrest of her new bedroom armchair with a sigh. She, Reeda, and Bindi were sitting in the newly renovated master suite after the inn's grand re-opening. They'd all agreed Kate could have the room as her own.

Bindi had opted to keep the room she'd slept in as a teenager on the second floor, and Reeda planned to travel back to Sydney as soon as things around the inn were running efficiently enough that she felt comfortable leaving them. She was sharing Kate's room in the meantime, sleeping on a narrow trundle bed. Her own, newly completed room was booked by a couple from Adelaide for the week.

"Today was crazy," muttered Reeda, a cup of tea clutched between her hands.

"I can't feel my feet," replied Bindi, squeezing her eyes shut.

Kate reached forward to massage Bindi's bare toes with

her fingertips. "Really? Because mine are throbbing with pain." Kate grimaced. "I've never worked so hard in my life."

"Well, we got it done. And I'm so proud of all of us," replied Reeda, grinning. "It was an amazing day, really amazing. I can't believe we had so many people here for the high tea and grand re-opening celebration this morning, not to mention the half dozen members of the local press. It was more than I'd expected that's for sure."

"You made a great speech," added Kate, nodding her head toward Bindi.

Bindi's face flushed. "Thank you. It was nothing really."

"No, it was wonderful. You're an amazing speaker and a gifted journalist. We're lucky to have you on our team, and I'm sorry if sometimes I treat you as though you're still a kid. It's hard for me to grasp how grown up you are, and that you really don't need us to take care of you anymore."

Reeda nodded. "Exactly, well said Katie; and congratulations Bindi on a rousing speech. I swear I saw tears in the eyes of some of our guests, and a couple of the hardened journalists who covered the event. Those things you said about Nan and her generosity of spirit were spot on and really touching."

Bindi dipped her head toward Reeda. "Thank you both, that means a lot. And with that, I'm off to bed while I can still walk." Bindi stood with a grimace and hobbled toward the door. "Good night."

They waved goodnight and Reeda swallowed the last of her tea. She set the cup on the dresser and stood with a yawn.

"Bed sounds perfect."

While she headed for the bathroom, Kate stayed put, sipping her own cup of tea, and listening to the quiet of the inn. Now that most of the guests were in bed, or at least tucked away in their rooms, the only sounds in the old building were the occasional creak of floorboards or the faint hum of a television set. It felt good to have a full house.

Kate walked to the window, pushed it open, and looked out. She rested her elbows on the windowsill and breathed in the still, hot, night air. Cool air escaped around her into the humidity.

There was movement on the lowest gumtree branch that brushed up against the side of the house. Cocoa waddled along the top of it and stopped close to the window. Kate grinned. She'd hoped the possum would come back to see her when she'd let her go early that morning. Her wounds had recovered nicely and would soon be healed entirely. She was ready to go back to her old life and seemed to like her new cubby. Kate had only to devise a better system for protecting the vegetable garden.

She pulled a small Tupperware container filled with slices of apple and kiwi fruit from the bedside table where she'd left it earlier in hopes she'd see Cocoa. Then tugged the lid free as she leaned out the window.

"Cocoa, come and get some apple."

The possum studied her, eyes gleaming, then stepped closer.

Kate held out a slice of apple and the possum took it in her mouth, then rested on her hindquarters to hold the apple between her front paws while she nibbled.

Moonlight glanced off the silver fur on the possum's underside. The sounds of her sharp teeth biting through the apple rang out over the hum of cicadas and the distant call of a sand plover.

Kate scanned the yard, then looked toward the stables. They lay dark in the distance; only the faint outline of the building was visible from where she stood.

Alex had been there this evening, taking guests riding along the beach. She hadn't seen him of course, but Bindi told her it was going well. The guests loved the new ponies and the three quarter horses Alex had picked out for them. All the while, the older horses, including Ginger, grazed peacefully in the paddock.

Tomorrow was Saturday, so he'd be at the stables all day long, helping their guests to experience the beauty of Cabarita beach on horseback. Perhaps she should wander down to say hello, check things out. After all, it only made sense that she understood how things were working. The horses were new, and she should make sure they were gentle with the guests and easy to ride. She couldn't do that from the kitchen where she'd spent most of today baking scones, Anzac biscuits, profiteroles, mini pavlovas, and the succulent roast beef they offered for a special, grand re-opening meal.

From now on they'd only be serving breakfast and morning and afternoon teas. Guests would have to forage for their own lunches and evening meals. But today they'd put on a full, four-course menu for every meal in celebration of the re-opening, and it'd been fulfilling and satisfying for Kate in a way that working for Marco never had been. If she were being honest, she'd never felt that kind of thrill working for anyone else. The fact that it was her own menu, served the way she wanted it, and at her own inn, filled her with excitement and pride as the meals were taken out to the dining room by their brand-new wait staff.

Maybe this was what she'd been looking for. She'd always dreamed of opening her own restaurant but had never wanted to take the risk while she had a prestigious job as head chef at one of the most renowned restaurants in Brisbane. But now everything was different.

She wished she could talk to Alex about all of this. She longed to hear what he thought about it all, to share her heart with him and hear his. But she couldn't — it wouldn't be fair to him now that they'd broken up. Still, she missed him.

Missed talking to him, hearing his deep voice as he studied her, amusement in his sparkling eyes. Missed the feel of his full lips against hers, the scent of saddle oil and old spice tickling her nostrils.

Cocoa finished the piece of apple and her head bobbed up and down, then side to side, as she searched for more. Kate handed her another piece, and this time she carried it in her mouth down the length of the tree branch and sat in the darkness to eat it.

Kate watched her go, then pulled the window shut and headed to bed.

❧ 33 ❧

FEBRUARY 1996

CABARITA BEACH

Kate slung the dish towel over her shoulder and smiled. It was the day after the grand re-opening, and everything at the inn was running like clockwork.

She and Mima had served a full hot breakfast to the guests. The wait staff served with a smile, then ferried all the dirty china and silverware back to the kitchen where a single kitchen staff member washed and stacked it all away again.

Each time one of the dishes from the buffet in the breakfast nook was emptied, a waiter returned with it for Kate and Mima to refill. And finally, the last guest had left, the last dish had been washed and it was time for Kate to do the rounds, to make sure everything else was as it should be at the Waratah.

She almost whistled as she walked around the inn, checking on linen supplies, the progress the cleaner was making on the rooms where the guests had already left for the day, and the menu.

Mima had gone to her room to lie down. Kate hoped the cook would have the energy to keep up with the pace of the newly minted inn. Now that it was full to the brim with guests, it might be more than Mima could manage. Thankfully, Kate was there to help for now. But when, or if, Kate returned to Brisbane they'd have to consider hiring a replacement.

Kate stood by the back door and looked out through the small, square window in the top half of the door. A line of horses walked past the stables and on toward the trail that would take them to the beach. Alex rode Ginger at the head of the line. Kate swallowed, her heart skipping a beat.

The bell at the front door chimed and she hurried to answer it. She met Reeda and Bindi, both rushing to the door as well, and laughed.

"I guess we'll have to figure out who answers the door, so we don't all drop what we're doing every time someone rings the bell," she said, then stopped with her mouth agape when she saw who it was.

"Howard Keneally," offered the man, sticking out his hand toward Reeda. "But you can call me Howie."

REEDA'S LIPS PRESSED INTO A STRAIGHT LINE AND BINDI hovered behind her, both hands linked together. Kate sat across from Howard, her eyes darting between his face and her sisters.

The last thing they needed on the second day of operation was a visit from the developer who wanted to level the inn and build a resort. They had work to do, guests to tend to, an inn to run. She'd forgotten all about Howard and his resort for a time and thrown herself into managing the

Waratah. And she'd had more fun doing it than she could remember.

"I hope you received my offer for the place," said Howie, glancing around the small office. "I like what you've done, although, I think you'll find my offer will more than compensate you for the work you've put in." He grinned, revealing a set of gleaming, white teeth that contrasted with his deep orange tan.

Kate opened her mouth to respond, but Reeda interrupted her. "Thank you so much for your offer, Howie. We appreciate it and we're happy to be neighbours. Please let us know if you ever need to borrow a cup of sugar or a glass of milk. But as for buying the Waratah, well I'm afraid it isn't for sale; not now, and not ever."

Bindi's eyes widened and Kate's stomach did a flip. Was she hearing things? Did Reeda just declare that they'd be keeping the inn, that they had no intention of ever selling it?

"Reeda... do you mean it?" asked Bindi, a smile disrupting the worry lines that'd formed above her nose.

Reeda squeezed Bindi's hand. "I do. We've done something amazing here. Honestly, I wasn't sure we could pull it off. I was pretty certain we *wouldn't* manage it, that we'd fight too much or run out of money, or that no one would want to holiday here after all the construction work we'd done. But that's not what happened. We worked well together, we're a great team. I have loved almost every single minute of this project with the two of you." She reached for Kate's hand as well and the three of them smiled at each other, every set of eyes glimmering with unshed tears.

Kate's throat ached. "I've had the best time as well."

"Me too," declared Bindi.

"And this is Nan's inn. We're not going to get rid of it. I believe in it, and I believe in us. Nan knew we could pull this off, and she was right." As Reeda finished her speech her voice trembled.

Kate squeezed her hand. "After running from it all these years, and the pain of being here after everything with Mum and Dad, I can honestly say that the Waratah feels like home to me now. Especially after finding Nan's diaries, and reading about all she went through, I'd hate to give the place up. There's so much of her and Pop here, in every room, every squeaking floorboard, and so many memories..."

Howie cleared his throat and stood to his feet. "Well, I guess that's it for me then." He laughed. "Never mind. You can't blame me for trying. All the best, ladies." He touched two fingers to his forehead, as if in salute, then showed himself out of the office.

Reeda stood and pulled Kate and Bindi into a group hug. Kate wound her arms around her sisters and pulled tight. Tears streaked her face and the faces of her sisters, as they grinned at each other.

Bindi shook her head. "I can't believe it. I'm so happy."

Kate laughed. "Me too, although I never would've imagined that keeping the Waratah Inn would be the thing to bring me that happiness."

"So, what are you going to do?" asked Reeda. "Are you going to stay or go back to Brisbane."

Both sisters watched for her reaction. Kate's heart rate accelerated. She knew exactly what she was going to do, what she longed to do with everything inside her. She'd turn the inn's kitchen into the restaurant of her dreams. She'd make it everything she'd hoped to achieve, and she'd do it with family by her side.

She smiled through a veil of tears. "I'm staying."

Reeda cheered and Bindi bounced up and down in place, jostling both her sisters. "Yay!"

She couldn't wait to tell Alex. Wait. Alex — if she was

staying there was no reason to keep him at arm's length. Unless he didn't want her. Unless he was settling for her because he couldn't have the one he truly loved. But maybe Mima was right — Nan had loved Pop. She'd grieved Charlie and then spent a long and happy life with Paul Summer. They'd raised a family together, then grandchildren. They'd weathered the highs and the lows of life and they'd done it side by side. Wasn't that what she wanted? Someone to share her life with? Someone she could love, who'd love her back? Maybe Alex could love her the way Nan had finally loved Pop. Maybe it wasn't a second-class kind of love, but a real, passionate love that could weather the storms of life with two people coming together as one.

She let go of her sisters, her heart racing.

"What is it?" asked Bindi, her brow furrowed.

Kate sucked in a quick breath. "Alex — I've got to tell Alex I'm staying."

Reeda's lips curved upward.

Kate flung the dishcloth onto the bench as she ran by. She slapped the back door open with the palm of her hand and kept running. The horse-riding group had returned from the beach. She could see them, milling about, helmets in hand as they chattered and giggled over their adventure. Horses relaxed around the yard, reins looped over fence posts and heads lifting and dropping as they reached for the handfuls of hay scattered on the ground in front of them.

Where was Alex?

He stepped out of the stable and across the yard, then reached out to stroke Ginger's neck.

"Alex!" she called, huffing into the yard.

He faced her with a start, eyes wide. "What's wrong? Are you all right?"

She leaned her hands on her knees, catching her breath as thoughts tumbled about inside her head. He reached her in two long strides and lifted her chin with the tips of his fingers until she was staring into two, deep hazel eyes.

She sighed and linked her hands with his, winding her fingers through his own, strong calloused ones. A crease formed between his eyes.

"What's going on?"

She smiled. "I'm staying."

"What?"

"I'm staying here, at the Waratah. I've decided not to go back to Brisbane, I'm going to run my own restaurant here at the inn."

"You're staying... for good?"

She nodded.

His lips curved into a half-smile. "Is that so? Well, I'm happy for you."

"And I was hoping, since I'm not leaving, that you'd maybe give me another chance."

He huffed. "Oh? I don't know... you kind of broke my heart." Her pulse quickened. She'd hurt him? She hadn't realised his feelings for her ran so deep.

She cocked her head to one side. "I did?"

"Yeah, cause I'm in love with you. If you didn't know that already."

Her heart leapt into her throat and she inhaled a sharp breath. He loved her? He loved her. Why had she pushed him away?

"I was worried..." she began.

His eyes narrowed. "Worried about what?"

It sounded stupid now, even in her thoughts. It was immature, childish. She sighed. "That you'd never love me the way you loved your wife."

His eyes widened. "What? Why would you...? That's crazy."

"Is it? You loved her, she died, and it shattered you.

Understandably of course. I mean, I get it. But what if you're never able to love me the way you loved her? I don't want to be the one you settle for."

He shook his head. "It's official. You are crazy." His eyes twinkled. "I love you. I'm not settling... you've given me hope that I can be happy again. I am happy when I'm with you. You've given me a second chance at life. It doesn't change how I felt about her, it doesn't erase the past. But my future is with you, if you'll have me."

Relief swamped her. She laughed, and threw her arms around his neck, standing on tiptoe to reach for his lips. "I love you too."

✵ 34 ✵

CABARITA BEACH

Kate brushed the hair from her eyes and rested her hand above her forehead as she peered out through the inn's front door. Reeda's hire car waited in the driveway, engine idling as Jack wrested an enormous suitcase into the boot.

"I'm going to miss you," said Reeda, her arms wrapped tight around Bindi's thin frame.

Bindi sobbed. "I'll miss you too. It's been amazing having you here for such a long time, but I know you must miss Duncan. Please tell him thank you for lending you to us."

Reeda nodded and released Bindi, then dabbed at her eyes with a tissue. "I don't know how I'm going to settle back into my life in Sydney after this. It's been exactly what I needed."

Kate's throat was too tight to speak. She'd asked Reeda a few times over their months together at the Waratah how things were going, but apart from some marital conflict, which Reeda assured her was completely under control, and some issues at work, she'd been close-lipped about what might be bothering her. Perhaps that was all it was. Sometimes a girl only needed to get away and swim in the ocean with her sisters.

"Will you visit?" asked Kate.

Reeda nodded as she slung her purse strap over her shoulder. "Of course I will. You won't be able to keep me away."

"Good. Wait here a moment."

There was something in her room she'd been meaning to give to Reeda but had forgotten in the frantic grand re-opening celebrations and the weeks that followed. The inn had been chock full since opening and was already taking bookings for the Christmas holidays.

She pulled the timber box out from beneath her bed, wrapped her arms around it and carried it out to where Reeda stood waiting. Reeda's face lifted like a sail in a breeze.

"I wanted to give you Nan's journals," said Kate, handing her sister the box.

"I can't take them. You and Bindi should keep them here at the inn," objected Reeda, handing the box back to Kate.

Kate shrugged. "I asked Bindi about it, and she said you could have them. She'll take them next. We can pass them around and each have a turn with them. It's kind of like having Nan visit each of us."

Reeda met Bindi's gaze and Bindi nodded, her eyes wet with tears. "It's fine. You have them, and when you're done, I'll read them. Honestly, I don't mind."

Reeda nodded and tucked the box under her arm. "Well, if you think so... I really would love to take a look at them."

"Great, it's settled then. And besides, I need a break from reading about Nan's heartache. It's hard to discover all the things she went through, things she never spoke about," said Kate with a sigh. "Poor Nan."

"Yes, poor Nan. I wish she'd talked to us, or at least to someone," said Bindi.

"She shared her heart; don't you worry about that." Mima's voice turned all their heads as the cook emerged from the kitchen drying her hands on the green leafy apron tied around her ample waist.

She smiled. "I was there through thick and thin. She had a shoulder to cry on, and she made it through. She was a tough old bird, your Nan."

Reeda ducked her head and Kate embraced Mima with a chuckle. "Yes, she was, just like you, Mima. You lived through enough heartbreak of your own as well."

"And she was there for me when I needed her, too. It was a tough time for a lot of people, the war. When it was over, so many of us weren't sure what to do with ourselves. Where to go, how to act, how we should live... our families had been torn apart, a lot of us had to give up our jobs for the men returning from battle. We had nowhere to go, nothing to do, it was as though the rug had been pulled out from under our feet. But we made it through, like people have done since the beginning of time. Somehow you find a way."

"Was Nan happy, do you think?" asked Bindi, wiping her eyes with her fingertips.

Mima laughed, a big booming laugh. "She was as happy as anyone can be. Paul was a good husband to her — the best, really. And a true friend to me as well. When she and Paul built this place, it was a dream come true for both of them. They'd wanted to fill it with children, but that wasn't to be. Still, they had Keith and then you girls, and it was enough. For all of us."

"I'm glad she found happiness," added Reeda. "I don't think I could bear to know Nan was unhappy. It wasn't something I ever thought much about when she was alive. She was always there, she was Nan. I never considered whether or not she was fulfilled, because she always had a smile on her face and took care of everyone around her as though it was the most natural thing in the world."

Kate nodded. Why had they waited until she was gone to get to know their grandmother? Why hadn't Kate come home to the inn more often, asked Nan if she was happy, done something to bring joy to her life? Tears choked in her throat and she pressed her lips together to hold them at bay.

"You girls are too hard on yourselves," said Mima softly, watching Kate's face. "Nan loved you all, and she was proud of you. You brought her a lot of joy, and she wouldn't have changed a thing... except of course losing Keith and Mary — that broke her heart into pieces, that did." Mima's mouth puckered and she swallowed hard.

"Us too," whispered Bindi.

Mima cleared her throat. "Yes, it was a hard time for all of us. But you've each made a life in spite of the tragedy, and Edie would've been so happy to see you come together and restore the inn the way you have — it's truly beautiful. She wanted so badly for the three of you to be a family again, to love each other the way she loved you, and look at you — you're a family."

Mima beamed and wiped the corners of her eyes with the edge of her apron.

Kate reached for Mima and drew her into a hug. "Thank you, Mima."

When they waved goodbye to Reeda, Kate's chest hurt and her eyes smarted. She'd miss her sister, though she couldn't help feeling excited about her plans for the Waratah Inn. She'd already spoken to Reeda and Bindi about opening the Waratah Restaurant at the inn and received their approval to add on an extension if the restaurant did well enough to pay for it.

Things were finally turning around.

❧ 35 ❧

CABARITA BEACH

Bindi poked her head through the office doorway. Kate saw her out of the corner of her eye, but she was too busy to stop what she was doing. She opened the oven door to check on the lamb shanks and a delicious smell crept out to fill the kitchen. She braised each shank with a few spoonfuls of the gravy that bubbled around them, then grinned. She'd been serving the lamb shanks once per week as part of their new evening menu, and every single time, she got rave reviews on the little feedback cards they left on the reception desk for guests to complete.

When she shut the door, she pressed her hands to the small of her back with a grunt. Too much leaning forward and bending over had given her a backache. She'd have to go and see someone; a chef couldn't afford back problems. Maybe there was a chiropractor in Kingscliff.

"Hey Bindi, do you know if there's a chiropractor or physiotherapist in Kingscliff?" she asked, without turning around.

"I'm sure there would be."

Bindi was hovering. Kate faced her with a smile. "Is there something I can help you with?"

"I don't want to bother you, but wondered if you knew how to fix a paper jam in the fax machine?" Bindi offered a wry smile.

Kate sighed. "Maybe, I guess I can take a look at it, but don't let me forget about the potatoes. They're roasting and I don't want them overdone."

By the time she wrested the paper from the bowels of the fax machine, the potatoes were ready. She slid them from the oven, her oven mitts warming on contact with the pan, then set the pan on two heat pads on the counter. Just as she was about to put the next batch of potato pieces into the oven to roast, she saw Cocoa at the kitchen window. She was perched on top of a chair, her eyes peering in through the glass directly at Kate.

Kate laughed and tapped a fingernail on the pane. "I can't hold you right now, sweetheart, I've got to get tea cooked for all our hungry guests, but I promise you, I'll be out as soon as I'm finished, and I'll bring an apple."

As if she understood, Cocoa jumped down from the chair. Kate heard the thud of Cocoa landing on the verandah floor boards, then the scamper of her toenails scratching out a rhythm as she pattered off to occupy herself elsewhere until Kate was done.

Kate laughed, basted the potatoes with one last coating of oil, then slipped them into the oven. She'd given Mima the night off to play Bingo in Tweed Heads with a group of friends. It was good to see Mima relaxing and enjoying life. She'd worked hard for so long, and it was time she had a break to enjoy herself. Life was too short for anything less.

The ring on her pinky finger caught her eye. It wasn't as dull or tarnished as it'd been when she found it in Nan's wooden box. Still, it had small dents and scratches and wasn't exactly high fashion. Kate never took it off. Every time she caught sight of it, memories of Nan flashed through her head and made her smile. She spun it around her finger, her lips curling upward.

The back door swung open and Jack stepped into the kitchen. He slipped off his mud-covered boots and set his Akubra hat on a peg set into the wall.

"That smells about as close to divine as we'll get in this lifetime," he said with a grin, sitting at the end of the kitchen table.

"I hope it tastes as good as it smells," replied Kate with a wink, as she snipped the ends from a handful of beans.

"If it's anything like last week's, it will."

Kate's lips pursed. "We have new guests here every week, so it's been fine to offer the same meal once per week, but maybe I should give you, Bindi, and Mima a bit more variety," she said. "When we open the restaurant to the public, I promise, you'll have more of a selection to choose from."

Jack laughed and slapped his knee, his eyes sparkling. "Honey, I've never eaten so well in all my life as I have been lately thanks to you."

Kate's heart warmed. "Thank you, Jack. I'm glad I could bring your tastebuds some joy."

"And my waistline," he quipped, pointing to his slender waist.

She laughed. "Your waistline hasn't changed a bit in all the time I've known you."

"I guess that's been a few years now," he replied.

She did the calculation in her head. He'd moved to the inn the year before Mum and Dad's accident, which meant...

"Fourteen years," she said.

He scratched his head, his grey hair flopping onto his forehead. "Is that so? Well, those years have flown by."

After dinner, Kate let the staff clean up and she slumped

into a chair on the verandah to listen to the cicadas and the sighing of the ocean. The cool autumn breeze dried the sweat on her face and as she sipped a cold glass of water, she remembered all the times she'd sat in the same spot with Nan or Pop by her side. The chairs were new, the view was the same.

Alex's truck crunched down the drive and stopped when he spied Kate through the front windscreen. He climbed out and offered her a wide smile.

"Hey honey, you're a sight for sore eyes."

She laughed. "You too. I would get up... only I can't. This whole chef thing is harder than I remembered. Every muscle in my body aches all the time. And I'm so bone tired..."

He chuckled and leaned down to kiss her lips, his were soft and warm and drew her in, until her breath was shaky, and her head swam.

He lowered himself into the chair beside her and took her hand in his. "Well, there are worse ways to end a long day."

She leaned her head on his shoulder. "How about this view?"

He stared at her, eyes sparkling and nodded. "It's breath-taking." Then he faced the sunset. "And the landscape isn't bad either."

She laughed. "Did you make up that line?"

He shrugged. "It works on all the ladies..."

"Oh, does it?" she punched his arm and he feigned injury.

"Ow!" he said, rubbing his arm. "I wanted to go for a surf, but we've started up with soccer training again."

She studied him, the curve of his cheeks, his deep hazel eyes, the way his hair fell across his forehead. Having him beside her filled her with warmth and made her heart light.

"Maybe we can go together in the morning. It's Saturday and I have the morning off, since I showed Bindi how to make breakfast and she insisted I take a break," said Kate.

He grinned. "Perfect, I can't wait."

He leaned forward until their lips touched, then lifted her neatly into his lap. She squealed against his lips, then relaxed against his chest as he deepened the kiss.

In the distance a curlew sounded out its mournful cry and the last of the kookaburras called their goodnights. The soughing of the waves as they crashed onto the shore and drew back into the ocean beat a steady rhythm, and a cool breeze rustled gum leaves overhead as stars twinkled in the sky above the Waratah Inn and everyone who was settled and warm within its sturdy walls.

EPILOGUE

SYDNEY

Reeda leaned against the white timber door frame, her arms crossed over her chest. A cardigan draped around her torso and hung low, reaching toward the floor. Her bare feet were almost buried in the plush, beige carpet.

She stared into the yellow-tinted room, lost in thought.

It was strange to be back in Sydney. She'd been almost manic by the time she'd left home all those months ago to travel north for Nan's funeral. She was running from everything: from her life, her husband, her pain, for far too long. Still, running away had given her a chance to think, to gain some clarity on everything she'd been through.

Was she sane? She felt sane, and yet sometimes...

How long could someone undergo fertility treatments before she lost her mind entirely?

She'd certainly come close.

Her lips tightened.

Duncan didn't understand. He'd never understood what it meant for her to have a child. Even now, he was in surgery, taking care of other people's problems and completely oblivious to the emptiness of her life, to what she was feeling. He'd always been that way — if something was complicated it was too hard for him to face. He'd rather bury himself in work than address the fact that they may never have children, that it might be the two of them for the rest of their lives, and that she couldn't cope.

She'd run to Cabarita, and he'd hidden himself away in his operating theatre, hadn't even attempted to make it to Nan's funeral. That had been the death knell for their relationship as far as she was concerned. Nan had been important to her, one of her few remaining family members, and he hadn't been able to drag himself away from his precious surgeries for a day to support her at the funeral. She'd been alone again, like she had for so much of their decade-long marriage.

Since her time in Cabarita, her friends had continued with their lives, and she hadn't made much of an effort to reintegrate into her old social circles. She didn't feel like meeting for coffee or eating at fancy restaurants. Even getting dressed up seemed too hard.

She padded across the carpet and lay her hand on the cream sheet that covered the cot she'd bought five years earlier but never used.

A mobile jutted up beneath the sheet, almost grotesque under its cotton tent. Something else that'd never been used. Maybe never would be.

Duncan's answer to all her pain was, "Why don't we adopt? There are plenty of children in the world who need parents. We could have one of those."

But she didn't want to adopt. She wanted to carry a child in her womb and raise it with all the love in her heart. Why couldn't he understand that?

Still, she couldn't blame him, she supposed. She hadn't exactly been rational with all those fertility hormones rushing through her body turning everything topsy-turvy for months on end. Perhaps adoption was the answer. Though she hadn't gotten to that stage yet. Agreeing to it seemed like giving up, and she wasn't ready for that yet. At least she hadn't been.

Since Nan died, she'd taken the opportunity to spend time up north with her sisters, to get away from the fertility treatments, the quiet, empty house, and the load of expectation she'd carried on her shoulders for so long.

The rug beneath her feet felt coarse. The natural fibres tickled her flesh. She'd picked it out especially for that reason. No bleach, no artificial dyes, nothing dangerous or toxic, like every other item in the nursery. She'd chosen each with such care. And now it all sat idle beneath old sheets to protect her hopes and dreams from the gathering dust and the reach of the sun's damaging rays through the window. Not that she ever drew the blinds open anymore. It was too depressing to see dappled rays of sunlight dancing across the floor in an empty room.

She sank to the ground, knees bent to her chest, chin resting on her knees. No doubt her jeans would be covered with those natural fibres when she got up. One of the hazards of a rug like that, but at this point she didn't care. What did it matter if her jeans were covered with the stuff when no one would see it but her?

With a sigh she pushed to her feet, took one last glance around the room, and shut the door behind her. She padded to her office and slumped into her desk chair.

The white timber desk had a clear surface, just the way she liked it. She always put away her work when she was finished, leaving only a neat stack of papers pushed up against one edge of the desk.

Before she'd gone to Cabarita, the latest project had been a downtown loft for a multi-millionaire businessman. The catalogues she'd been perusing for the perfect leather armchair still sat in that neat pile. She'd handed the job over to her best designer, Karen Nguyen, when she'd decided she'd stay awhile in Cabarita, instead of returning a few days after the funeral like she'd originally planned. The designer had run things while she was gone, run them so well Reeda wasn't sure she was needed at her own company any longer.

Still, she loved it — loved pulling together a design, seeing the warmth it could bring to someone's home or office. It brought her so much pleasure — at least it had. Now she wasn't so sure. Nothing seemed to bring her joy anymore. She missed the Waratah, missed her sisters and the beach, Jack, Mima, and that ridiculous possum Kate had adopted and that'd stolen a peach right from under her nose when she wasn't looking one day out on the verandah. She'd tipped her head back and shut her eyes for a few moments' rest, and when she opened them the peach was gone and all she could see was the scampering rear end of that darned possum.

She chuckled at the memory and wiped a hand over her face with a groan. She missed it all. Why had she come home?

The Refidex book of maps sat on the bottom bookshelf beside the desk. She pulled it free and set it on the empty surface in front of her. With one hand she wiped the dust from its plastic jacket, then opened it up to the index. Her red-painted fingertip ran down the listings until she found the word she was looking for.

Bathurst.

She flipped the book open to the right page and stared at the town's outline. Then, she flicked to another page and measured the distance within the lines of the grid to see how far it was from Sydney. Not far, less than three hours' drive. That was doable; definitely doable.

She'd read almost all of the first of Nan's diaries since she arrived back in Sydney. So far, there wasn't anything to shed light on whether Nan found out more about Charlie Jackson's fate. He'd been shot down, that much she knew, missing in action, still, surely there was more to it than that? Perhaps he still had family in Bathurst.

From what she remembered, Nan didn't have anyone left. Her parents had died years earlier, and her brother was killed in the war. That much she knew. But perhaps there was still someone in Bathurst who knew something about Charlie Jackson. She'd tried calling Mima to pump her for information, but the cook was being particularly evasive on the subject, and Reeda couldn't tell if she was avoiding the subject intentionally or she really didn't know anything more.

She shook her head and stared at the map. Then, she took a Post-It note and stuck it on the page, marking her place, before slapping the book shut.

A day to drive out there, a few days to try and locate anyone left alive from Charlie's family tree, and a day back. That meant missing another entire week of work, but she doubted Karen would mind. She was in her element, ordering staff around, meeting with clients, and generally acting as though she were the top dog at the design firm. Let her relish it a while longer, Reeda had other things on her mind.

Charlie was her biological grandfather. Surely, she'd be able to discover something to give her insight into her family heritage. It was too tragic that he could disappear, never to be seen or heard of again. No wonder Nan hadn't ever told Dad about him — it would only have saddened him. And besides, Pop was a great father to Dad and a wonderful grandfather to the three of them.

Still, Dad and Pop were gone now, and so was Nan. It was just her, Kate, and Bindi left, and they deserved to know the truth about where they came from and what had happened to their grandfather, the man Nan had loved so passionately and waited for so patiently all those years ago.

A car door slammed, and she startled, then stood to her feet, wiping her damp palms down the front of her jeans.

In the kitchen, she found Duncan drinking milk from the bottle, the fridge door hanging open. He returned the milk to the fridge door and faced her with a surprised expression.

"Oh, hi, I didn't realise you were home."

"I parked on the street," she replied.

"Oh, okay."

She pushed a smile onto her face and linked her arms around him, kissing his cheek with soft lips. "It's good to see you," she said.

He tugged free of her embrace. "You too. I'm exhausted. I'm going to grab a shower."

She watched him go, her heart aching. He smelled of antiseptic and Old Spice. He'd withdrawn further and further from her over the past year. She didn't know how to bridge the gap between them, it had drifted too wide. She felt so alone.

THE END

ALSO BY LILLY MIRREN

Liz Cranwell is divorced and alone at Christmas. When her friends convince her to holiday at The Waratah Inn, she's dreading her first Christmas on her own. Instead she discovers that strangers can be the balm to heal the wounds of a lonely heart in this heartwarming Christmas story.

EMERALD COVE SERIES

Cottage on Oceanview Lane

When a renowned book editor returns to her roots, she rediscovers her strength & her passion in this heartwarming novel.

GLOSSARY OF TERMS

Dear reader,

Since this book is set in Australia there may be some terms you're not familiar with. I've included them below to help you out! I hope they didn't trip you up too much.

Cheers, Lilly xo

Terms

Bex - strong compound analgesic

Bloody - mild swear word with similar meaning to *damn*

Boot - car trunk

Chemist - another word for pharmacy or pharmacist

Chook - another term for chicken (the bird, not the food)

Echidna - a small spiny anteater

Eisteddfod - competition or festival of literature, music and performance

Pavlova - a meringue based dessert piled high with whipped cream and slices of fresh fruit.

Lift - elevator

"*Love*" - a word used affectionately for friends and lovers alike

Old fogey - elderly invalid

Righty-oh - Slang that means similar to 'alrighty-then'

Ringtail possum - adorable, furry marsupial with a curling tail, grey-brown coat, big eyes and small pink nose.

Tea - used to describe either a hot beverage made from leaves, or the evening meal

Tim Tams - chocolate covered cookies with frosting in the middle

Ute - A utility vehicle: a pickup truck with a cargo tray.

Unit - apartment or condo

Wagging - skipping school

Wowser - an insult, meaning puritanical or teetotaller

DISCUSSION GUIDE

Book Club Questions

1. Kate left Cabarita as soon as she was able to after graduating from high school. Do you think that her decision had more to do with her parents' death and the pain associated with that time in her life or because she was excited to begin a new chapter? A combination of both?

2. Was Charlie was the love of Edie's life, or was Paul?

3. Was the tension between the three sisters justified by the tragic events of their lives or had did they let a lack of communication make it into more than it was?

4. In what ways was Alex better suited to Kate than Davis?

5. In what ways did Kate grow and change from the first chapter to the end of the book?

6. Was Kate reading Nan's diaries an intrusion into her privacy, or would she have wanted her granddaughters to know about her life?

7. What did each of the sisters have in common? How were they each different to one another?

8. In what ways did the sisters hide from the pain of their past?

9. Why would you like to visit the Waratah Inn?

10. Which character did you most relate to?

ABOUT THE AUTHOR

Lilly Mirren lives in Brisbane, Australia with her husband and three children.

Lilly always dreamed of being a writer and is now living that dream. She is a graduate of both the University of Queensland, where she studied International Relations and Griffith University, where she completed a degree in Information Technology.

When she's not writing, she's chasing her children, doing housework or spending time with friends.

Lilly is also a bestselling romance author under the pen name *Vivi Holt*.

Sign up for her newsletter and stay up on all the latest Lilly book news.

And follow her on:

Website: lillymirren.com
Facebook: https://www.facebook.com/authorlillymirren/
Twitter: https://twitter.com/lilly_mirren
BookBub: https://www.bookbub.com/authors/lilly-mirren